BURDEN

JOHN J. SPEARMAN

DEDICATION

For Joe Piacquad, the best friend a man could ever ask for,
who encouraged me to write this book many years ago.

For Alicia, who is responsible for giving me everything good in life.

OTHER BOOKS BY THIS AUTHOR

The Halberd Series

Gallantry in Action

In Harm's Way

True Allegiance

Surrender Demand

The Pike Series

Pike's Potential

Pike's Passage

Pike's Progress

Pike's Purpose

The FitzDuncan Series

FitzDuncan

FitzDuncan's Alchemy

FitzDuncan's Enlightenment

FitzDuncan's Fortune

FitzDuncan's Gambit

FitzDuncan's Hope

FitzDuncan's Inheritance

FitzDuncan's Navy

FitzDuncan's Beginning

The Perseverance Andrews Series

The Defense of the Commonwealth

The Courage of the Commonwealth

The Resolve of the Commonwealth

Mercenary Navy Series

Rawlins' Redemption

Swiftsure Ascendant

ACKNOWLEDGMENTS

Great thanks to my editor, Martin Roy Hill, who makes me a better writer, and to Thea Magerand, whose cover designs bring my characters to life and never cease to amaze me.

And thank you, dear readers. You are the purpose of this and all my books. Thank you for reading. If you like what you have read, please leave a positive review on amazon.com or goodreads.com. If you did not like it, I apologize.

1

Throbbing pain from the back corner of his head woke him. Cold … wet … he could hear men arguing. It felt like wet sand under his face. He opened the eye not on the sand. It was darkish—twilight or morning, he couldn't tell. He could hear the susurrus of surf. The men weren't arguing any longer.

"Here, friend," came a voice from above his head. "Have some water."

He tried to move his head. The throbbing pain spiked and he winced. His mouth was dry. Water sounded good. He opened his mouth but didn't try to lift his head any further. Some water squirted in. With the water, now he could taste … seawater, vomit, sand, salt. He retched. The spasm sparked an outburst of pain and he lost consciousness again.

When he next woke, it was dark. There was a flickering of orange light—a fire. He still could hear the surf as waves came ashore. The throbbing from the back of his head was still there. He moaned.

The soft sound of feet moving through sand grew closer. "Ah, friend," came the voice. "You're back with us. More water?"

He grunted. The stream of water entered his mouth then played over his lips. His mouth was full of the foul taste from before but he was ready for it. He swirled the water around and spat it out, holding his mouth open for more. The water streamed in. He swallowed and opened again. "Thank you," he croaked.

When he woke next, he was somewhere else, inside. It was daytime. His head still hurt but less than before. He was in a bed, covered by a thin blanket—more than a sheet but lightweight. He had felt fabric like this before, but the name for it wouldn't come to him. He realized he had no clothes on. That bothered him. When he tried to move his head, the throbbing pain increased, so he stopped. There was a window and a doorway. The window had no glass. The door was open, and there was another room on the other side. A pleasant breeze came through the window.

He heard the sound of soft footsteps. A young woman came to the foot of the bed. She had long hair, light brown, tied back. Her eyes were blue. She was beautiful, he thought. "You're awake," she said. "I'll go fetch Da." She turned and left. A few minutes later he heard footsteps again.

"Welcome back, friend," came the voice he'd heard before. A man, older judging by the gray hair, in a simple shirt, with trousers held up by a hempen belt, came and sat next to him. The man's accent was odd, but it was a lilt he had heard before. It did not prevent him from understanding his speech.

"You need water, friend," the man said. "I will help you sit up so you can drink."

The man leaned over and reached under his arms, and began to pull him upright and towards the back of the bed. Moving made his head pulse with pain, but he did not lose consciousness. The man fussed behind his back and then gently pushed him into something soft that held him upright. 'Pillows' he thought.

The man poured water from an earthenware jug into an earthenware cup and gave it to him. He lifted it to his lips. The water was cool and pleasant and he realized he was thirsty. He drank the cup dry and held it out with a shaky hand for more. He drank two more cups greedily before remembering his manners. "Thank you," he said.

"You're welcome," the man replied. "Tell me, friend, what's your name?"

He thought. The man knew he had a name, but what it was puzzled him. He frowned slightly in concentration. Nothing came to him. Bewildered, he said, "I don't know."

"You took a nasty blow to your head," the man explained. "I've heard that people can lose their memory for a time when that happens. It will come to you in time. Or not. When we were carrying you from the beach, my friend Quentin called you a 'damned burden.' Quentin is a good man but prone to complaining. We could call you that," he teased, "for the time being."

"What is your name?" he asked, "and where am I?"

"My name is Caleb Gauthier," he replied, "and you are in my home. We are on Daubmer Island in the middle of the Eastern Ocean. You washed ashore a few days ago. How long you were on the beach, I don't know, but you have been in my home for three days now."

"The Eastern Ocean is vast," he said, reciting the fact like a school child. He didn't know how he knew that.

"Yes," Caleb responded, "the Eastern Ocean is enormous. We think we are more than five hundred leagues from Auster, or Boreas, or Skamorra—wherever you come from. Though, now that I hear you speak, your accent sounds Borean. Regardless, if you had not landed here, you would have kept drifting for weeks."

"Auster," he recalled. "I was going to Auster."

"Well, friend, you're not likely to get there in this lifetime," Caleb chuckled sadly.

"Why not?"

"The trade winds blow against us," Caleb explained, "and our island is surrounded by shoals that would rip the keel off any ship big enough to attempt the journey. People have tried, of course, but I don't think any have ever succeeded."

"Then how did you get here?"

"Same as you," Caleb replied, "shipwrecked. Blown off course by a storm and carried by the trade winds. I was on a merchantman bound for Varenna..."

"In Boreas," he blurted.

"Yes, in Boreas," Caleb continued. "We were making the last run of the season, and a storm caught us from the west. By the time the storm let up we were dismasted and taking on water. We rigged a couple of spars up to hoist sail, but we couldn't tack into the wind. After a few days, we caught sight of this place. We could see the combers breaking on the shoals. We got as close as we could, dropped anchor, and rowed ashore. We found we weren't the only ones here."

"How long ago?"

"About twenty-five years now," Caleb answered.

"So, your daughter was born here," he said.

"She was. There are a hundred and sixty-four of us … a hundred and sixty-five, counting you. Cia is one of thirty or so who were born here." Caleb pronounced her name 'Sha.'

"What happened to your ship?"

"Another storm came and drove her onto the shoals. There was nothing we could do except watch as it was smashed to bits."

"And now you can't get back."

"No," Caleb said, shaking his head. "The only way would be for a ship to sail here on purpose and anchor outside the shoals. They'd have to know where the island was and that there were people who needed rescuing. Since none of us had any idea this island existed before we got here, that doesn't seem likely to happen. Every so often, someone gets the idea of taking one of the fishing skiffs and trying to make it back. We wish them well but never see them again. Since a ship still hasn't shown up, we figure none have ever made it. As far as the people back home, they likely reckon we went down in a storm."

"What happened to my ship?"

"I don't know," Caleb admitted. "All that was left of it when Quentin and I found you was some debris washed ashore. That's usually all we find. We found you as well. Something hit your head quite hard—you have a nasty gash where the skin split and probably a cracked skull underneath. You're going to need to go easy for a bit until you mend some and recover your wits."

"My clothes?"

"I'll have Cia get them. Maybe they'll help you remember more," Caleb commented.

Caleb left, and a few minutes later, Cia came in carrying what the man guessed were his clothes. There was a pair of breeches, a white shirt, and a blue jacket with brocade decorating it. All were covered with smears of tar. There were also high boots and a sword with its scabbard attached to a belt. The thing that interested him most was the sword.

"Cia," he asked, "would you please hand me the sword?"

When she did he looked at it. Somehow, he knew about swords and knew this was an especially nice one. He lifted it, then withdrew the blade from the scabbard. He noticed rust spots from having been soaked in seawater. He would need to attend to those. The weight of it felt familiar and there was a sense of rightness in its balance and length. He closed his eyes.

He remembered picking himself up off the floor as someone told him, "Footwork, John, don't forget your footwork. Philip caught you off-balance, and that's why your butt hit the floor. Try again."

He opened his eyes and looked at Cia. "My name is John," he said uncertainly, "I think."

"My name is Cia," she replied, making a small curtsy, "short for Patricia."

"Thank you for taking care of me. I hope it wasn't too much work," he said.

"Getting the sand off you was the most difficult part," she said. "Other than that, you've just been lying there so you haven't been any bother at all."

"You bathed me?" he asked, surprised.

"Of course, you were covered in sand. Oh…" she said, realizing he was embarrassed by the color in his cheeks. "Don't worry about that. You needed help and … I'm sorry. You're embarrassed. I'll go get Da."

John wanted to ask her not to leave, but the words didn't come out in time. She was so pretty and seemed so nice. He wished he could talk to her for hours.

Caleb returned. "Cia tells me you think your name is John," he recounted.

"I think so," John replied. "Holding my sword brought back a memory from years ago when I was a boy."

"It looks to be a fine weapon," Caleb admitted. "I don't know much about them, though. Your clothes also seem quite fine. I'm sure you were some sort of gentleman in Boreas. Of course, that doesn't count for anything here."

"I don't know what sort of person I was," John admitted, "so I don't expect anything."

"That's for the best," Caleb stated. "Everyone is in the same situation here, so we're all just islanders."

"Tell me more about the island," John asked.

"You'll find that being stuck here is not the worst fate," Caleb said. "It's big enough that there is plenty of room for all of us. We grow crops for food and for cloth. There are plenty of fruit trees. We have flocks of sheep and goats, and we raise pigs, so feeding and clothing ourselves aren't problems and don't take much work from each of us. The weather is pleasant year-round. We've found enough ore that we can make some iron tools, and there are plenty of trees for wood—

we have everything we need for a nice life. The only negative is that we're stuck here and can't leave. If you can adjust to that, you'll be pretty happy. Most of us are."

"You said that sometimes people try to leave," John commented.

"I did," Caleb said nodding, "and strangely enough, it's usually ones who were born on the island and never knew life back where we came from. They have a longing to see those places. Those of us who came from there realize how much more pleasant and easy life on the island is compared to what we knew, so we're content to stay."

A woman entered. She looked like an older version of Cia. "Ah, you're awake," she said.

"My wife, Phoebe," Caleb said. "Phoebe, this is John—at least, he thinks that might be his name."

"I'm pleased to meet you," John said politely. "I apologize for disrupting your household."

"You're quite welcome," she replied. "You certainly had no choice in how you arrived here. You'll find people on the island pull together to help one another quite readily."

2

A sense of something wrong stirred the king from sleep. He was awake in an instant. Years spent on the border with the Wardens had taught him that skill. In the dark of his bedroom, he perceived someone approaching stealthily. He grabbed the pillow from under his head and waited for the person to approach one more step while trying to free his legs from the sheets quietly. When he judged the man was close enough, he exploded up from the bed, the pillow his only weapon. He swiped with the pillow where he thought the man's sword would be and was pleased when it wrapped around, and he was able to yank it from his grasp. He followed that with a punch to the man's face and a shout.

He felt the crunch as his hand hit the man's jaw. He turned to the door of the antechamber and burst towards it. Tearing it open, he saw the chancellor. "Mark," he gasped, "attac—"

He had run right onto the sword in the chancellor's hand.

"—kers," he finished, almost with a sigh, as he realized who had betrayed him.

"Guards!" came the shout. Lieutenant Fitch snapped awake. Rolling out of his bunk, he pulled on his trousers and boots in seconds. Grabbing his sword belt from the hook by his door, he charged into the hall. "Guards!" came another shout. It originated from the corridor leading to the Royal Chambers. Fitch ran.

He sprang into the antechamber, his sword drawn. Standing there was the chancellor with his own sword out, dripping with the blood of what looked like a Skamorran who lay at his feet. A pace away was the body of the king. Fitch groaned. "The queen?" he asked.

"Dead," the chancellor replied calmly, "and the baby and nurse. There's another Skamorran in there too. I killed him as well."

Lieutenant Barthlemy charged into the room, leading with his sword. Fitch motioned to him to stand easy. Taking a candle, Fitch went into the bedchamber. The queen's face was frozen in shock, and the blankets were blood-soaked. He went through the room to the nursery. Another Skamorran lay on the floor in a pool of blood, his throat slit. In the corner, the corpse of the nurse, curled into a ball. She died trying to protect the baby with her own body, but the Skamorran had stabbed right through her repeatedly and killed the baby as well.

Returning to the antechamber, Fitch saw the two guards. They had fallen face-first into what must have been their dinner. He went and checked. They were both dead. Fitch nearly staggered from the shock of what he had seen. More guards had arrived. Barthlemy was keeping them in the corridor.

"A dirty Skamorran plot," the chancellor stated, "that succeeded. I need you to get to the bottom of this, Fitch. They obviously poisoned the guards. I'd start questioning the kitchen staff to see who was their accomplice. I'm thinking it was that simpleton."

The chancellor strode out of the room. Barthlemy and Fitch looked at one another. "Immortal gods," Barthlemy hissed under his breath.

"We need our wits about us," Fitch warned.

He began breathing heavily, trying to flush the adrenaline from his system. Barthlemy saw what he was doing and began the same procedure. After a few minutes, Fitch felt as calm as he believed was possible under the circumstances. He nodded at his friend.

They started by looking at the two guards who had been stationed in the antechamber, both poisoned by the look of it. They sniffed the food and the wine in their cups. Looking at the meat on the plates, Barthlemy wet his finger and touched it. He then touched his finger to his tongue. Fitch looked on apprehensively.

"Spicy," Barthlemy commented, "very hot."

"To make them drink the wine, even though it didn't smell right," Fitch commented.

They continued to examine the scene. They noted the position of the king's body and that of the dead Skamorran in the antechamber. They went into the bedchamber. Both saw the pillow on the floor on the king's side of the bed. In the nursery, they inspected the body of the Skamorran, turning him over to see his throat slit nearly from ear to ear. They returned to the antechamber.

"Is it just me," Fitch commented, "or do you feel some things simply do not add up?"

"It's not just you," Barthlemy agreed.

"First of all, how on earth did Skamorrans not only make it into the kingdom but even manage to reach the Palace?" Fitch asked.

"And without being detected," Barthlemy added. "That took some resources to arrange. The resources of someone rich and powerful."

"And how did the chancellor, whose swordplay is amateurish at best, manage to kill two Skamorrans?" Fitch inquired.

Barthlemy went back to the bodies of the guards. Reaching down to one's waist, he held up a set of keys. Fitch nodded in agreement.

"Both doors to the antechamber are normally locked," Barthlemy stated, "so even if the assassins tricked the guards into opening the outer door, they would have needed to take the keys to open the bedchamber. The keys are still on Jack's belt, so—"

"So, someone else with keys to the bedchamber opened the door," Fitch said. "I only know of six keys to the bedchamber—you and I each have one, there's one on the guards' keyring, the king and the queen each have their own and—"

"The chancellor," Barthlemy whispered. "Immortal gods!"

"That explains how the Skamorran's throat was slit. He wasn't expecting an attack from someone who was helping him."

"And the look of surprise on this fellow," Barthlemy said, nudging the Skamorran's body at his feet. "Not to mention how the chancellor overcame them all. Look at the wounds. He stabbed that one in the back."

"So, how do you think it unfolded?" Fitch asked.

"Well, from the chancellor's insistence that the kitchen was involved, I'm going to guess that they had nothing to do with it. Dougie, the simple one, likely brought the food up just as he does any other night," Barthlemy stated. "I'm going to guess that the chancellor put some sort of pepper sauce on the meat and poisoned the wine."

"How did he distract the guards to do that?" Fitch inquired.

"Hm. That's tricky," Barthlemy mused. "One would be feasible. Both? I don't know."

"Maybe Dougie didn't deliver their dinner," Fitch suggested. "Maybe when he arrived, the chancellor was here and told him he would do it. We could always ask him."

"Right," Barthlemy responded with heavy sarcasm, "and how do you think Dougie will respond?"

"Dang," Fitch sighed, "you're right. He'll be rattled because he didn't actually deliver their dinner, and he doesn't want to get in trouble. He's also scared to death of the chancellor, so he won't want to mention him. He'll be confused and act guilty."

"This is exactly what the chancellor would want, to make it look like Dougie was involved. So, the chancellor takes the food from Dougie and waits for Dougie to leave. He puts the pepper sauce on the meat and poisons the wine. He comes to the antechamber, and the guards open the door. Then what?" Barthlemy asked.

"Then he stays or leaves—doesn't matter," Fitch said. "If he leaves, he comes back to check to make sure it worked. It did. He finds the assassins somewhere in the palace and brings them in. He opens the bedchamber door, and the assassins go in."

"The king wakes up and gets past the one coming for him. He runs to the antechamber, where the chancellor kills him. The assassin who was supposed to kill the king runs in a second later, and the chancellor kills him too," Barthlemy explained. "The one who killed the queen then goes to the nursery and kills them. As he's doing it, the chancellor slits his throat from behind."

"The chancellor then comes back out here," Fitch stated, "opens the outer door and starts shouting. He positions himself to make it look like he just killed the assassin in the antechamber."

"Gods below and above," Barthlemy muttered. "What happens now?"

"With the king and his son dead, Prince John inherits the throne," Fitch recalled. "Prince John was sent to Auster for some negotiations regarding the Skamorrans, even though the normal sailing season was over."

"Yeah," Barthlemy agreed. "And who was insistent that John leave right away, even though the typhoon season had begun?"

"The same guy who would control the government in his absence," Fitch stated, "the chancellor. I wonder if the prince's ship didn't meet with an 'accident' on the way to Auster—perhaps some Skamorran corsairs? Or maybe assassins waiting for him in Auster? If the prince is missing, what happens?"

"We move to a three-year period of interregnum," Barthlemy said, "with the chancellor in power while the line of succession is determined. Right now, the next in line after Prince John is Lord Halverd. After him, it's a bunch of second and third cousins."

"Halverd is almost ninety and so addled he doesn't even know his own name," Fitch protested. "It would drop to the cousins."

"And there are at least two who would have a decent claim to the throne," Barthlemy concluded, "and both would want it, leading to civil war. The nobles would want to avoid that."

"So, they might just leave the chancellor on the throne," Fitch stated. "They'd argue that he was treated almost like a son by the Royal family. He was brought up alongside King Philip and Prince John, so he'd be an easy choice if they wanted to avoid bloodshed. They never realized what a jerk he was."

"He was always careful in their presence," Barthlemy recalled, "from the time he arrived. Anyone subordinate always knew his true color though—black as the deepest of the known hells."

"He has this whole thing sewed up, doesn't he?"

"Except for you and me," Barthlemy responded. "The question is, what are we going to do about it?"

They paused for a moment, both thinking.

"One of us has to go look for Prince John," Barthlemy stated. "If he is still alive, we need to find him and protect him. If he's not, we need to find out what happened if we can."

"One of us needs to stay here," Fitch offered, "and act stupid so that someone is keeping an eye on the chancellor. If possible, whoever stays behind needs to reach out to some of the nobles and share our suspicions—quietly, discretely. That's probably you, by the way."

"For the acting stupid part," Barthlemy asked, "or the talking with the nobles?"

"Only you could try to find humor in this whole mess," Fitch said, shaking his head. "So that means I need to go."

"As soon as you leave," Barthlemy counseled, "the chancellor is going to say you're running away because you're somehow involved. He'll send me and the rest of the Guard to grab you and bring you back. You'd probably never make it."

"Hmm," Fitch mused, tapping his finger on his lips while he thought. After a couple of minutes, he snapped his fingers. "Got it," he said urgently. "If he wants to paint me as a traitor, let him. It'll make things easier for you—instead of trying to claim you don't know what I'm doing, you can act righteously indignant and betrayed. I'll head for the Skamorran border."

"How in the world will that get you to Auster?" Barthlemy demanded.

"Remember the goat track?"

"The goat track?" Barthlemy asked, puzzled.

"Off the road to the border, just in the foothills," Fitch reminded him. "Where we surprised the smugglers."

"Oh yeah," Barthlemy recalled.

"It leads to the coast," Fitch stated. "There are a couple of fishing villages there. It's where the smugglers were based, too. I'll bet I can find someone willing to take me to Auster for the right price. If I head south to Varenna or one of the other main ports, the price will be much higher, and you guys will likely get there before I'm able to negotiate passage."

"It's going to make you look guilty as hell," Barthlemy cautioned. "There will only be three people who know you're innocent: you, me, and the chancellor."

"And you have to pretend you think I'm guilty and betrayed everything we stand for," Fitch advised.

"Well," Barthlemy suggested, "if you're going to be a criminal, you should go all the way. Go to my quarters and grab my purse, then take my horse with you when you leave. I'll come charging after you."

Fitch nodded. "Try to give me as much of a head start as you can. If you can give me three or four hours?"

"I'll do my best."

3

A few days later, John felt strong enough to get out of bed. When he suggested it, Cia mentioned that his head wound needed to be cleaned. They had only done a quick job of it before. She led him outside to a set of flat stones. Above was a water barrel on a raised platform above head height.

"When you tug on this rope," she taught him, "it moves that disk off to the side. There are small holes in the bottom of the barrel, and the water will fall down onto your head. You get yourself wet, then pull this other cord to move the disc back in place. Wash yourself, then pull on the first one to rinse the soap away."

John nodded in understanding and stood there, waiting for Cia to leave and give him some privacy. She was waiting for him to take off the long linen shirt they had given him to wear. "Do you need me to explain it again?" she asked.

John shook his head gently.

"Then what are you waiting for?" she asked.

"Some privacy would be nice," John suggested.

Cia smiled. "How will I be able to clean your wound if I'm not here?" she responded. "You can't do it yourself."

John's face reddened with embarrassment. He had not reckoned on being naked in front of her. Just the thought of it began to arouse him. That made his embarrassment worse. He decided to just make the best of it and reached up and pulled the shirt off. He stood naked in front of her. She smiled as she looked him up and down, then started to laugh.

"I'm sorry," she said, covering her mouth with her hands. "I shouldn't look, but…"

John turned his back to her, pulled the rope, and the water poured out from above. It was cool enough to make him gasp, though it wasn't cold. He made sure his hair was thoroughly wet, as well as the rest of his body. He pulled the other line, and the water stopped. Cia handed him a cake of soap, and he began to lather himself, starting with his feet and working his way up. When he reached his face, he reached out with the soap to hand it back to Cia. His eyes were closed to keep the soap out.

He felt her fingers lathering up his hair. As she began to work carefully around where his wound was, she pressed herself against his back. He thought she did in order to get a closer look at it—he hoped that was the case. He realized she was not wearing any clothing.

"Rinse," she warned.

She pulled the rope, and cool water cascaded over them both. As it did, she was working her fingers on the edge of his wound.

"Again," she cautioned as more water came down. She moved her fingers through his hair to remove the soap suds.

"Lift your arms and turn around," she instructed.

As he did, he felt her hands wiping suds off his face, shoulders, chest, and back as the water trickled from above.

"Done," she announced.

John turned away slightly, too well aware that they both were naked. She handed him a towel to dry himself. He concentrated on that. When he finished, he wrapped the cloth around his hips before turning to face her. By the time he did, she was already dressed again.

"Sit," she told him, pointing to a chair nearby. "I'll be back in a snap."

When she returned, she had a bowl of steaming water, a small brush, and a razor. He realized she was going to shave his beard. "I can do that myself," he protested.

"Nonsense," she replied, "it will be my pleasure."

She dipped the brush into the hot water, then rubbed it on the cake of soap. When she had worked up a lather, she applied it to his face. With swift, deft strokes, she shaved his face, dipping the razor into the bowl to rinse off the soap and whiskers. When she finished, she wiped his face with a towel, pronouncing, "All finished. You look almost civilized."

She walked him back to his room. Two sets of clothes were laid out. One set was the clothing he was wearing when he washed ashore. The other was like what he had seen Caleb wearing.

"Which do you recommend?" he asked.

She pointed to the simple clothing. "It's comfortable, durable, and easier to wash. Besides," she added, "you don't need to impress anyone here. Not that you would in your old clothes. We can't get the tar off."

Observing the redness of his cheeks, she told him, "I'll be out here. Come get me when you're dressed. I'll take you on a walk."

When he was dressed, he met her outside. He offered his arm as he was accustomed to do. She grasped him at the elbow, smiling. They headed down a path through some underbrush. When they emerged into the open, they turned onto a larger path in an open area dotted with several houses. They saw Phoebe coming towards them.

"My, John, you look much better now that you're shaved. You were beginning to look a bit disreputable—like a pirate," she laughed. "Cia, did you look at his wound?"

"Yes, Ma. I washed it just like you said. There was quite a bit of dried blood and sand."

"Good. And now you're showing him off—I mean, showing him around," Phoebe said, teasing her daughter.

It was Cia's turn to blush. She and John continued along this broader path. There were twenty-two houses facing one another. They were single-story, built of stone, and painted with a variety of pastel colors. The roofs were all white. All the houses were dotted with small windows with wooden shutters. There was no glass in them.

"This is the main settlement on the island," she explained. "About half of us live here. There's another group of fourteen houses about a half-day's walk away. There are a number of houses that are scattered all over—the farmers and herders live in those."

"What do you call this town?" he asked.

"You'll laugh," she replied.

"No, I won't," he promised.

"Yes, you will," she said. "We call it Town."

John tried but a small chuckle escaped him. "I'm sorry," he apologized, "it's only logical. It's not like there are any others. Who lives in Town?"

"People with different skills and abilities," she explained. "Weavers, a smith, a potter, the miller, carpenters, a stonemason, a cooper, a tanner, a baker, and a couple of fishermen. At harvest time we help bring in the crops. We work together and share the results. The land is fertile, there are plenty of fish, there are more sheep and goats than there are people, there are plenty of trees for wood and fuel, and the climate is pleasant year-round. Everyone needs to work, but no one needs to work too hard."

"It sounds like a dream," John commented.

"That's what Ma and Da say," Cia remarked. "To me, it's just dull. You washing ashore is the most exciting thing I can ever remember happening. Every year or two, someone has a baby, and that's interesting. I've already read every book on the island. The only men my age live out in the countryside, so my future is to be a farmer's wife or a herder's wife. It's not a lot to look forward to."

John did not know how to respond. They walked, and Cia named who lived in each house and what they did. As they strolled, people who were outside said hello to Cia, and she introduced them to John. By the time they reached the end of the row of houses, John felt his head begin to hurt. He mentioned it to Cia, and they returned to her parents' house.

She followed him into his bedroom. When he looked at her questioningly, she shushed him. She gestured for him to lie down. When he did, she arranged herself behind him.

"What are you doing?" he hissed. "Your father will kill me if—"

"He will do nothing of the sort," Cia answered. "As for what I am doing, I plan on holding you until you fall asleep. Once you do, I will leave."

"But—this is highly improper," John protested.

"Says you," Cia replied.

She reached over his body and began stroking his temple. Despite his misgivings, he admitted to himself it felt lovely. He tried to protest again, but Cia shushed him. Before he realized it, he was asleep.

Cia felt herself drifting off. Just as she was about to close her eyes, she saw the door swing open slightly. Her mother was on the other side. Phoebe shook her head and beckoned Cia with a crooked finger. Moving gently so she would not disturb John, Cia got up and followed her mother.

"Don't overwhelm the poor man," Phoebe cautioned.

Cia's response was to blush and look at the floor.

"He is as handsome," Phoebe said, "as you are pretty. The two of you make an attractive couple. Go slow, my dear. The poor man isn't even sure of his own name. He's vulnerable. Let him begin to chase you until you catch him."

"What? That makes no sense, mother."

"Cia, darling, you have no rivals for his heart," Phoebe said. "Be patient. He's not blind."

"I suppose," Cia muttered.

"You helped him bathe today. I assume you were both naked?"

"Yes," Cia admitted grudgingly.

"And now you feel as though you're burning up inside," Phoebe remarked and laughed.

"It's not funny, mother."

"To you? No. To someone who has experienced the same feelings, it is amusing for me to see."

"You cannot know the way I feel," Cia protested sharply.

"Oh, but I do," Phoebe replied. "I felt the same way about your father when I was your age. Even now, it does not take much for that fire to be rekindled. Just remember, there is more to love than just a person's appearance. It's what rests in the heart that matters most, and that requires a bit more patience."

"John is a good man," Cia asserted.

"As far as we know," Phoebe said, "considering we know next to nothing. Great gods, girl—he isn't even sure what his name is!"

"He is a good man. I can feel it."

"You want him to be a good man," Phoebe said, "but give it time to make sure. One good thing about his lack of memory is that he probably lacks artifice. He can't show anything other than his true nature. Even so, slow down. Good things come to those who wait."

4

Fitch hurried to the barracks. First, he stopped by his quarters and threw a change of clothes into a leather bag. Then he went into Barthlemy's room and quickly found his purse. He dumped the coins into his own and tossed the empty leather pouch onto the bunk. Finally, he went to the Guards' stables and found one of the grooms.

"Saddle Buckets and Hammer for me," he ordered.

The groom did so quickly and brought the two horses around when he finished. Fitch flipped the groom a copper as he usually did and mounted his own horse, Buckets, leading Hammer by the reins. He rode out of the Guard compound at a sedate pace. Once outside the walls, he spurred Buckets, riding recklessly through the crowded streets of the capital towards Westgate. He left commotion in his wake.

When he reached Westgate, he shouted, "Clear the way! Clear the way!" as he barreled through.

He kept Buckets at the gallop until he was out of sight of Westgate. He then slowed to a trot. After an hour, he switched mounts and climbed on Hammer. He continued at a trot. He kept this pace up all morning, reaching the hamlet of Simpson. He stopped at the inn there. He rode around back to the stable and found the groom. He asked the groom to wipe down and water the horses, then went inside.

"Ralph!" the innkeeper cried. "What brings you my way?"

"Nothing but trouble, Captain," Fitch answered. "Nothing but trouble. What's hot and ready to eat? I'm in a bit of a rush."

"I can carve you a few slices off the roast and slap them in some bread. Sound good?"

"If I can drink a mug of cider while I'm waiting, it does," Fitch agreed.

The innkeeper, a former captain in the Wardens, drew a mug of hard cider for Lieutenant Fitch and then disappeared into the kitchen. He returned within minutes with the sandwich wrapped in waxed paper as Fitch was draining the last of the mug.

"What do I owe you, Captain?" Fitch asked.

"Your life," the innkeeper replied, "several times over. But today, slap a silver on the bar, and we'll call it even."

Fitch did just that. He took the sandwich and went out back. The groom was just finishing with the horses. Fitch flipped him a copper, mounted Buckets again, and set off.

Barthlemy made his way to the kitchens slowly after Fitch left. He found the one they knew as Dougie. He took Dougie outside. Dougie was a large man. He had been apprenticed to a farrier years ago, where he had been kicked in the head by a horse. Since then, Dougie had been weak-minded. He was employed in the palace kitchen and given the simplest tasks—peeling vegetables, sweeping up, cleaning pots and pans, and delivering dinner to the guards on station in the anteroom of the Royal Bedchamber.

"Dougie," Barthlemy began, speaking gently as to a spooked animal, "do you remember handing the guards' dinner to the chancellor last night?"

Dougie's eyes flicked back and forth.

"It's not a problem, Dougie," Barthlemy said calmly. "The chancellor told me he wanted to do it."

Dougie stopped looking back and forth, realizing he wasn't going to get in trouble. The words spilled out of his mouth then. "He asked if he could help me and take them their dinner and I told him no that's my job and I don't want no trouble and he said it was fine and that he knew Namie's kittens opened their eyes that morning and he knew I wanted to play with the kittens now that they eyes was open and I dint want to get in no trouble and to just lets me take the food like always and he says he's gonna do it so I can hold the kitties and I lets him."

"That's exactly what he told me, Dougie," Barthlemy lied. "Thank you. You helped me a lot."

"I ain't in no trouble?" Dougie asked, incredulous.

"Not at all," Barthlemy lied. "You go on back to work now."

After Dougie went back inside, Barthlemy sighed heavily. He knew the chancellor would kill Dougie the first chance he had. He returned to the Royal bedchambers, moving as slowly as he dared. He wanted to use up as much time as he possibly could. When he reached them, he walked up and down the outside corridor, trying to figure out from which direction the Skamorrans had come. In one direction lay the rest of the castle, so he walked past the anteroom in the opposite direction.

The corridor came to an end at another, perpendicular corridor. At one end lay steps down to the throne room. At the other were the quarters of various palace functionaries, including the chancellor's apartments. Barthlemy retraced his steps and made his way out of the building. He took his time as he went to examine the outside of the palisade. He knew he would find a rope dangling from a window. The room would belong to someone else the chancellor would accuse falsely, someone else who would die although he was innocent.

By now, it was midday. Barthlemy was somewhat surprised he had not already been summoned. He went to the Guards' mess and sat down to eat lunch. He had just begun a helping of shepherd's pie when a page came bursting into the mess, red-faced with exertion. The page saw him and ran over.

"Lieutenant Barthlemy," he gasped, "the chancellor needs to see you immediately."

Barthlemy nodded, swallowed his mouthful, and got up slowly. The page took off at a run. Barthlemy did not run but did walk at a pace faster than he had used all morning. The page was waiting for him when he reached the chancellor's office.

Barthlemy composed himself, adopting a mask of urgency, then knocked on the door. "Enter!" came harshly from within.

"Report!" the chancellor barked as soon as Barthlemy shut the door.

"Sir, I've interviewed Dougie," Barthlemy said. "He tried to tell me a fantastic story involving you. He's clearly lying. In addition, I found out how the Skamorrans entered the castle. There's a rope dangling from the window of an apartment. I believe the apartment is assigned to a young man on your staff. Gilchrist, I think his name is. I believe that Dougie poisoned the guards' wine and treated the guards' dinner with something that made them crave drink. Gilchrist let the three assassins in—"

"Three?" the chancellor queried.

"Yes, three," Barthlemy responded. "After they killed the king and queen, I suspect the assassins had a falling out. The third one killed the other two, then made his escape."

"I know the identity of the third assassin," the chancellor said smugly.

"Who is it?" Barthlemy demanded.

"Lieutenant Fitch was seen leaving the city a couple of hours ago, at a high rate of speed, heading on the road to the Skamorran border."

"I'm sorry, sir, but I find that hard to believe," Barthlemy replied.

"What's more," the chancellor added, "he took your horse with him."

"He took Hammer?" Barthlemy said, incredulous. Displaying growing anger, he cried, "The bastard!"

"I took the liberty of ordering a search party," the chancellor said. "They're waiting for you in the courtyard. Go get Fitch and bring him back to face justice."

"Yes, sir!" Barthlemy replied.

He spun on his heel and moved quickly out of the room. When he reached the corridor, he began to sprint. He wanted the chancellor to believe that he had accepted the lies. He would give the appearance of a man responding with the fury of one betrayed. He knew the chancellor had a low opinion of soldiers, thinking all of them were dunces. The chancellor knew an ordinary person would have trouble believing that a comrade of two decades would suddenly turn traitor. Even an ignorant soldier would have difficulty accepting the news, although the authority of the chancellor would influence him somewhat. But for a stupid soldier, the theft of his horse would remove all doubt of the suspect's guilt. He was going to act just as the chancellor expected a stupid soldier to act.

He ran to his quarters, seeing the empty purse on the bed. This would give him another reason for righteous rage. He jogged into the courtyard, finding ten men mounted and waiting. A horse was saddled and ready for him. He mounted quickly and told the men to follow him. He spurred the horse and galloped out into the streets. They headed for the Westgate, forcing their way through the normal city traffic. When they finally got out of the city, he brought them back down to a canter. In an hour and a half, they reached Simpson and the inn. He stopped briefly to allow the men to water the horses.

"Two in one day," the innkeeper said jovially, "first Fitch, now you."

"It's a bad business, Captain," Barthlemy said, shaking his head. "Fitch is on the run. We think he was involved in the assassination of the king last night."

The innkeeper noticed Barthlemy had laid his finger aside his nose as he spoke. This had been an old signal in the Wardens that things were not as they appeared. "The king was assassinated!" the innkeeper exclaimed, his shock unfeigned. "Fitch didn't say a damned thing about it."

"Well, seeing as how he was a part of it," Barthlemy stated, still rubbing the side of his nose, "I don't think he would. How long ago was he here?"

"A couple of hours ago," the innkeeper answered.

Barthlemy whistled, the signal for his men to remount. "We're gaining on him, men," he called as he swung into the saddle. "Thanks for the information, Captain. I hope to tell you more later when this is done."

Barthlemy and his troop set off at a canter again. If he had really wanted to capture Fitch, he would not have pushed the horses so hard. Fitch, knowing he had a head start, would have set a slower pace, alternating between trotting and walking, switching between mounts regularly. Barthlemy was hoping he would catch up to Fitch just as his squad's horses reached the limit of their endurance while Fitch's mounts still had plenty of stamina. If the men were able to report back that they had nearly caught Fitch, it would put Barthlemy in the chancellor's good graces.

The faster pace also meant Barthlemy's horses would be spent and would need at least a day of rest before continuing onward. He would take the squad all the way to the border looking for Fitch, then return to the castle after nearly a month away to report their lack of success to the chancellor. By then, he hoped Fitch would be in Auster.

Fitch continued at his controlled pace through the day. As the shadows grew longer he began to wonder whether Barthlemy would catch sight of him. He had no idea of how long Barthlemy had been able to delay. He still had a few hours more to ride before he reached the goat track that would take him to the coast. He was changing mounts when he noticed Bucket's ears prick up. He looked back to the west and saw the squad of men riding after him, about a mile away. He climbed into the saddle and set off at a canter.

Fitch would allow them to close the distance gradually. He suspected that the horses of his pursuers were nearly blown while his still had plenty of energy. He watched the distance carefully. By the time the squad was within a half-mile of him, he saw two of the troopers drop back, their horses clearly exhausted. By the time the remainder of the squad had closed to within a quarter-mile, three more had fallen back. By now he could see the sweat lathering the chests of the horses pursuing him. The road began to climb up a long gradual hill.

By the time Fitch reached the crest, only Barthlemy and one member of his squad were still in pursuit. They had closed to about a hundred and fifty yards. He nudged Buckets to a gallop on the downhill slope. He started to pull away from Barthlemy. "You damned horse-thief bastard!" he heard Barthlemy yell. He looked back. Barthlemy and the trooper had both dismounted, their horses spent.

Fitch waited until he was out of sight again before allowing Buckets to slow to a walk. He reached into his saddlebag and retrieved the rest of the sandwich he had purchased earlier. As he ate, he tried to consider why the chancellor had killed the king.

Mark, the chancellor, had been the son of a distant cousin of King Seamus. Seamus was the father of the recently deceased King Philip and the missing Prince John. When Mark's parents died mysteriously, there were no other close relatives who could take the orphan in. Queen Sophie decided to bring Mark into the family. He was raised alongside Philip and John. To all appearances, he had seemed a dutiful son to the king and queen and a faithful brother to Philip and John. Away from the royal family, he showed quite a different side: petulant, arrogant, snotty, and heartless. The servants feared him. For his part, Mark despised the servants.

Unlike Philip and John, Mark never served as a soldier, claiming his health was too delicate. Queen Sophie took his side and King Seamus did not force the issue, since Mark was not in the line of succession. Philip and John both served several years with the Wardens patrolling the border with Skamorra. Their willingness to share in the hardships the Wardens endured, and their rough and ready sense of humor had earned them the Wardens' respect and many men were proud to call them friends.

Fitch thought back to when he first met Prince John. He had been a soldier in the regular army for two years and had just qualified to join the Wardens, considered the elite part of the service. Newly arrived at camp that evening, he went looking for the commanding officer to report in. The first person he saw was a man sitting on a camp stool, looking at some maps spread on his cot. The man was somewhat disheveled in appearance and bore no sign of rank.

"Have you seen the commander?" Fitch had asked. "I need to report in."

"Haven't seen him all day," was the reply. "You're reporting in?"

"Yeah," Fitch had answered. "How is he?"

"For a royal, he's not so bad," the man replied. "All the handmaidens and attendants are kind of a pain in the ass, though. They follow him around everywhere—that's how you'll spot him."

Fitch was just about to thank him when someone else came up and addressed the man sitting on the stool as, "Your Highness." Fitch remembered turning bright red from embarrassment. When the other man left, Prince John had laughed at Fitch's predicament.

The chancellor never displayed a sense of humor that Fitch had ever heard of. He developed a reputation as someone to be avoided if at all possible. The royal family was oblivious to his darker side. He was careful to act always as a dutiful and faithful adopted son or brother.

5

Just before twilight gave way to night, Fitch found the goat track. If he had been a few minutes later, he would likely have missed it in the darkness. There was a stream nearby, so he watered the horses. He tied them up and groomed them carefully before laying out his bedroll for the night. He grew cold in the middle of the night and retrieved his cloak to use as a blanket.

In the morning, after feeding and watering the horses, he let Hammer go. He took the horse back to the road, pointed him back towards the city, and gave him a swat on the butt to get him started. With any luck, Barthlemy would have his horse back by the end of the day.

The path may have begun as a goat track, but it was a little better than the name might indicate. There were several fishing villages on the coast. This path was the quickest way for them to reach the nearest town, Hanville, which was another few hours' ride down the road toward Skamorra. It was also the path that smugglers used to bring goods up, and for that reason, it was difficult to spot from the road unless you knew where to look. It took Fitch two days of walking to reach the coast. He needed to walk Buckets since the path was narrow and skirted the edges of the spur of the hills that continued along the coast. Eventually, this rolling terrain gave way to the foothills of the Neyesper mountains that formed the border between Boreas and Skamorra.

He arrived in the late afternoon. There was a row of houses set well back from the beach, comfortably above the high tide line. In front of each of the homes, a fishing boat had been pulled ashore, also above the high tide line. Lines stretched from the boats to their anchors, carried further up the embankment on which the homes stood. Some of the boats had nets draped over their sides. At the third boat, there was a bald man mending the nets, his back to Fitch.

The man didn't turn his head as he spoke. "It's the wrong time of year for the tax man," he said, "and they usually show up in greater numbers. Plus, you're wearing the livery of a lieutenant in the Palace Guard, and they don't collect taxes—at least, not that I've heard of. What brings you here, stranger?"

Fitch recognized the voice but couldn't place where he knew it. It didn't seem to match with the bald head. He decided to take a chance. "If you'd turn around," Fitch suggested, "maybe you wouldn't find a stranger."

The man turned around slowly. He looked Fitch up and down. Fitch looked at him and knew who it was, though the man hadn't been bald when he knew him.

"Young Fitch," the man said in an amused tone. "Never thought I'd see you again. And all dressed up like a lieutenant in the Palace Guard. Who'd you steal the uniform from, son?"

Fitch laughed. "Sergeant Gunnar! What happened to your hair?"

The two men clasped hands and thumped each other's backs. "When you left the Wardens," Fitch said, "you told us you were going to help out your sister, and she lived over by Varenna. What the heck are you doing here?"

Sven Gunnar put down the needle he had been using to repair the net. "It's not a long story," he said, "but I'm tired and thirsty, and it's getting to be suppertime. I have some fish stew that ought to be enough for both of us, and some cider. We can sit and tell some lies."

Sven led him up the embankment to the house and pointed out where Fitch could tie Buckets and the cistern where he could fetch a bucket of water for the horse. Fitch took care of his mount first, then went inside. Sven was stirring a pot, but he gestured to the jug on the table and two mugs beside it.

"Pour us both a drink, Ralph, and tell me what brings you here."

"Sergeant, my story is not so pleasant," Fitch replied, "so I'm thinking it might wait until we have a mug or two of cider inside us. Tell me how you ended up here."

"Fair enough," Sven said, wiping his hands on his shirt. "When I left the Wardens, I went to help my sister, just like I told everyone. That first winter, though, she up and married again. Her new husband didn't need my help, but it turned out his brother needed exactly the kind of help I could provide."

"What sort of help is that?"

"Oh, someone a little intimidating, good with his fists, handy with a blade, and who knew how to keep his mouth shut even when he got drunk," Sven answered.

"Gosh," Fitch teased, "I hope he found him."

"Ha-ha," Sven answered sarcastically. "So, the brother—Paul's his name—has a fishing boat, but he doesn't try to catch many fish, if you gather my meaning."

"Smuggling, in other words," Fitch stated. "If you don't fish, why were you mending the net?"

"Seven hells, son! That net didn't need mending. I was there to see who the heck you were, coming down the goat track, dressed all fancy. Paul operates out of here, far away from the King's revenue cutters by the big ports. Paul should be due back tomorrow. He just took our last shipment of the season up to Hanville. Anyway, I've been here for the last five years, working with him. Now, what brings you down here? Ain't exactly normal for someone to wander this way."

Fitch grimaced and told him the whole story about the King's assassination. He mentioned his and Lieutenant Barthlemy's belief that the chancellor was behind it. He related how he had ridden away from the capitol and how Barthlemy had played it.

"I need to sail to Auster immediately," Fitch said earnestly. "I know it's the wrong time of year, but if Prince John is there, I need to protect him. If he's not or if he's already dead, I need to get word back to Stan Barthlemy."

"How do you expect to convince anyone to sail to Auster during storm season?"

Fitch thumped his heavy purse on the table, with both his and Stan Barthlemy's entire savings in it. "With this," he said.

Sven asked, "Do you mind?" and loosened the drawstring and peered inside. He whistled softly. "Less than half of that is still more than a year's earnings for Paul and me. Let's wait until he comes back tomorrow, but I think he'll be willing to give it a try. Take half of that money and hide it in your saddle bag.

We don't want to let on how much you've got, or the price will go up. Also, Paul ain't the patriot you and I are. I may tell him a different story about why you need to get to Auster so quick."

The next afternoon, Paul Escamil returned, leading a dozen mules. Escamil was a black-skinned, barrel-chested man with black hair and a full beard. Sven pulled Paul aside after the mules were taken care of. He told Fitch to wait outside until he called him in.

"I understand you need to get to Auster," Escamil said. "Put a bun in the oven of some nobleman's daughter, did we?"

"His men showed up at the palace a couple of days ago, looking for me," Fitch said, making it up as he went along. "I took off as soon as I could after that."

"Sven tells me you can pay for your passage," Escamil said. "Let's see your money."

Fitch put his purse on the table, reduced by half thanks to Sven's advice. Escamil loosened the drawstring and dumped the coins on the table. Escamil quickly sorted through them, separating the gold crowns from the silver florins from the copper pennies. Escamil scooped all the gold crowns and half of the silver florins to one side. He picked up the remaining florins and the pennies and returned them to the leather bag.

Escamil handed the purse back, now greatly reduced in weight, saying, "You're going to need to start a new life for yourself in Auster. Should be enough in there to see you through until you make a new beginning."

From what Fitch could figure, the coins Escamil left would enable him to obtain a room at an inn and feed himself for three or four months. He found himself unexpectedly touched by the man's relative lack of greed.

"We'll leave the day after tomorrow," Escamil continued. "Sven and I need to get the boat in the water and tend to a few things, mostly stores for the trip. Sven, get him some clothes. The ones he's wearing make him stand out too much. If you don't have enough, I can ask around."

"No," Sven answered, "I can do it."

After Escamil left, Sven went to a dresser and pulled out some shirts and trousers made of homespun fabric. He also found a pair of rope sandals. Fitch put on a shirt and pants and the sandals and packed away his uniform and boots into the leather bag he brought from the palace. He also retrieved the other half of his money and put it back in his purse, burying that in the middle of his clothing.

The next day, Fitch and several other men helped Escamil and Sven launch their boat. They dragged it down to the water's edge during low tide. While they were waiting for the tide to come in, Escamil and Sven went off. They came back later with full water barrels. Escamil also brought a barrel of salt pork, which he said they'd eat only if the fish weren't biting. He loaded tins of biscuits and several casks of hard cider. One of the men agreed to take care of Fitch's horse.

"If I'm not back in a year," Fitch told him, "sell it and keep the proceeds for your trouble."

The next morning, several men came aboard and helped step the mast. The next time the tide came in, Escamil Sven and Fitch climbed aboard, and four other men shoved the boat the rest of the way into the water. Escamil waited until the breeze changed from a sea breeze to an offshore breeze, then had Sven hoist the sail.

While waiting for the breeze to change, Fitch had already begun to feel nauseous from the motion of the boat on the waves. As they began to move forward, the forward up-and-down motion was augmented by a side-to-side roll. A few minutes later, Fitch vomited over the side of the boat.

He spent the next three days vomiting over the railing, even when there was nothing to bring up except the water Sven and Escamil forced him to drink. He was of no use to them, curled in a ball below the railing. On the fifth morning, he woke. That was new—he hadn't slept more than a few brief periods between his bouts of nausea. For the first time since boarding the boat, he felt hungry. More than hungry, he was starving.

He stood and stretched. Sven was manning the wheel. "Back to the land of the living?" he inquired.

Fitch gave him an uncertain look. "I don't know about that," he said, "but I just realized that's the first sleep I've had, and now I am hungry enough to eat a bear."

Sven laughed. "Seasickness is what they call it. You had it pretty bad. Give me a minute to lash the wheel, and I'll help you out."

When Sven lashed the wheel, he made Fitch strip out of his vomit-encrusted clothes. Sven manned the pump and made Fitch hose himself off. Fitch cursed as he danced under the rush of cold seawater coming from the pump. Sven made him continue until he was thoroughly clean. Sven then made him hose the area of the deck and the railing where his vomit had splattered. Last, he made Fitch hose off the clothes he had been wearing. Fitch left the wet clothes on a line and went to his bag below to find dry stuff.

Sven then went below and returned with a tray of biscuits, cheese, and fruit, along with a jug of water. "Go slow on eating," he cautioned. "You haven't had anything solid in your stomach for a few days. I want to see you drink that whole jug of water, too. I'd start with the fruit."

Fitch took an apple and bit into it. He thought he had never tasted an apple as good as that one. When he finished it, he drank some water. When he felt the water in his mouth, he realized how thirsty he was. He drank more until Sven warned him to take it easy.

Escamil came up an hour later and laughed to see Fitch back to himself once more. "You were in rough shape, sonny," he cackled. "Glad you're back on your feet. Sven and I have been going four hours on and four hours off since we started. It'll be nice to have a third hand to share the watches."

Sven and Escamil taught Fitch the basics of how to steer and stay on course. When he asked what to do if the wind changed direction, they told him not to worry about anything else since they'd know in their sleep if the wind changed. They explained they had a little over a week left before they reached Auster—so far, the wind had been steady and the weather fair.

Sven told Fitch that while Fitch had been sick, he had shared with Escamil the real reason for him needing to get to Auster. Surprisingly, Escamil was fine with it. Sven commented that although Escamil wasn't much of a patriot, he had no love at all for the chancellor since the chancellor was responsible for the revenue cutters that made Escamil's life more difficult.

Three and a half days later, as Fitch was manning the wheel at night, the rhythm of the waves changed. The slow and steady rise and fall began to feel more like the sea was slapping the boat. Within a minute, Escamil and Sven were both on deck. Without any conversation, they began reefing the sail, reducing the amount of canvas exposed to the wind.

"If anything changes," Sven told Fitch, "we'll be back up. Just keep the wind on the bow like you have been, and everything will be fine."

A few hours later, Escamil took over from Fitch. In the morning, when Fitch came on deck, he noticed that the slapping of the waves had become a little more insistent. Sven was on the wheel.

"See those clouds," Sven pointed. "They're called mare's tails. Always a sign that weather is coming."

"Is it anything to worry about?" Fitch inquired.

"Not by itself," Sven replied. "If we see mackerel scales later, then we'll know."

"Mackerel scales?"

"Another type of cloud," Sven explained. "Mare's tails are a sign, the change in the rhythm of the waves is a sign, mackerel scales are a sign. Just the gods' ways of letting us know what's coming. Don't worry about it because you can't do a darned thing to stop it. We figured we'd get some weather on the trip."

6

As the day wore on, the high, wispy clouds that Sven had called mare's tails gave way to low-lying bands of clouds. Sven explained these were called mackerel scales and Fitch could see a slight resemblance. The waves were slapping the boat a little hard on the side, and the boat was rolling more in response.

At one point, Escamil dropped a chip attached to a line alongside. When he dropped the chip, he tilted a small hourglass. He watched it as the line played out. When the sand in the glass ran out, he grasped the line and pulled the chip back in, counting the knots in the line. When he saw Fitch looking at him with curiosity, he explained, "I just measured how fast we're sailing. Even with the sail reefed, we're scudding right along."

As the afternoon wore on, Escamil and Sven kept Fitch on the wheel. The wind was now coming directly from the west. Escamil and Sven began attaching lines to some stanchions near the helm and the mast. In the front of the boat, they both worked on something that looked like a large child's kite, about six feet tall. The frame of the contraption was made of iron. They slid the iron bars of the frame into the sleeves of a large piece of double-thick canvas. Then, they fastened the frame pieces together and joined them to two struts that crossed in the middle. Unlike a kite, where the fabric is drawn tight to the frame, on this, the canvas was loose and would form a deep pocket. They fastened lengths of chain to the corners. The chains ended at an iron ring. They attached the anchor cable to the iron ring. Finally, to one corner, they attached a number of floats.

When they finished, Sven came to tell Fitch what they'd been doing. "There's some bad weather coming—I'm sure even you have figured that out.

How bad it will be, I don't know. We've been making good progress and there's a good chance we'll outrun the worst of it. You can tell because the wind is now directly abeam."

"When do you think it will hit us?" Fitch asked.

"In the middle of the night," Sven replied, shaking his head with a grimace. "Figures. Anyway, we rigged these lines," he said, pointing to the lines attached to the stanchions, "to tie around our waists so we don't go overboard. That up there," again, he pointed, "is a sea anchor. If the blow gets real strong, we'll take in the sail and drop the sea anchor off the bow."

"What does it do?"

"It will keep us pointed into the sea," Sven replied. "That way, we won't get swamped by the waves catching us sideways. Some of the waves will likely be pretty steep, and, like as not, they'll be crashing over the bow. The three of us will stay up top, and we'll keep all the hatches battened down tight."

Fitch looked concerned. Sven noticed and chuckled. "Don't worry, Fitch. She's a damned sturdy boat. A couple of years ago, Escamil and I got caught in a typhoon, and she was completely underwater four times. All four times, she bobbed up like a cork and the only damage we took was when the mast broke off. When the storm was over, we went below, and she was dry as a bone. We'll have a bad night of it, for sure, and a rough tomorrow as well, but we'll make it through." Sven took his leave then, explaining that he needed to help Escamil make sure everything below was tied down tight.

When they finished below, they reefed the sail again. That evening, Escamil grilled fish they caught. He explained to Fitch that it was likely the last hot meal they'd have for a couple of days since a cooking fire would be impossible in heavy weather. He and Sven traded stories about the storms they'd been in, trying to help Fitch's confidence.

Escamil laid out for him what was likely to happen. "When it starts getting bad, we'll tie up to the lines. Sven and I will handle getting the sail down. All you have to do is make sure we're pointing into the wind. When we get the sail down, then we'll set the sea anchor. After that, just relax and let it blow out."

"Relax?" Fitch replied with a snort.

"A figure of speech," Sven answered with a grin. "If you can't relax, praying helps pass the time. If you aren't much for praying, cursing might make you feel better."

Fitch went below to try to get some rest while he could. It was no use, though, since the boat was rolling so sharply by now that he was tossed about. He gave up after an hour and went back to the deck, making sure to fasten the hatch behind him. Already, the sky had changed, and no stars were visible. The wind had picked up quite a lot. Sven went below and returned with oilcloth coats and hats for them. He instructed Fitch to tie the hat securely under his chin.

Escamil had questions for Fitch, asking him when Prince John had sailed for Auster, nearly shouting to make himself heard over the wind's roar. When Fitch counted back the days, Escamil thought for a moment and turned to Sven. "That was when we were homebound."

Sven nodded. "Rog came in two days later," he recounted. "Said there was a storm down south coming from the west that chased him back."

"Also mentioned he thought he saw three Skamorran corsairs heading south by east," Escamil added, "which he reckoned was peculiar. Corsairs ain't much for heavy weather. It was at quite a distance, though, and he wasn't entirely sure that's what they were. From what you've told me, now I'm guessing that they were corsairs for certain and that they were aiming to intercept Prince John. The timing's about right."

"I hate to say it, Ralph," Sven added, "but you might be on a fool's errand. If the storm got him, or the corsairs, or both, the Prince is likely dead."

"Maybe so," Fitch replied, "but I have to make sure anyway. Plus, it's not like I can go back to Boreas."

Escamil chuckled with black humor. "I reckon so. You're in worse shape than if you had knocked up some nobleman's pride and joy."

The seas grew rougher as the minutes passed, and the wind was strong enough that further conversation was impossible. The boat was pitching from side to side more steeply. Escamil turned the boat away from the storm, and the side-to-side motion was replaced by slow rises up and steep falls down. The three men tied themselves to the lines, reminding Fitch that if he had to move, he needed to hang onto something. Sven tied Fitch to the line nearest the wheel while Escamil and Sven tied themselves to the lines fastened amidships.

Rain came. At first it spat at them from behind, stinging when it hit bare skin. Before long, it began to come down more heavily. Within an hour, it was the worst downpour Fitch had ever experienced. The rain was cold and Fitch realized that without the oilcloth coat and hat he would be chilled to the marrow. Lightning flashed. The thunder could not be heard over the storm.

Escamil leaned in close to Fitch's ear. "I'm going to go about and stick us into the wind," he yelled. "Then you're going to take the wheel and keep us pointed that way. The wheel's going to buck and try to yank out of your hands, so hold on tight."

Escamil tapped Sven on the shoulder and pointed forward. When Escamil wrestled the wheel over, Sven was busy with the ropes controlling the boom of the sail. The boat turned broadside to the wind and waves, rolling steeply back and forth. Sven had braced himself against the base of the capstan around which the boom line was wrapped, fighting to make sure it had some purchase against the wind. All of a sudden, the violent side-to-side motion dropped off, replaced by pitching forward and back.

Escamil motioned for Fitch to grab the wheel. Fitch took the wheel as Escamil went forward. Escamil began lowering the sail quickly. When it was fully lowered, both men started furling it to the boom as fast as they could. When they finished, Escamil fastened a line to the boom to secure it and prevent it from swinging wildly.

Fitch was holding onto the wheel with his knuckles white from strain. As Escamil had warned him, the wheel was bucking and shuddering in his grasp, almost like a wild animal trying to get away. He watched as Sven and Escamil wrestled with the sea anchor, fighting against the wind, slipping and sliding. They struggled as the gale tried to rip it from their hands. They made it to the side of the boat and lowered it down.

After a few moments, while Sven and Escamil got out of the way, the anchor cable began to play out. Slowly at first, then with gathering speed. At a nod from Escamil, both men leaned against the brake lever, slowing the cable's progress. When they had it stopped, they quickly secured the capstan, locking it in place. Fitch felt the effects in the wheel as soon as they put the brake on. The wheel's violent jerks subsided.

Escamil headed back. Sven stopped to reconfigure the line holding the boom in place. Just as he finished, an enormous wall of water came over the bow of the ship. It hit Fitch like a giant fist. He realized he was underwater, his feet straight out behind him. Somehow, he managed to hang onto the wheel. When the water subsided, he could see Escamil with his arm wrapped around a stanchion. He could not see Sven.

Escamil skittered over to the side of the boat and grabbed the line that trailed overboard. Bracing his feet against the railing, Escamil hauled the line in hand over hand. A few seconds later, in a lightning flash, Fitch saw two hands grasping the railing as Sven pulled himself back aboard. The two stumbled and lurched back to Fitch. "Now's the time when praying might be comforting," Sven yelled in Fitch's ear, "or cursing."

Fitch hadn't been particularly religious since he was a boy but found himself mumbling the prayers that he remembered to the sea god. He made up new ones, too, as other waves came over the bow of the ship, submerging them and nearly washing them all overboard. The tempest pummeled them through what Fitch knew was the longest, most frightening, and most miserable night of his life.

Daybreak brought no relief except for being able to see the occasional huge wave that thundered down on the boat. It was roughly midday when Fitch noticed that the storm seemed slightly less violent than it had been. As the afternoon went on, it became clear to him that the worst was over. Just before twilight, Escamil and Sven went forward to inspect the mast. Over a dozen huge waves had submerged the boat during the worst of it, and they needed to make certain the mast was not damaged too much.

"It'll get us to Auster," Escamil stated, "but I'll need to replace it before we head home."

He went below and returned with apples, cheese, a skin of water and a skin of cider. The three of them ate and drank in silence. Fitch found his fingers were stiff from clutching the wheel all night. The rain tapered off and the wind dropped. After Escamil stowed the remnants of their meal, he explained to Fitch what they needed to do next.

"Right before dark, we're going to raise the sail again. You and Sven are going to haul the sea anchor in. When you get it aboard, you're going to sit on it so the wind doesn't take it. Sven will haul the sail up and then square the boom away while I bring us back on a southerly course. Sven will come, and you'll take the sea anchor apart and stow it. After that, we'll all get into some dry clothes."

Escamil and Sven unfurled the sail from the boom. Escamil came and took the wheel, and Fitch went forward. Sven made sure Fitch was holding onto the brake before he unblocked the capstan. Sven went to the bar opposite where Fitch was and nodded for him to release the brake. Sven staggered back two steps before Fitch was able to grab his bar and begin to push.

Slowly, they hauled the anchor cable in. When they had brought it close enough to the boat that the sea anchor lifted from the water, the capstan began to turn so easily that Fitch nearly fell on his face. When the iron ring reached the railing, Sven quickly blocked the capstan in place, and he and Fitch lifted the sea anchor onto the boat. The wind was much less than it had been when Sven and Escamil set it, so it was not nearly as much of a fight.

Following instructions, Fitch sat on the sea anchor. The wind was still strong enough that it wanted to pluck the wet canvas and toss it around. Sven trotted back and hoisted the sail, tied it off quickly, and unfastened the boom. On a nod from Escamil, he allowed the boom to swing out slightly as Escamil turned the wheel. The boat heeled over as the sail caught the wind. The waves were striking on the quarter of the boat now, giving it a corkscrew motion.

Sven returned to Fitch. He showed Fitch how to take the sea anchor apart. He opened the hatch and stowed the various pieces as Fitch unfastened them and handed them over. The canvas was the last. Sven just wadded it up and dropped it, explaining, "We'll have to dry this properly tomorrow before we stow it."

Escamil sent them below to don dry clothing, then gave Sven the wheel so he could do the same. Darkness fell, and shortly after, stars began to appear in the west. Escamil took the first watch. Fitch went below and fell asleep in an instant.

7

By the end of the next day, it was hard to believe the storm had ever occurred. The sea had settled down and the sky was blue, with occasional clouds. Escamil and Sven kept busy checking lines for damage and replacing a couple. Fitch commented that it was hard to believe they had lived through the gale.

Escamil laughed. "Well, now that you have, you're just an old sea dog, like Sven and me."

"I don't think so," Fitch replied. "I never prayed so hard in my life, and I'm lucky I didn't piss myself a couple of times."

"That was a bad one," Sven commented. "You were right to be scared. By the known hells, I was! By the way, Paul, thanks for hauling me in."

"I just didn't want to deal with your sister if I'd lost you," Paul joked. "She's got a temper."

Escamil explained to Fitch that the storm had likely blown them off-course to the east, and so they were now keeping a southwesterly heading. They'd continue to sail until they saw the coast and then figure out where they were. On the morning of the fourth day after the storm, Fitch could see a smudge on the horizon. He mentioned it to Sven when he came to take the wheel.

"That's land, sure enough," Sven agreed. "We'll have to get a bit closer before we can tell where we are."

"How will you know?" Fitch asked.

"We've sailed a fair part of the coast before," Sven explained, "and if we don't recognize it, we have charts that will help us identify it."

After mid-day, while Escamil had the wheel, he exclaimed, "Shoot! I know right where we are. Sven, see that headland?"

Sven squinted, then nodded his head in recognition. "Yup," he confirmed. "Hector Grimble's place is about five leagues west. Storm didn't blow us as far east as I thought."

After warning Sven what he was about to do, Escamil hauled the wheel over and began tacking into the wind. "We'll be in Chartage in about two days," Escamil informed Fitch. "It's not that far as the crow flies, but we're going upwind."

They sailed within sight of the coast for the next two days. That morning, Sven pointed out a smear of land ahead of them. "We're in what's called Sunit Bay—see how the land curves to the north? It's a fairly tall headland and Chartage is on the other side. Chartage is the main port for Auster, bigger than Varenna by about half."

They continued their slow progress. As they drew closer, Fitch could see that the headland Sven had pointed out was actually a steep set of cliffs of white rock. Above the cliffs was a gray smudge. He didn't know if that were normal so didn't mention it.

An hour later, on an inshore tack, Escamil said, "Do you smell smoke?"

Fitch hadn't noticed it before, but now that Escamil had brought it up, he could identify a faint tang of smoke. Sven looked forward towards the cliffs. The gray smudge was much more prominent now.

"What in the known hells is that?" he wondered.

They switched to an offshore tack and stayed on it to clear the headland. As they came nearer, the gray smudge grew larger. As they came close to rounding the headland, Escamil suggested that Sven should climb the mast to get a better look. Sven clambered up and looked out. A few minutes later, he shouted, "Immortal gods! Put about Paul! Now!"

Escamil waited for Sven to reach the deck and spun the wheel. "What is it?" he asked.

"Chartage Harbor is full of corsairs!" Sven blurted. "The whole damned city is on fire!"

With the wind at their back now, the little boat scudded right along. Sven kept an anxious watch behind in case a corsair had spotted them and was giving chase. While they sailed, they tried to puzzle out what was happening.

"The Skamorrans likely came over from Dalusia after the storm," Sven suggested, "so they haven't been here long. I'd guess they arrived just at first light. I'm surprised they'd do that. It means war with both Auster and Boreas since they have been allies for decades. They'd have to know that Boreas would honor our treaty obligations."

"Unless the king were dead," Fitch said glumly, "and Prince John was missing. Even if John is alive, he's likely in the capital by now, and he'll be cut off. He'd have to get through the damned Skamorran army to get back to Boreas. That damned bastard!"

"Who?" Escamil asked, "Prince John?"

"No, the chancellor, may all the gods curse him," Fitch spat. "He probably set this whole thing up with the Skamorrans. He arranged to have Prince John leave for Auster at a dangerous time of year to sail and maybe even had the Skamorrans tipped off to try to intercept him. Even if he makes it to Auster, he's out of the kingdom and out of contact for four or five months. Even if Auster manages to get word to Boreas that they are being attacked, the chancellor, who is now the head of the government, won't respond. Auster will be on their own, and I'm willing to bet the Skamorrans caught them completely by surprise."

"What do you want to do now?" Escamil asked Fitch. "You're the one who chartered this boat."

"You mentioned you know someone down the coast?" Fitch suggested.

"Yeah, Hector Grimble," Escamil confirmed.

"Is there a way from where he is to the capital?" Fitch queried.

"Pretty sure there is," Sven answered. "It won't be much—sort of like the goat track you took until you get to a main road. Hector is a … uh, a business associate of ours. He trades with some inland towns the way we do business with Hanville, Shawton, and Pergo."

"If it's all the same with you," Fitch suggested, "let's head there. I'll ask if they can give me a guide, and I'll head inland to get the word out about the Skamorrans. Damned Skamorrans will likely be slowed down a few days at Chartage, so maybe I can mobilize some resistance and get the word to the capital in time that they can pull together an adequate defense. Do you think your business associate will help?"

"Hector has pretty much the same feelings towards his government that I do," Escamil smiled. "But we both despise the Skamorrans. He probably hates them worse. His son-in-law was killed when he was attacked by corsairs."

At nightfall, Escamil suggested they drop anchor. They were close enough to Hector Grimble's little community that he worried they'd sail well past it in the night. Sure enough, when the sun rose and they set sail, they only had an hour before they reached the cluster of houses past the headland. Fitch went below and changed into his uniform. He explained to Sven and Escamil that he was now doing his duty and wouldn't feel right without it. His leather bag had straps and could be used as a pack. In it he had his purse and a change of uniform. His sword was strapped to his waist.

There was a small cove and they headed for it. They dropped anchor right in the middle. A group of people was watching them. A boat rowed out and the three men climbed over the side into the skiff. When they reached shore, a burly man with sandy hair was waiting. Escamil handled the introduction of Fitch, introducing him as a lieutenant in the Borean Palace Guard.

"What's someone like you doing here?" Hector wanted to know.

"It's a long story," Fitch replied, "and this isn't the time for it. We were heading for Chartage and saw massive amounts of smoke coming from the city and the harbor full of corsairs. I need a guide to lead me to the nearest towns so I can try to mobilize some sort of resistance and get word to the capital. It would help if the guide were known and his or her word was respected where we're going."

"I'll do it, Da," said a young woman standing behind Hector Grimble.

Fitch glanced at her. She was tall and slender, only a couple of inches shorter than he was. Her raven-black hair was tied behind her head and fell down her back. Her skin was tanned, and she had a dusting of freckles across the bridge of her nose. He noticed her eyes were hazel. *Immortal gods*, Fitch thought, *she's a beauty*. Fitch yanked his eyes away from her to look Hector in the eye. Hector thought for a moment, then nodded.

"I'll be right back," the girl told Fitch.

"That's my daughter, Mira," Hector stated. "If anything happens to her, I will skin you alive. Do you need anything before you set out?"

"A water skin," Fitch answered. "Do any of the towns nearby have a stable where I could get us horses? And what about an inn, further along? If there's no inn, we'll need bedrolls."

"Once you get up the path," Hector responded, "you'll be in the highlands—horse and cattle country. You won't have any problem getting a horse. Let Mira do the talking or you'll get fleeced. As a matter of fact, you'd best stay out of sight until she's done. You have money?"

"He does," Paul Escamil said, handing Fitch a purse. "I took enough out to pay for a new mast and to keep Sven and me for the winter, but I don't feel right keeping your money under the circumstances."

Fitch thought about protesting, but only briefly. "Thank you," he said gratefully.

Fitch took off the pack and stowed the purse inside. He unbelted his sword and lengthened the strap so he could fit the belt over one shoulder and have the sword hang down his back. As he was strapping the pack on again, someone handed him a skin of water.

"You and Mira should be able to get as far as Alica by nightfall," Hector said. "There's an inn. Again, let Mira do the talking. You'll have another day's ride before you reach the King's Road. There's a town there, Baust, with an inn. If the Skamorrans were leaving Chartage right now, you'd still reach Baust nearly a day ahead of them. Have Mira get a map in one of the towns you reach today. If you can get enough people together, there's a place on the King's Road before they reach Baust where you might be able to slow them down a bit. There's also a spot on the other side of Baust that might work. Beyond that—you'll need a good map."

Mira reappeared wearing leather moccasins, a blue skirt and a sleeveless tunic. She had a water skin and a small pack. Her father explained quickly what he had just told Fitch. Mira nodded in understanding and then started off at a jog. Fitch followed.

8

Shortly after they left the cluster of homes by the cove, the path started to climb. Fitch tried to keep pace with Mira but was finding it difficult. She seemed to glide effortlessly along the path, her hair swinging behind her. Fitch, on the other hand, seemed to find every occasional root or rock to stumble over.

"Mira," he said, in between breaths, "I'm going to slow you down. I'm sorry. I just spent the last two weeks on a boat, and before that, most of my exercise was horseback riding or with the swordmaster."

"Your wind sounds good," she replied, not turning her head. "As long as your wind isn't bad, you can keep up. You just need to focus on something other than the pain."

Easier said than done, Fitch thought. Focus … focus. Gods forgive him—he decided to focus on the wiggle of Mira's hips as she trotted ahead of him, the muscles flexing in her shapely legs and her hair swinging back and forth. He felt guilty because he didn't know her; in fact, had just met her and was staring at her backside. As they kept going though, he found that having something on which to concentrate did make it easier. He wasn't particularly short of breath, but his leg muscles were complaining about what he was doing. Focusing on Mira helped him ignore the pain.

The path kept swerving in a zig-zag pattern as they went up the side of the rise. Fitch stopped worrying about how long they would run or when they would reach the top and just kept pounding behind her. As he began to sweat, he loosened his tunic and used his sleeve to keep the sweat out of his eyes. Meanwhile, Mira kept trotting along at the same pace at which she began, showing no sign of effort other than occasionally wiping sweat from her brow or squeezing a quick drink from the water skin she carried. *At least the weather is cool,* he thought.

From what Fitch could tell, it was about an hour past midday, judging by his views of the sun through the leaves of the trees. He noticed they weren't climbing any longer and had been heading in the same direction for the last few minutes without turning. They came to a split in the path, and Mira headed right without hesitation. A little further, and they again went right at a split in the path. At the third split, they went left. Five minutes later, Mira held up her hand and slowed to a stop.

"Where's your purse?" she demanded, holding out her hand.

Fitch shrugged off his pack and dug through it to find the purse that Escamil had given to him. He handed it to Mira. She opened it, peered inside, and dug out some coins. "You don't have any Austerian?" she asked.

He shook his head no. She shrugged, then dug a couple more coins from the purse and handed it back. "Stay here. I'll be back in a little while. I'll whistle for you. In the meantime, stay on your feet and walk around. Don't let your legs seize up."

"Are you sure you have enough money?" he asked. The amount she had taken was less than half of what his horse Buckets had cost.

"If I took more, they'd try to overcharge me," she responded. "If I show them this is all I have, they'll take it. They're going to overcharge me as it is since the coins are Borean. I need tack for both mounts, and I'm in a hurry."

She trotted off again, leaving Fitch behind. He followed her advice, continuing to walk back and forth along the path. He could feel his leg muscles seizing up and realized he likely had a blister or two on his foot. Other than that, he felt better than he would have thought, based on how he felt shortly after they set off.

It took Mira long enough for Fitch to begin feeling impatience when he heard her whistle. He went down the path and found her sitting on a roan mare, holding the reins of a dapple-gray gelding. She had changed out of the skirt she had worn during the run to a similar-color blue pair of trousers. Her moccasins had been replaced by boots.

Fitch was pleasantly surprised at the horses. Based on the amount of money Mira had taken, he was expecting two broken-down nags. Both these horses looked healthy and sound. The closer he got, the more impressed he became. The saddle and the reins were also of a much better quality than he had expected.

Mira could tell he was impressed. She decided to rub it in. She held up two gold crowns, showing him. "I managed to keep these out of sight," she teased.

"Immortal gods, Mira," Fitch exclaimed. "You're amazing!"

"Yes, I am," Mira cracked.

"You keep them—finder's fee," Fitch told her. "Plus, then you'll have some money if we get separated later."

"You plan on deserting me later?" she asked, teasing him.

Not if I can help it, Fitch thought. *I think if I had my way, I'd never leave your side.* "No," he answered, "it's just, who knows what we'll find the further we go. Anything could happen, and I don't want you to be left in the lurch."

Mira enjoyed teasing Fitch. *Gods*, she thought, *he's handsome—much better looking than my late husband. And after only a brief complaint, he'd kept up with me the whole way, and I'd been trying to make him quit. If he can ride and fight,* she mused, *and has a sense of humor, I might have to try to make him stay in Auster.* She watched him check the girth and then admired the easy way he swung himself into the saddle.

She nudged her horse with her heels, and they set off through the field. They reached a broader path with wheel ruts, almost a road. Seeing the ease with which he rode and his confident posture, she smiled as she felt one of her questions was answered. She was interrupted from daydreaming when he asked her a question. She hadn't caught what he said.

"Pardon me?"

"What's his name?"

She chuckled. "Bob," she answered.

"Bob?"

"Yep, Bob," she confirmed. "Not the most imaginative. She's called Shasta," she said, gesturing at her mare.

"Sounds like more of a proper name for a horse," he stated.

A couple of miles down the road, they stopped to check the girths since their weight on the saddle might have loosened them a little. She noticed he was addressing Bob by name, murmuring to him, stroking him gently. She figured the lieutenant and his mount would have the beginnings of a relationship by nightfall. She had no worries about her mount. She'd ridden Shasta before on many occasions and had been dreaming that one day she'd be able to buy her. All of a sudden, this handsome stranger from Boreas showed up, and Shasta was hers.

On top of all that, he brought with him news of a crisis—the Skamorrans had invaded. Now, they were riding to raise the alarm and mobilize the countryside. And just last night, she had been complaining to her cousin about how boring her life was and promised to be. Her father was planning on arranging another marriage for her to one of the men in the next community down the coast. Worse, he was a fisherman, so even the small bit of excitement from Hector's illicit smuggling would be lacking. It would be a dull life of tending the vegetable plot, mending nets, and raising children. She counted herself lucky she hadn't already had children from her first marriage.

It did not take long for them to reach the first community, called Dostin. Fitch noted to himself that it was smaller than Hanville but larger than Simpson back in Boreas. Mira rode straight to a home near the center of the gathering of houses along the road. She dismounted, went to the door, and knocked. An older woman answered.

"Good afternoon, Ma Petten," Mira greeted her rather formally. "Is Pa Petten home? We have important news."

"I'll get him."

An older man came outside. Mira continued with her formal tone. "Good afternoon, Pa Petten. We have important news," she said.

"Who is this?" he asked.

"This is Lieutenant Fitch of the Borean Palace Guard. He was sailing to Chartage on an important matter of state. Would you like to speak with him?"

The old man nodded. Fitch dismounted and crossed to him. "Good afternoon, Pa Petten. Lieutenant Fitch," he said, introducing himself.

The man nodded, indicating Fitch should continue with his news. "Yesterday, when we pulled within sight of Chartage, we saw plumes of smoke rising from the city. As soon as we caught a glimpse of Chartage Harbor, we saw it was full of Skamorran corsairs. We reckon they left Dalusia as soon as the recent storm passed, which means they'd likely just landed in Chartage that morning. Miss Grimble and I are riding to raise the alarm and mobilize the countryside. We hope to gather as many soldiers as we can at Baust the morning after tomorrow. Do you think you can help us?"

"Immortal gods, son! Skamorrans, you say! Damn me!" the old man said agitatedly. "Yes, yes, I'll get the word out. Tomorrow morning next, at Baust? Daybreak?"

"Yes, sir," Fitch replied.

"Consider it done. You and Mira go spread the word," he said, making a shooing motion with his hands before turning back into the house.

Mira nodded at Fitch, and he mounted Bob. They rode away. As they were leaving town, they heard a bell begin to ring.

"The bell is in the cupola of his barn," Mira explained, "that's the signal for everyone to gather."

"How many will come from Dostin?" Fitch asked.

"About two dozen, all mounted," Mire responded. "Mostly archers. You did well with him. Only two small mistakes, which you wouldn't have known, being Borean."

"What did I say wrong?"

"You called me Miss Grimble," she answered. "That would imply that you and I are betrothed. You should have called me Mira Grimble—using both my first and last name. That implies we are only acquaintances and is the more proper address."

"And the other?"

"You called him 'sir' instead of Pa," she explained. "The word 'sir' is reserved for members of the nobility. He's not. He's the head man for Dostin, so 'Pa' is the proper address."

They reached the next town two hours later. This was larger, about the size of Hanville and was named Tarpot. Here, Mira rode to a large building on a central square in the village center. She indicated that Fitch should dismount and follow her into the building. She crossed to a woman at a desk.

"Mira Grimble to see Ma Ratledge on an urgent matter," Mira stated.

The woman looked past Mira to Fitch. She nodded and got up from her chair, knocked on the door behind her, and went in. Moments later, she returned. "Go on in," she said.

Waiting behind another desk was a white-haired woman. Mira crossed to in front of the desk, making a subtle hand gesture to Fitch that he should accompany her. "Ma Ratledge," Mira began, "we have important news. This is Lieutenant Fitch of the Borean Palace Guard."

"Ma, I was sent to Auster on important state business even though it was past the sailing season," Fitch stated. "Yesterday morning, when we neared Chartage, we saw smoke rising from the city. When we rounded the headland, we could see Chartage Harbor, which was full of Skamorran corsairs. My captain believes they embarked from Dalusia as soon as the recent storm passed, putting their arrival in Chartage shortly before we saw them. My captain sailed down the coast to the nearest safe harbor, which is where Mira's father is. Mira Grimble volunteered to be my guide so I could raise the alarm and mobilize the countryside. We hope to gather as many soldiers as possible at Baust by the morning after tomorrow. Will you please help us?"

By now, Ma Ratledge had already risen and was moving to the door. "Gods, yes, Lieutenant," she replied. Opening the door, she told the woman at the desk to ring the bell. The woman moved quickly to the stairs. "Mira, thank you for helping this young man," Ratledge said. "Lieutenant, as many as we can muster will be at Baust tomorrow morning next, at daybreak, I assume?"

"Yes, Ma," Fitch replied.

"Some excitement for you at last, eh Mira?" Ratledge said. "Now go on. You've still got hours to go to reach Alica."

Fitch followed Mira out of the building. The bell was already ringing before they got outside. They mounted and headed down towards Alica. The path had now become a dirt road, wide enough for two wagons most of the way.

"Any mistakes?" Fitch asked.

"Nope," Mira replied.

"Some excitement at last?" Fitch queried.

"Ma Ratledge is like an auntie," Mira explained. "She's my father's cousin, not an aunt, but she's always had an interest in me, and she's always been someone I could talk to about anything. I suppose you think it's silly, but growing up in such a small community wasn't very exciting. The prospects aren't much better up here in the Highlands or further down the coast. My father married me to a sailor before. He was killed by Skamorrans not long after. Now, he wants me to marry a fisherman. If I do, I'll be trapped in a life of dullness. It's probably a life that would satisfy most, but it horrifies me."

"Believe it or not," Fitch responded, "I understand. I'm the son of a farmer. It's not a bad life—my father and mother both seemed quite happy. It just wasn't for me. If I'd stayed, I'd eventually inherit the farm, and my younger brother would have ended up apprenticed to some tradesman. My younger brother loved farming, and I didn't. First chance I could, I ran away to town and joined the army."

"What did your father say?"

"He hasn't said anything to me," Fitch replied, shrugging his shoulders. "I wrote and tried to explain. About a year later, I got a letter from my brother. He thanked me and told me that father was so furious with me that he refused to allow my name to be mentioned in the house. Mother spent nights and nights crying."

"That's awful!"

"I feel bad for my mother," Fitch admitted. "I would never have wanted to make her unhappy. My father was just stubborn—is still stubborn. I write to my brother every so often, and he reads my letters to my mother when my father isn't around. I apologized to her for causing any unhappiness and she's forgiven me. She and my brother are secretly happy for me, since up to now I've had a promising career."

"What's a promising career for a Borean soldier?" Mira inquired.

"After I joined, I went through training and spent a couple of years patrolling our northern border, keeping the northmen from raiding. It was a hard life but no harder than being a farmer, and certainly not as predictable or boring. I was promoted to corporal and applied to join the Wardens. The Wardens are more of an elite unit. They patrol the border with Skamorra and man the forts in the passes."

"Sounds dangerous."

"It was," Fitch confirmed. "When I joined the Wardens, I had to give up my promotion and start all over as a trooper. I didn't mind. I served in Prince John's unit, at least, until he returned to 'official' life, so I spent six years under him. Two years later, he recommended me for the Palace Guard, so I transferred again."

"So, you started over again as a trooper," Mira commented, "and now you're a Lieutenant?"

Fitch chuckled. "I guess I'm not very smart about these transfers. I was a captain in the Wardens. I was promoted when I took over command of Prince John's unit. When I moved to the Palace Guard, I had to drop down to lieutenant. The pay is the same, though."

"Who is the captain of the Guard?" Mira asked.

"There hasn't been one for a few years," Fitch explained. "Stan—Lieutenant Barthlemy, who is my best friend—he and I were competing to be the next captain."

"Didn't that bother you? Having to compete against your friend for the same post?"

"A fair amount at first," Fitch admitted. "It bothered both of us. One day, I realized that I hadn't spoken to him for nearly two weeks, except for what duty required. We went out that night and got so drunk we ended up beating the stuffing out of each other. The next morning at roll call, King Philip happened to come by and saw we were all battered and bruised, plus being hung over. The King had also served in the Wardens back when his father was still alive and knew us from then, and knew about our situation. Anyway, King Philip called us aside after roll call and asked us if we'd gotten it out of our systems and whether we'd figured out who the better man was. We assured him we'd gotten it out of our systems. He asked us again who the better man was. 'He is,' we told him, pointing at each other."

Mira laughed. When she recovered, she asked, "Isn't life at the Palace boring compared with the Wardens?"

"Compared with the Wardens, just about anything is boring," Fitch confirmed, "but it's not dull. We accompany the King or Queen or Prince John when they appear at official functions. We're their bodyguards. There have been some exciting things that have happened. I get to train a lot—my swordsmanship has gotten pretty good, with all modesty. The best benefits are that I get to sleep in a bed every night with a roof over my head instead of on a cot or on the ground, get hot meals, and get to bathe daily."

9

It took time for John's wound to heal. Caleb had explained that whatever had hit John had fractured his skull bone and likely bruised the brain underneath. John had a difficult time grasping the idea that his brain could be bruised like a muscle. Caleb said that he hoped that John's memory would return as the bruise healed.

Another storm came through. They suffered two days and a night of torrential rain and howling wind. After it passed, John helped the people of the little village pick up the many branches that had fallen from the trees. A handful of trees had been uprooted and blown over, and some of the men were cutting and splitting them. They explained that two of the trees would be used for lumber, but the others would be chopped up for fuel. John attempted to help, but strenuous labor still made his head hurt.

Phoebe and Caleb were gracious hosts and asked nothing of John other than that he continue to heal from his injuries. John felt guilty about not being able to help, but they assured him that his time would come. Cia took John on walks, gradually increasing in length as his head healed. She did not rejoin him in bed.

John had additional flashes of his memory. After being shown his sword, he knew that being dunked in seawater would damage it. The scabbard, fine though it may have been, was ruined. The blade was already showing rust. He asked Caleb for a whetstone, some oil, and a piece of cloth. On his daily walks with Cia, he kept his eyes open for other less abrasive stones he could use to remove the rust and polish the blade.

Sitting and working the stones over the sword, slowly removing the rust, brought back glimpses of memory of other times he had cleaned and polished this same sword. Many of these were of him sitting outside on some sort of low stool, surrounded by roughly dressed men. Other glimpses were in an indoor setting. It took a full day before John was satisfied that he had cleaned and polished the sword thoroughly. He gave it a light coating of oil before wrapping it in rags.

There were times when John sat, holding his sword and touching the clothing he had been wearing when he washed ashore. He was hoping that would stir other memories. The harder he tried to think about it, the more frustrated he became since the memories came when they came, and he didn't seem able to force the process. When the typhoon rolled through, he remembered some strange images of himself on a ship in a similar storm. They were like pictures of an instant, lit by a flash of lightning, and were disjointed and jumbled.

Phoebe explained to him that the clothing he had been wearing was of extremely high quality and very expensive, even though they were ruined with smears of tar. She told him that the clothes indicated he had been a man of some wealth and likely importance. It meant nothing to him. He commented that, since the sword felt so comfortable in his hands, perhaps the fine clothes merely indicated that he was a successful bandit who waylaid travelers on the highways.

Caleb, Phoebe, and Cia left him alone for several days. It was harvest time for certain vegetables and fruits, and the little village emptied as everyone went to help gather them in. As Caleb had explained, everyone pitched in when someone needed help. The harvest benefited everyone, so of course they all helped bring it in. No one person had to work too hard, but everyone needed to do something. There was plenty for all. They had no money. When you needed something from someone, you asked. Depending on what it was, they might simply give it to you or ask for your help with a task in return.

John stayed behind because he was not capable of much physical exertion. If he walked too far, his head started to hurt. It bothered him that he was unable to help.

Caleb had explained that it often took newcomers to the island a bit of time to adjust—that many, when they first arrived, tried to take advantage of the generosity of their fellow castaways. He mentioned that it typically didn't last too long. Since no one was greedy, selfish or entirely lazy, acting that way stood out and most abandoned that behavior of their own accord. There had been a few, he said, who had stubbornly refused to contribute, in which case they were denied access to the supplies the rest of them shared. Eventually, they wised up.

In some ways it was like a mythical paradise. The weather was generally pleasant. It rained regularly but not for long, except when the typhoons came through. The days were warm and the evenings were cool.

Day by day, John felt better. When the harvest and haying were finished, Cia took him on longer walks out in the countryside. Since the time she had cleaned his wound, there had been no further physical intimacy between them, other than Cia clasping his hand once they had left Town on their walks. She took him to the beach so he could see how the men fished. They had built skiffs, and they rowed out and cast nets from them. It rarely took them long to finish. She showed him the vegetable gardens outside of Town, which they all worked on.

It was peaceful and pleasant. Yet, as the days passed, John became convinced there was something he was supposed to be doing that didn't involve anything on the island. He began to feel as though he was failing in his duty, though he had no idea what his duties were wherever he had come from. He also began to agree with Cia that island life was dull. Each day was similar to the day before. Caleb had explained that it was generally like this, except now during the season of typhoons.

Though the weather was generally pleasant, about every ten days or so a storm would roll through. The storms would last for two, sometimes three, days, with torrential rain and howling wind. John asked if these were typhoons. Caleb told him that they were but not the full extent, just fringes of one that passed. John asked what it would be like if one hit the island. Caleb grimaced.

"I hope we don't find out anytime soon. The last one knocked houses down."

During the storms, the only thing to do was to stay inside and wait it out. Caleb and Phoebe had a couple of books that John would read until he developed a headache. He was able to last longer every day, which he felt was a good sign. The third book he picked up began to seem familiar to him. He didn't remember ever reading it, but he knew every plot twist in advance. Of course, the more he tried to think of how he knew this, the further the knowledge seemed to recede.

One day, John had the sudden impulse to grab his sword and go outside. He found himself stepping through a slow-paced movement drill. When he tried to think about what he was doing, he would falter and forget, needing to start over again. When he didn't think about it, the movements flowed one into another. He felt the creak of unused muscles as he stepped through the drill. Cia came outside to see what he was doing, and he faltered and stopped.

"Please," she requested, "keep going. You're very graceful."

John smiled ruefully. "Thank you. I don't think I can do it with an audience, though."

"Why not?"

"Well, if I think about it while I'm doing it, I don't know what to do next," he explained. "If I don't think—sort of like the opposite of concentration—then my body remembers the movements. I'm guessing this is something I did many, many times, though right now my body is complaining that I've stretched things that haven't been stretched in too long."

"You were moving so slowly," she commented. "I thought sword fighting would be fast and violent."

"I suppose it is," he shrugged. "This drill is for footwork and control."

As he told her this, a memory flashed into his mind. "We do this to develop our balance and learn to control every muscle in the body," he remembered someone telling him. "When you are in a fight, your body needs to remember these movements without thinking. This ability gives you a powerful advantage over someone who can't."

"John?"

He looked at her, his reverie broken.

"You just remembered something, didn't you?" she asked.

"Um, yes, I did."

10

It was twilight when Fitch and Mira reached Alica. Mira went immediately to a large house facing the town square. She knocked on the door, asking for Sir Gerald. When Sir Gerald arrived, she introduced Fitch who explained what he had seen.

"I'll not ring the bell at this hour," Sir Gerald told them. "I don't want anyone riding in the dark here and then home. Better first thing in the morning. May I ask you to delay your departure until after you've had a chance to share what you saw with everyone? You should still be able to reach Baust before nightfall."

Fitch and Mira agreed. She then led Fitch to the inn. They went behind to the stables. She handed Shasta to the inn's groom. Fitch wanted to groom Bob himself. "I'll get us rooms then," she said.

Fitch asked the groom if he would have the two horses ready at first light and then busied himself grooming his horse. Bob appreciated the attention. Fitch had never minded grooming his horses and felt it was important in establishing the bond between horse and rider. He was just finishing when Mira returned.

"I have good news, better news, and some news you might not like," she announced. "The good news is that they have a room for us. The better news is that they will draw us a hot bath and will also wash our clothes. The last news is that they have only one room, with one bed."

Fitch's legs were still and sore from the run in the morning and then riding. A hot bath sounded perfect. Washing the sweat and dirt from his uniform sounded good, as did the opportunity to wash the salt crust off his skin that he'd gathered during his two weeks on the ocean. Sharing a bed with Mira troubled him as he remembered her father's threat to skin him alive if anything happened to her. In addition to her outward beauty, she had shown she possessed a quick and clever mind, a wicked sense of humor, and carried herself with a natural grace and poise beyond her years.

"That sounds great," he responded, "except for the one bed part. I'll take the floor, then."

"Suit yourself," she said with a saucy smirk. "When you're finished, there's dinner."

"I'm finished now," he told her, putting the brushes away.

He asked the groom to make sure Bob had food and water, then followed Mira inside. The common room of the inn was full. Mira found them a seat in the corner at a small table. A serving girl came and asked if they wanted dinner and something to drink. They both agreed to dinner. As far as drink, Fitch asked Mira.

"Which is better here at this time of year? Ale or cider?"

"We're not much for cider in Auster," Mira smiled. "Must be a Borean thing. The ale at this time of year is marvelous, though."

Within minutes, the girl returned with two plates and two large mugs. Dinner was a slice of roast beef with potatoes and a green vegetable that was unknown to Fitch. He took a sip of the ale while he waited for Mira to begin eating. The ale was as good as Mira had indicated.

Mira made no move to begin eating. Fitch, hungry as he was, waited for her. After a few minutes, he asked her if she were hungry.

"I'm starving," she replied.

"So am I," he echoed.

"Then why aren't you eating?" she asked.

"Because I'm waiting for you," he answered. "In Boreas, it's good manners to wait to eat until after the ladies at the table have begun."

She laughed. "In our family, we wait for Da to start eating. I don't think he has any manners."

"Please begin," Fitch asked.

When Mira picked up her knife and fork and began to eat, Fitch then followed suit. The meat was tender and juicy. It was the first thing he'd eaten in two weeks that wasn't fish, cheese, or an apple. He relished every bite.

"That meat," Mira said, "probably walked into town this morning. Cattle are being collected to drive for sale. That's why there was only one room. Some of the ranch hands are spending the night."

"We'll have to tell them to take the cattle back in the morning," Fitch suggested. "We don't want to make it easy for the Skamorrans to forage for food along their way."

Mira nodded in agreement. A few minutes later, she looked up with a twinkle in her eye. "So, you think I'm a lady, then?"

Fitch's handsome face flushed. "Hm," he cleared his throat. "Yes, you are," he said quietly.

Mira grinned in response, then let out a loud belch. Fitch started to laugh hard. Mira joined him.

As they were finishing the last of their dinner, the innkeeper entered. Spotting Mira, he came over. "The bath is ready in your room," he said. "Just leave your clothes outside the door, and we'll give them a quick wash and dry them overnight. They'll be outside your door by sunup."

Fitch and Mira finished and went up to the room. Fitch's legs ached and he was looking forward to soaking them in a tub of hot water. While Fitch was closing the door, Mira cautioned him, "Don't turn around."

He heard the faint sound of her feet stepping into the tub. "I'm going first, by the way," she stated. "You just spent two weeks on a boat, and you'll get the water all salty and dirty."

Fitch heard her settling into the tub. He glanced over and was relieved to see her back was to him. He sat facing away from the tub. He heard her go underwater and then come back up. A minute later, he could hear her stand. Despite the very great temptation, he kept his back to her.

"It's okay," she announced, "I'm decent."

Fitch turned slowly. Mira was wrapped in a towel. She smiled at him. "Your turn," she said.

"Fine," he replied, "turn around."

"Spoilsport," she muttered, but turned around.

Fitch quickly stripped. As he stepped gingerly into the tub, he noticed Mira had swiveled back and was examining his naked form. He blushed. She winked. As he eased himself into the hot water, it felt heavenly on his aching legs.

"By the fourteen major gods and all the minor ones," he sighed, "this feels wonderful."

Mira stepped past him, now wearing a linen shift. She gathered up his clothes along with her own and left them outside the door. She sat on a stool close by looking at him. Fitch was busy washing the salt and grime of two weeks off his body. He slid down and dunked his head under the water, scrubbing his scalp vigorously. When he finished cleaning himself, he stayed in the water, enjoying how the heat was affecting his legs.

When he noticed the tips of his fingers wrinkling, he warned, "I'm going to get up now."

Mira was sitting with her chin in her hand, looking at him. "Okay," she replied.

"Turn around, please, young lady," Fitch said with mock sternness.

"Why? I've already seen everything you have to offer," she teased, "and I've enjoyed the view."

Fitch shook his head, stood, and quickly dried his upper body, then wrapped himself in a towel. Fitch quickly found a pair of underclothes and slipped them on under the towel. He then whipped the towel off, and began to dry his hair.

"I wish I had a razor," he commented.

"Why?"

"I never like the look of a beard on myself," Fitch replied. "Plus, I want to touch it all the time. It's irritating."

"I don't have a razor, but my knife is sharp enough," Mira said. "I'll shave you."

"You don't have to," Fitch protested. "I can do it myself."

"I want to," Mira said. "It's fascinating."

She made Fitch wet his face again, then come sit on the stool by the candle. Mira knelt between his legs and began scraping the whiskers from his face. Fitch was acutely aware of how close she was. He could feel her breath on his face. It was all he could do to keep from grabbing Mira and kissing her.

When she finished, Mira stretched out on the bed. Fitch stayed on the stool, pulled some things out of his pack, and began cleaning and oiling his sword. She watched him for a bit.

"Lieutenant," she commented, "you were right. You do look much better without a beard."

"Thank you."

"Lieutenant, what was the 'mission of state' that was so important that you sailed during the typhoon season?"

"My first name is Ralph, thank you very much," he teased, "not lieutenant. Besides, I'm probably not even a lieutenant any longer."

"Why not?" she inquired.

Fitch told her the whole story—the assassination of the King, his suspicion (and Stan Barthlemy's) that the chancellor was behind it, and the plan he and Stan had concocted on short notice to try to find Prince John. He told her of his extraordinary luck in finding Sven Gunnar and, through him, Paul Escamil. He told her about being seasick, then the storm and how scared he had been. He summed it up by mentioning what they saw at Chartage.

"So, you're looking for Prince John, and if he made it to Auster, he's likely at the Palace in Austeria, the capital. If he made it, there would likely be Skamorran assassins looking for him and you're going to try to warn him and protect him. If he didn't make it, if he was caught by the storm or by the corsairs, or if he's already been killed, what will you do?"

"I'll keep looking until I'm convinced he's dead or I run out of money," Fitch answered. "Even if I run out of money, I'll try to keep looking somehow. I didn't think about it at the time Stan and I came up with our crazy idea, but I can't go back to Boreas without the prince. I sentenced myself to exile."

"There are worse places to be than Auster," she advised.

"I know," Fitch admitted. "Speaking of which, from the towns we've been through and the ones we'll visit tomorrow, what sort of forces are we likely to gather?"

"Between six and seven hundred, I think," Mira estimated, "all mounted, mostly archers. About a hundred lancers, and most of those will likely come from Baust. After Baust, as we head towards Austeria, it will be more lancers and a few cataphracts."

"What's a cataphract?" Fitch asked, "I've never heard of such a thing."

"Cataphracts are heavily armored cavalry," Mira explained. "They use great lances, bows, and a variety of personal weapons."

"Great gods!" Fitch exclaimed. "How many?"

"In the whole kingdom, around fifteen hundred, I think. Sir Gerald is a cataphract. They're usually held in reserve to fight on the plains outside the capital," she told him. "We have a saying in Auster, 'It's down to the cataphracts.' That means we're out of other options. How many Skamorrans are there, do you think?"

"Sven only got the quickest look at Chartage Harbor," Fitch said. "He said he guessed there were around a hundred and fifty corsairs—maybe as many as two hundred. I don't know how many men they can pack into a ship that size. All I know is that a corsair is a lot smaller than the galleons that Auster and Boreas use for trade, and smaller than our war galleys as well. Paul Escamil or Sven would know. Speaking of which, why weren't Auster's war galleys able to defend Chartage?"

"I have no idea," Mira replied.

"That's a good question to ask when we reach the capital," Fitch commented. "Anyway, the Skamorrans likely won't have much cavalry except for mounts they capture. I'm going to guess they will have between six and ten thousand men—enough that they can take and hold Chartage, then bring more soldiers over."

"Yet you think they will march on Austeria?"

"I think they'll march until they meet organized resistance," Fitch advised. "If Auster is able to gather its defenses, the Skamorrans will likely turn around and sit tight in Chartage until their reinforcements arrive. As for this group, if Auster isn't able to oppose them in any meaningful way, they'll continue to the capital and possibly stage an attack. They don't have the numbers to be successful unless they catch the capital by surprise but they will cause enough commotion to set Auster back on its heels and give Skamorra more time to reinforce. Speaking of all this, I need a bow."

"I will too," Mira agreed. "Baust is going to be the best place. We can ask Sir Gerald tomorrow morning also."

"You can shoot?"

"Having fish for dinner every night gets a little tiresome," Mira joked. "Yes, I can shoot."

Fitch had finished cleaning his sword. He sheathed it in the scabbard and returned the stone, rag, and oil he had been using into a pouch he put back in his bag. He slapped his hands together and stood.

"Please hand me a pillow and a blanket," he said.

"What?"

"If I'm going to sleep on the floor, I'd at least like a pillow and a blanket," Fitch stated.

Mira rolled her eyes. "You're not sleeping on the floor, Ralph."

Mira rolled to the right. She lifted the covers and slid underneath. She patted the empty space on the left.

"Are you sure?" he asked. "Your father swore he'd skin me alive if anything happened to you."

"I'd be totally worth it," she joked. "Don't worry. I'll behave."

She waited for Fitch to lie down. "I think I like you, Ralph. I think you like me. And when I say 'like,' I mean in the way men and women like each other. I've been flirting with you, and you've been flirting back, but only a little. I wouldn't mind if you flirted harder. We're going to be sharing a bed tonight and even though I won't let anything happen, that doesn't mean I'm ruling it out in the future."

Ralph was stunned at her candor. His mouth opened and closed a couple of times as he thought about replying. Finally, he said, "You are just about the most direct woman I've ever met in my life, Mira. I mean that as a compliment."

She smiled.

11

They were awakened the next morning by the bell ringing from across the square. Fitch noticed that Mira had snuggled up to him in the night and had thrown her arm over his chest. "Sir Gerald is a man of his word," Fitch commented, rolling out of bed. He went to the door of the room and opened it. "So is the innkeeper."

Their clothing had been washed, dried, and folded neatly. Fitch handed Mira her tunic and skirt. He took his clothes and faced the corner, slipping them on quickly. He sat in the chair to pull on his boots. Thankfully, Mira had dressed quickly. They gathered their packs, checked the room to make sure nothing was left behind, and headed downstairs.

Breakfast was already being served. They ate quickly. Fitch gave Mira some money to pay the innkeeper. He went back to the stables to collect Shasta and Bob. They were saddled and ready, tied up and waiting for him. Fitch thanked the groom and asked if he had any treats for horses. The groom offered him carrots. Fitch gave the groom a couple of coppers, then fed each horse a carrot.

He led the horses to the front of the inn where Mira was waiting. They crossed the square on foot, tying their mounts to the rail in front of what appeared to be the town hall. Sir Gerald was waiting for them.

"Thank you, Sir Gerald," Fitch said. "We heard the bell."

"There are a handful here already," Sir Gerald responded. "We must give it some time for the rest."

"I would imagine it takes some people a little while to drop what they are doing to get here," Fitch replied with a smile.

"Only about half our troopers will actually show up," Sir Gerald explained. "The other half will soon get word from their neighbors."

"How many will Alica provide?"

"Nearly a hundred," Sir Gerald replied. "A handful of lancers, mostly archers and one cataphract."

"Mira told me you are a cataphract," Fitch said. Seeing the twitch of Sir Gerald's eyebrow, Fitch realized he likely had erred by referring to Mira by her first name only. "I apologize, Sir, and I apologize Mira Grimble," he said quickly, turning to her. "I am Borean, and customs are different. I did not mean to imply anything by such casual address."

"I understand, Lieutenant Fitch," Sir Gerald responded.

"I would like to ask you, sir, if it's possible," Fitch began, "it occurs to me that a bow would be useful for both me and Mira Grimble. I was planning on buying one when we reach Baust but Mira Grimble suggested you might be able to help in this regard."

"Indeed, I can," Sir Gerald answered, "and provide you with a better weapon than any you could buy in Baust. It would be my pleasure to give you the means to kill some Skamorrans. Now, if you'll excuse me, I must greet my people."

During the brief conversation, eight more men and women had arrived. Sir Gerald went off to speak with them. Fitch turned to Mira with a sheepish expression.

"What does it mean, here in Auster, when I use only your first name?"

"That we are family," Mira giggled, "or long-time friends. Since Sir Gerald knows we are not otherwise related and only met yesterday, the only likely family relation we could have would be husband and wife. That's a bit quick, even for me."

Fitch slapped himself in the forehead. "I'm sorry."

"Just wait until Sir Gerald learns we shared a bed last night," Mira teased, "and he will learn—since nothing happens in Alica that he doesn't know about, sooner or later."

"All the known hells," Fitch muttered. "I'll be skinned alive."

Sir Gerald called them over. People had been arriving in ones and twos. There were about four dozen gathered. Sir Gerald introduced Fitch and Fitch told the people what he knew. There were gasps of surprise and mutters of anger. Fitch concluded by telling them that he would like them to be at Baust, armed and ready, by first light tomorrow.

One person asked how many soldiers they would face. Fitch replied that he guessed there were no more than ten thousand and likely as few as six thousand. "With Mira Grimble as my guide," Fitch stated, "we began raising the alarm in Dostin yesterday. Mira Grimble estimates we will likely gather about six hundred mounted soldiers. That will not be enough to stop them, but it will be plenty to slow them down and harass them. When we reach Baust, we will also send riders along the King's Road to raise the alarm all the way to Austeria. The further the Skamorrans travel past Baust, the greater our numbers will be."

The meeting broke up shortly after that. Sir Gerald asked everyone to spread the word to absent neighbors and to gather in the square at midday, prepared to spend at least a couple of weeks on the road. He also asked everyone to have family members drive their livestock to more distant pastures. As people left, there was an excited buzz from them.

"Right," Sir Gerald said to Mira and Fitch, "bows. Arrows with bodkin points. Quivers. Come with me."

They followed Sir Gerald to his house. He led them through to a room in the back. When they entered, they saw it was his armory. A Sir Gerald-size suit of mail, along with a metal helmet, stood on a rack. There was a rack of swords of different lengths, widths, and styles. There were a half-dozen bows. "Take your pick," Sir Gerald said expansively, waving at them.

Fitch looked the bows over. He picked one, strung it, and tested the draw. He unstrung it and put it back, choosing another. He strung the second one, tested the draw, and nodded. He unstrung it and looked at Sir Gerald, who pointed at a couple of leather tubes leaning in the corner. Fitch took one and slid the bow inside. Mira also took a bow, strung it, and tested it. She didn't like it, so she unstrung it and put it back. She tried two more before finding one she liked. She, too, took a leather tube. In the meantime, Fitch had found two quivers and was filling them with arrows stored in a small barrel. Mira then did the same. It took them less than ten minutes.

"Much obliged, Sir Gerald," Fitch said appreciatively, offering to shake hands.

"My pleasure," Sir Gerald replied, clasping his hand. "I'll see you tomorrow."

Mira and Fitch rode off. They visited two other towns and spread the news, riding away to the sound of the alarm bells ringing. When they reached Baust, they found the town buzzing with activity. They called on Dame Kapiste, a tall, slender black woman.

"Please make this quick," Kapiste urged, "I'm up to my armpits in alligators."

"We come bringing news of the Skamorran invasion of Chartage," Mira said, "but it looks as though you heard already."

"Yes," Kapiste confirmed. "A rider pulled in a couple of hours ago. Now, if you'll excuse me…"

"We've ridden up from the coast, starting at Dostin," Mira blurted, "spreading the alarm. We're expecting five hundred or more at first light tomorrow."

That caught Kapiste's attention. "Thank the fourteen major gods and all the minor ones! I haven't even sent riders back that way yet, just up the King's Road. That is welcome news."

"This is Lieutenant Fitch from Boreas, a member of their Palace Guard, who also served as an officer in their Wardens guarding their border with Skamorra," Mira added. "He is the one who brought us the news."

"Excellent," Kapiste commented. "Come."

She walked over to a table covered with maps, gesturing for Fitch to stand beside her. "Here is Baust," she pointed. "The Kings Road … Chartage is this way. Based on what the rider was able to tell us, the Skamorrans set up camp for the night five miles away in the village of Guter. They should reach us by mid-morning tomorrow at the latest, sooner if they double-time."

"They'll likely move at double-time," Fitch advised, "speed is their ally."

"I agree. They made it to Guter by double-timing. They'll be coming out of the forest before eight o'clock then," Kapiste mused.

"How many are there?"

"The dispatch rider told us there were a hundred and eighty corsairs in Chartage Harbor. Our best guess is that each ship could hold forty to fifty soldiers, so we're looking at between seven and nine thousand total, less however many they leave to hold Chartage."

"What is this marking here, east of the King's Road?" Fitch asked.

"A slight swale," Kapiste replied. "In the rainy season, it provides drainage but right now it's still dry. It's about a hundred and fifty yards from the road."

"And here to the west," Fitch pointed, "the forest continues?"

"For a couple of hundred yards, it parallels the road," Kapiste instructed, "at a distance of roughly fifty yards, then stops and gives way to open ground."

"How deep is the swale, and how steep are the sides?" Fitch inquired. "Could we hide a hundred lancers there, and could they climb the bank easily?"

Kapiste smiled. "I like the way you think, Lieutenant Fitch. Archers in the trees?"

Fitch grinned. "Have the lancers show themselves, coming up out of the swale and with the morning sun at their backs. The Skamorrans will scramble and change formation for that, and then the archers hit them from behind. Once the arrows fly, have the lancers charge once, then retreat up the King's Road. The archers should retreat once the lancers' attack hits the Skamorrans. We'll regroup further up the road and look for a place to hit them again."

"You said the troopers coming up from Dostin and the other towns are due at first light?"

Fitch nodded. Kapiste told them, "Get a room at the inn before they're all booked. Tell Marty to make room for you even if they are and let him know I need the private dining room in…" She paused to think of all she had to do. "An hour. I'll meet you there with a couple of other folks, and we'll figure out what to do."

Once again, Fitch stayed with the horses at the stable and groomed Bob. Mira went inside the inn. She returned while Fitch was still grooming Bob. "Bob's a damned fine horse," he commented. "If I ever get to go home, I'd sure like to take him with me. Thank you."

Mira laughed. "I should be thanking you. I've known Shasta since she was born and ridden her many times. I dreamed of buying her for years but never had the money. Then, you showed up and made my dreams come true. Too bad you brought the damned Skamorrans with you."

"Let's not be too hard on the Skamorrans," Fitch teased. "If it weren't for them, I'd be halfway to Austeria by now, and we would never have met."

"Then I suppose I ought to be glad they killed my husband, too," Mira cracked.

"I'm sorry," Fitch flushed as he spoke, "I didn't mean…"

Waving her hand in dismissal, Mira said, "Don't … I was trying to make a joke, but it came out all wrong."

"Did you love him?"

"I barely knew him," Mira commented. "I suppose I would have grown to love him. He was a decent man, not mean at all. A little dull, maybe."

"You didn't know him?"

"Da picked him for me. I met him for the first time at our wedding. We were married, spent a week together and then he shipped out for three months. Another week at home and he shipped out again. He didn't make it home."

"That's awful," Fitch commented.

"What's awful?" she replied, "That he died so soon or that my father married me to a man I didn't know?"

"Both, I guess," Fitch answered, shrugging his shoulders. "Where I come from, arranged marriages are pretty common, but I would likely have known the girl before I married her. Though I suppose whether I liked her wouldn't have mattered much. But it's a shame you didn't have a chance to get to know him better."

"It made it easier when he was gone. I couldn't grieve what I didn't miss. That sounds cold-hearted—I mean that since I hadn't spent that much time with him and barely knew him, his death didn't mean as much to me as it might have. The worst part was that I had to move back home. I had an apartment in Chartage, and I liked being in the city, even though the apartment was just one tiny room. I was working for a seamstress, but without any income from my husband, I couldn't stay in the city."

"For what it's worth, I don't sense you're cold-hearted, at least, not yet," he said, finishing up.

"I'm not," she replied. "I got us a room. No bath, and I had to use Dame Kapiste's name to get the room. They're full up with the alarm. Marty, the innkeeper, will have breakfast ready and waiting for everyone before sun up. He's going to send his girl around before that to make sure everyone is awake."

They entered the inn and went to the room. It was the highest room of the inn, in what must have been the attic. It was tiny, with room for not much more than the bed. Even though the outside temperature was cool, it was quite warm in the room. There were only two small windows to catch any breeze.

"I don't think they let this room out very often," Mira commented.

They stowed their weapons in the corner and returned down to the common room. Marty, the innkeeper, found them. He indicated that they should follow him to the private room Dame Kapiste had requested. He offered them ale while they waited. They both agreed.

They didn't wait long before Dame Kapiste arrived with three others, two men and a woman. One of the men was carrying maps rolled up under his arm. Mira and Fitch had seen the other man a few hours before. Pa Sully was the head man in the last town before Baust. Kapiste introduced the man with the maps as Willum Gergel and the woman as Sergeant Middleton. Kapiste spread out the map Fitch and Mira had seen in her office.

"We agree with your ideas about putting the lancers in the swale and the archers in the trees," Kapiste confirmed, pointing to the spots. "We will have emptied Baust of people by then and see no reason to defend it. People are already burying or carting away their valuables. Buildings can be rebuilt, and our neighbors will assist us until then." At this, Pa Sully nodded.

"After our initial foray against them, we will regroup here," she said, pointing on the map, "on the far side of town. From there we will ride. Get me the second map, Willum…" She spread it out and traced the line of the King's Road with her finger. "To here, on the far bank of this stream, Carter's Creek."

"How much of a bank?" Fitch asked.

"Enough that our burning the bridge will be a big pain in the ass for them," answered the sergeant.

"It's about ten feet deep and steep enough that we could defend against a crossing for a long time. Unless they're completely witless, though, I don't expect them to try to force a crossing there. There's a ford up here…" she pointed, "…where the old road was. The old road is overgrown, which will slow them some, but I think if we felled some trees on it, we could make it even more difficult," she said as she smiled grimly.

"The old road rejoins the King's Road here," she indicated, "and it's wooded on both sides. We'll drop some more trees along the way, as many as we can. After the forest ends, here, after another mile or two is the crossroads town of McGovern. We sent riders to warn them to pull out and to send their troopers to be here at first light. From McGovern, the King's Road continues straight on, while the intersecting road leads eventually to Bergin, a port on the east coast.

"If they make it past McGovern today—next map, Willum—there's a spot here that should be interesting. The King's Road skirts a lake and on the other side is a bit of a hill, gradual enough slope that it won't cause any trouble for horses, just high enough to block us from view, not a long enough ride that the enemy will be able to form up properly. I'm going to send all the lancers we have to push a bunch of 'em into the lake.

"Just past that is the town of Oldcastle. If they make it past Oldcastle by nightfall, then nothing we did all day will have worked. I think they'll be lucky to make it to McGovern," Kapiste said, summing up.

"Do you have any calcitrapae?" Fitch asked.

"Calci—what?" Kapiste queried.

"Calcitrapae," Fitch repeated. He looked to Sergeant Middleton. "Two nails, bent and twisted together, like so," he demonstrated with his index fingers.

"Similar to tribuli," Sergeant Middleton stated. "An excellent idea. For the ford?" she asked Fitch.

"And the overgrown part of the old road," he added.

Middleton quickly explained to Dame Kapiste what they were and how they were made. Kapiste had her draw it out on a piece of paper then gave the paper to Willum Gergel.

"Willum, get this to the two smiths in town right now and have them work on these all night. Report back to me with whatever help they need and I'll make sure they get it—if they need help making them or ensuring their families and possessions are safe, we'll do it. After you get back from that, you're going to ride to McGovern tonight, wake their smith up, and get him working on them too."

Just after Willum left, the innkeeper knocked and told them dinner was ready. After dinner, Dame Kapiste left. Fitch suggested to Mira that they try to get some sleep since tomorrow would be an exhausting day. They climbed back up to the room, finding it had not cooled off much. Fitch turned his back while

Mira changed into the linen shift she wore for sleeping. He stripped down to his underclothes. They pulled the covers of the bed back and snuffed out the light.

The warmth of the room was uncomfortable. Fitch lay there, staring up, trying to relax. After about a half-hour, Mira spoke up.

"Um, Ralph," she whispered, "are you awake?"

"Yes," he replied quietly.

"Are you scared about tomorrow?"

"Right now? Apprehensive," he admitted. "I'll be scared tomorrow when it's time to fight."

"You will be?"

"Of course. They'll be fighting back once they gather their wits. They'll have archers of their own and even though the Skamorrans are godless bastards, they do fight well. They'll be trying to kill us just like we'll be trying to kill them. Even though we have some good plans, there are still going to be a lot more of them than there are of us."

"So, it's okay that I'm scared?" Mira asked.

"It would be strange if you weren't."

"And you still get scared?"

"Of course," Fitch answered. "People will be trying to kill me. That's a good reason to be scared."

Mira was silent for a time. Then she whispered, "Ralph?"

"Mhm?"

"Can I ask a big favor?"

"Sure."

"Even though it's hot up here and we'll likely get all sweaty, would you please hold me? Just hold me?"

Fitch rolled towards her, reaching with his right arm under her neck and wrapping his left arm over her. Mira scooted back into him as he did. She put her left hand over his on her stomach.

12

Fitch lay holding Mira. In spite of the heat and the discomfort it caused, he noticed Mira's breathing slowed as she fell asleep. Sleep was more difficult for him to find. He was acutely conscious of holding a beautiful woman in his arms, uncomfortable with the heat and thinking about what the next day would bring.

He eventually did sleep but roused instantly when the knock came on the door. It was still dark outside. He rose and sparked the candle into life. Mira woke groggily.

Fitch turned to the wall and quickly put on his uniform. Mira was dressed before he finished. He buckled on his sword, hung the bow and quivers from his shoulder and grabbed his pack. He checked the room briefly and followed Mira out and down the stairs. A dozen people were already eating breakfast quietly. He and Mira ate quickly. He went to retrieve the horses while Mira found the innkeeper to settle up.

Fitch found their horses saddled and ready. He checked the girths and asked the groom if he had any treats. The groom handed him two root vegetables. Fitch asked what they were.

"Sugar beets," the groom replied. "Horses love 'em."

Fitch held one out for Bob, who quickly scarfed it up. Fitch smiled and gave the groom two coppers. Mira arrived, and Fitch handed her Shasta's treat.

"Oh, a sugar beet. That will make her happy."

After Mira fed Shasta her treat, they walked to the town square. Dame Kapiste was there, along with Sergeant Middleton. She waved them over.

"In a minute or two, I'm going to leave Sergeant Middleton to direct traffic to the north side of town on the King's Road. There's a field there that was just cut where we can assemble."

They waited for Dame Kapiste and followed her to the gathering point. Some of the locals were already there, as well as Pa Sully and his riders from Woolwich, the town of which he was the head. As false dawn gave way to sunrise, the number grew and grew. Fitch saw Sir Gerald arrive and pointed him out to Dame Kapiste. Kapiste told Fitch and Mira to join her and trotted over.

Using the maps, which she had carried with her, rolled in a leather tube, Kapiste showed Sir Gerald what their plan was. He suggested one enhancement, to add a hundred archers to the group of lancers that would be lying in wait in the swale. "If their archers are out of the forest, they will be firing at the lancers. If we add horse-mounted archers to the mix, it will force the Skamorrans to keep their heads down. I'll take command of the lancers. Dame, you'll take command of the archers. Lieutenant Fitch, where would you like to be?"

"Home in bed," Fitch replied with a smile, "but since that isn't possible, I'll stay with you, Sir Gerald."

"Mira Grimble, since you have no sword, I'm going to suggest you accompany Dame Kapiste," Sir Gerald offered. "You may go where you wish, though. Dame, I'm going to call for the archers to assemble on you. Pick a hundred to join me once you see what you have."

Mira nodded in agreement. She looked meaningfully at Fitch and shrugged. He smiled in return, nodding that it was the right decision. Sir Gerald then took his helmet off, stood in his stirrups, and began to bellow for the lancers to assemble on him. Dame Kapiste and Mira rode off to separate themselves, and Sir Gerald hollered for the archers to assemble on Dame Kapiste.

It took some time for the groups to organize themselves. Fitch stood in his stirrups and tried to get a rough count of the lancers. He figured there were a hundred and sixty, give or take—better than he had been guessing would show. A few minutes later, a group of archers rode over. When they arrived, Sir Gerald yelled for his group to move out. They had a ride of a couple of miles, then reached the swale that was their goal. The sun had been up an hour by then. Fitch could see Dame Kapiste's group only a couple of hundred yards away. They were dismounting at the edge of the forest and leading their mounts into the cover of the trees.

Sir Gerald called for his group to dismount and gather. When the group assembled within earshot, he explained what they were going to do. "When I give the first signal—" He stuck his index and pinky fingers in his mouth and gave a shrieking whistle. "I want you all to climb to the top, here, and mill about in an extremely disorganized manner. Do you understand? I want you to look like imbeciles."

Some chuckles greeted this. "At the second signal—" He whistled again. "We're going form ranks at a trot. At the third signal, we charge the Skamorran column, one pass only. When you break through the column, head south on the King's Road. Our rallying point is on the other side of Baust. Archers, unless you have a sword or other close-combat weapon, keep your distance but make sure you shoot everything you have in your quivers. We'll have resupply on the other side of Baust. Any questions?"

"Sir Gerald," came a voice from the middle of the group, "will I be home in time for dinner?"

The group laughed at that. "Maybe not tonight," Sir Gerald shouted back. "I hope your wife isn't too angry. I realize she's probably more frightening than the Skamorrans."

That received an even bigger laugh. Fitch thought Sir Gerald had handled that well. The men mounted up and began to converse quietly while they waited. Fitch dismounted and climbed to the top of the swale, lying on his stomach in the tall grass. Sir Gerald joined him a minute later. From where they were, Fitch tried to estimate how much of the Skamorran column would have emerged from the woods. They normally traveled in columns six men wide.

"I'd suggest we wait until at least a thousand of them have left the forest," Fitch offered. "That will put the head of the column right about there," he pointed slightly to the left. "When we charge, those nearest the woods may try to run for the trees. Those in front of where we hit will be cut off. After we charge, we can work them over from a distance as we pass. They won't normally have archers this far forward in a column—it will be infantry."

"You sound as though you've fought them before," Sir Gerald commented.

"I spent eight years in Boreas's Border Wardens," Fitch answered. "I've had my share of encounters with them."

"I didn't know," Sir Gerald answered. "I apologize if I gave any offense."

"None meant," Fitch shrugged, "none taken. If, for some reason, they do have archers this far forward, take the lancers straight for them. Though we'll take some hits, the lancers will go through them like crap through a goose. You mount up. I'll wave when it's time to give the signal."

Fitch waited patiently. He'd endured much worse when he served on the border. He had butterflies in his stomach. He wasn't scared yet, but his apprehension was growing. When it came time to charge into the enemy and their spears, then he'd be afraid. When he was a raw recruit, serving on the northern reaches, his sergeant had told him it was normal to be afraid. "Courage," he'd said, "is not the absence of fear but the triumph over it."

He saw the first Skamorrans emerge from the forest. They were traveling in a column six men wide, in their jog-jog-jog-jog-walk-walk-walk-walk pace that enabled the Skamorran infantry to cover ground so quickly. They could maintain that pace for an entire day from sunup to sundown and march at that rate for days on end. Fitch waited until he counted two hundred ranks, then scooted down the side of the swale and waved his arm at Sir Gerald.

Sir Gerald stuck his fingers in his mouth and whistled as Fitch was running to Bob. By the time Fitch mounted, he was among the last to reach the top of the swale. The Austerians were following Sir Gerald's instructions and milling about in a confused, disorderly mob. Some were gesturing wildly with their arms and yelling at their mates as though they were having arguments. In the meantime, the Skamorran column had stopped.

The Skamorrans turned to face Sir Gerald's riders, having unslung their black shields and readied their spears. Sir Gerald whistled again, and the Austerian riders quickly sorted themselves out into neat ranks and began to trot toward the Skamorrans. Fitch looked at where the troopers would hit the column—there were about thirty ranks of Skamorrans at the head of the column who would be cut off by the charge. As they closed the distance to the column, the archers in Sir Gerald's group, including Fitch, began to fire.

Almost at the same time, Dame Kapiste's archers hidden in the forest behind the column fired. The arrows from Sir Gerald's soldiers hit mostly shields. The arrows from Dame Kapiste's hit the Skamorrans in their lightly armored backs. Skamorrans began to fall. The Skamorrans on Dame Kapiste's side of the column turned to cover themselves with their shields against the barrage of arrows. They still fell, since the distance was short enough that the archers in the trees could hit the open face of their helmets above the shield, or legs below.

Sir Gerald whistled again, and the lancers began to gallop. Fitch joined them, putting his bow over his shoulder and unsheathing his sword. He'd been worried how Bob would respond to battle, but, so far, the horse seemed eager. As the distance closed, the archers in Sir Gerald's group dropped back and began to swing to the so-far-untouched head of the column. Dame Kapiste's archers began to emerge from the trees, already mounted, and they began to fire into the head of the column from their side.

At twenty yards, lances were lowered. The yelling of the Austerian lancers and the screaming of the Skamorrans created a cacophony of war. The Skamorrans tried to thrust with their spears, but the longer lances of the horsemen had the advantage. Fitch saw a rider slightly in front of him skewer two Skamorrans quickly. Fitch reached the column. A spear was thrust for his chest. He parried it with a backhand move of his sword and, with his return swing, took the man's head off. Another spear reached for him. He blocked it with his left arm and stabbed the soldier in the face. Then he was through.

He sheathed his sword and unlimbered his bow, turning Bob towards the front of the column. Skamorran discipline at the head of the column had broken and their soldiers abandoned the ranks, running for their lives. The archers were picking them off, and now, lancers were catching them from behind. Fitch pulled Bob up to look behind. What he saw was gratifying.

There were as many Skamorrans lying on the ground, wounded or dead, as there were still standing. Most of those standing were running or staggering for the woods from which they'd emerged. He only saw about a dozen Austerians had fallen. Sir Gerald was riding up with two unhorsed men clinging to his stirrups.

Fitch turned Bob again and looked for a target with his bow. There were none within range. He put the arrow back in the quiver and slung the bow back over his shoulder as he nudged Bob into a canter towards Baust. Riding through the town was eerie. When he'd departed that morning, it had been bustling with activity. Now the streets were empty except for the riders heading south. Many of the riders were watering their horses as they passed through. Fitch thought that a good idea and did the same.

On the other side of Baust there was a field, harvested down to stubble, like the one where they had gathered that morning. He saw Dame Kapiste, Sir Gerald, and Mira. He rode up to them.

"I have good news and bad news," Fitch said. "The good news is that we left over six hundred Skamorrans lying on the field, either wounded or dead. The bad news is that they're going to be angry and will likely put Baust to the torch."

Dame Kapiste shrugged and grimaced at the same time. "I already figured on the destruction. Doesn't mean I'm too chipper about it. Near as we can figure, we lost about fifteen. I like that we got many more of theirs but that's still fifteen families that will have a hard, hard winter."

"How many wounded do we have, men and horses?" Fitch asked.

"Twelve men, nine women, and seventeen horses," Kapiste replied, "as of last count. Three of the men and two of the women bad enough that I'm sending them home. Six of the horses need to be put down, but we have eight that we gained from the soldiers who died. Of the other eleven mounts, seven will need some time to heal and shouldn't be ridden; the other four just had nicks and scratches."

"It looks like the last of us just arrived," Sir Gerald commented. "Should we head to Carter's Creek?"

"Yes," Dame Kapiste confirmed. "Oh, and Fitch, good news for you. We have a couple thousand of those thingamabobs you wanted, plus whatever Willum convinced the smith in McGovern to make last night."

"The calcitrapae?" Fitch asked.

"Yes, those things," she confirmed. "They're in a wagon that's already on the way to Carter's Creek."

"Excellent," Fitch grinned. "I'll need a detail of soldiers to spread them over the ford and on the old road inside the forest."

13

After speaking with them, Fitch looked for Mira. He saw her off to the side, riding alone, her head down. He trotted up beside her to see how she was. When he drew even, he saw her cheeks stained with tears. He leaned over and took Shasta's reins from her hands, and stopped both horses. He swung down and went around Shasta. Mira dismounted, then turned and wrapped her arms around Fitch's neck. She began to sob.

Fitch let her cry. He put his arms around her and patted and rubbed her back, making soothing noises. Her face was buried in his shoulder. After a few minutes, she straightened slightly and he heard her sniff loudly.

"That was horrible," she told him, still gasping with emotion. "I've hunted. I've killed animals. I've watched their bodies go limp in that instant of death. I've never killed a person before, and today I killed three. Watching a person's body collapse to the ground like that was awful. It made me sick. I threw up after."

Fitch leaned forward and kissed her forehead. "I wish I knew what to say so I could comfort you. It's normal for you to feel this way. It doesn't mean you're weak."

"How do you do it?" she asked, still sniffing.

"It's easier to justify it to yourself when you're face-to-face and your enemy is trying to kill you," he said. "When you use a bow and shoot from concealment, it's more troublesome because it can seem unfair. We planned ahead to make sure that it would be unfair—as unfair as possible. It helps to remember that if the situation were reversed, your enemy would likely kill you. If they had not invaded, then none of this would be necessary. I know that's not very comforting."

"Does it bother you?"

"Sometimes," Fitch admitted, "but you need to think of the larger picture too. Every single one of their soldiers we kill is one less to fight, one less who will loot and pillage the countryside, and one more reason for them to stop marching, turn around, and return to Chartage. Keep in mind, too, that the soldiers you killed today likely were killing unarmed men and women in Chartage just a day or two ago."

"I guess," she said uncertainly, pulling her arms from his neck and stepping backward, pulling the bottom of her tunic up to wipe her face.

"I know that nothing I said will help you fall asleep more easily tonight," Fitch told her. "I also know that if you stay with us, you'll likely need to do it again before we're through. If you don't think you can, you should find another way to be useful or go home. I won't think any less of you if you do."

Mira nodded. She released Fitch's arms and climbed back on Shasta. Fitch mounted Bob. They hurried up to rejoin the group.

It was nearly three hours to reach Carter's Creek. Mira had pulled away from Fitch when they reached the others. Later, he noticed she had found Ma Ratledge and was talking with her earnestly.

Once they arrived at Carter's Creek, Fitch saw the wagon loaded with crates of the calcitrapae. Sir Gerald selected some men to help Fitch spread them. They drove the wagon along the bank up to the ford. The creek bed was covered with large smooth stones, arranged long ago to make the ford easier to cross, but now covered with a thin layer of dirt with some grass and reeds growing up in the cracks.

Fitch directed the men to spread the calcitrapae liberally, beginning at the bank closest to Baust. He explained to the men and women helping him that they did *not* want to step on one by accident—they would pierce right through the sole of a boot and into the foot. A few minutes later, one of the men misstepped and lost his balance. He staggered the wrong way and then shouted in pain. Fitch sent him back to the main road.

As they were scattering the calcitrapae, they could hear trees being cut in the woods. Fitch looked at how many of the sharp-pointed devices he had left and told his people they were finished for now. "Let's save the rest for where this old road meets the King's Road," he said.

They hauled the wagon around and headed back. Fitch saw Dame Kapiste. She was overseeing the destruction of the bridge over the stream. Men were hacking the supports with axes and others were chopping the beams. There were three barrels of pine pitch they would use to make sure the remnants burned.

"I was wondering whether those doodads were worth it until I saw Benton limping back," Kapiste commented. "He told me he stepped on one by accident, and it hurt like the tortures of the known hells."

"Make sure he gets the wound clean," Fitch counseled.

"Already had someone look at it," Kapiste answered. "You didn't use them all?"

"I thought it would be a nice surprise to have the rest of them waiting at the end of the old road, just before it joins the King's Road again," Fitch remarked. "Nothing so dismaying as one more obstacle when you think you've already made it through."

Kapiste smiled. "I'm glad—We're glad you're here, Lieutenant Fitch. We owe you and Mira Grimble a huge debt for getting the word out."

"Where is she?"

"Up ahead," Kapiste replied. "She's with Ma Ratledge, helping with the wounded horses."

Fitch rode ahead and caught up to the wagon with the remainder of the calcitrapae. Along the way, he saw Mira on the side of the road. She waved when she saw Fitch. She looked much less troubled. Ma Ratledge was nearby, looking at a gash on the flank of a horse. Ratledge had been talking to Mira and when Mira waved, Ratledge looked up and saw Fitch. She smiled broadly and waved as well.

Fitch continued with the wagon until he reached where the old road met the King's Road. Sir Gerald found him there. Behind Sir Gerald, Fitch saw smoke rising into the air.

"Looks like the bridge is down," Fitch commented.

"Quite right," Sir Gerald agreed. "Dame Kapiste tells me you're going to spread more of the whatsits here."

"Calcitrapae," Fitch corrected him. "I'm debating on whether to wait for the loggers to finish or to just spread them now and leave someone behind to warn the men not to tread on the old road."

"Spread them now and post someone," Sir Gerald requested. "I'd like you to wait with me by the stream. We have two hundred and fifty archers we'll spread through the tree line to convince them not to climb the banks. I've posted another hundred by the ford to get a few volleys off while the Skamorrans are tip-toeing on your doohickeys. I could use your cool head in either place."

Fitch issued the orders for men to stay behind and warn those Austerians coming from the woods about the calcitrapae. He returned to Sir Gerald. The remnants of the bridge were burning furiously. Sir Gerald had already divided the men into two groups for the right and left of the road. He gave Fitch the left side. Fitch went among his men to find out how many of them had swords or other close-combat weapons. Few did. He asked how many had axes. Several did.

Fitch borrowed one of the axes and strode into the forest a few yards. He found an appropriate-sized limb and hacked it from the tree. Where he had cut, it was about as big around as his bicep. He then cut it to a length of about three feet. He quickly stripped it of the smaller shoots. He pulled his men together.

He showed them the length of branch he had cut. Grasping it on the smaller end, he swung it against a tree with a resounding thwack. "There's always a chance one of them might make it up the bank," Fitch instructed. "I'd like you men to make about forty of these quickly, so if a Skamorran does climb up, we have something to keep him busy."

Those with axes quickly went into the woods to select branches of their own. Fitch took the one he'd made and went to demonstrate it to Sir Gerald's men. Sir Gerald heartily approved.

Fitch then picked his way along the bank to speak with the men and women Sir Gerald had posted at the ford. He showed them how to make a club from a tree branch and warned them about the calcitrapae at the end of the old road. "Don't be heroes," he cautioned. "When they arrive, they'll likely launch a few volleys into the woods. Stay behind a tree. When they start to cross the ford, get a couple of quick shots off and then get out of here. Try to regroup down the old road and find a spot where they'll be slowed down by one of the trees just felled. Get another shot or two off and run like hell again. If you can do it two or three times, that's great. If all you can do safely is get two or three shots here at the ford, that's fine, too."

Fitch went back to where the remnants of the bridge were still burning. About forty minutes afterward, Fitch could see the dust from the King's Road, indicating the approach of the Skamorran column. Beyond that, he could see smoke rising into the sky as the town of Baust burned. The Skamorrans had not spent much time in Baust. Though the town would be burnt to the ground, the valuables people had buried would likely still be where they'd left them.

A Skamorran officer stopped the column on the road just out of bow range. Sir Gerald had one of his men launch an arrow. It landed and stuck in the dirt about five yards short of the officer. The officer turned and peered into the woods. Other officers on horseback rode to the head of the column. There was a brief discussion, after which men began to fan out, jogging in both directions along the stream bed, being careful to stay out of range of any arrows that might come from the tree line on the far bank.

Less than ten minutes later, there was a shout as one of the men discovered the ford. The mounted officers rode over and quickly returned. Within a minute, the column marched off the road and towards the ford. Sir Gerald and Fitch quietly prepared their men to retrieve their horses and move out. Fitch could see that a unit of archers was now near the head of the column. The Skamorrans approached the ford carefully. They positioned their archers along the banks and advanced slowly. Their archers fired three volleys of arrows into the trees.

When no arrows came back in response, the Skamorran officers ordered the column to cross the ford. Fitch couldn't see the ford due to a bend in the stream, though he wished he could. He began to hear shouting and cursing, though, which made him smile. By now, the end of the Skamorran column no longer had a view down the King's Road. Sir Gerald ordered his men to pull out. Fitch did the same. Word was passed quietly down the lines, and men and women went to retrieve their horses.

Fitch waited for the men and women who had been at the ford at the place where the old road joined the new. They were chattering excitedly though quietly. One of them called to Fitch. "Sar, it were the funniest thing I seen in a spell. They goes marching into the ford, then they starts yowling and yalping. An officer rides up to holler at 'em and gets throwed from his horse right in the water. They keeps crossing, though real slow and shuffling, like. Then, we loosed a volley. Hit more'n fifty of 'em. Got less with the next one and then their archers fired so we skedaddled." Fitch smiled.

"Did you regroup later?" he asked.

"About a half a mile down, there was a tree down," the man replied. "Some of the ones afore was so big the Skamorrans woulda had to go around 'em, but this one they could climb over. So we waited and got mebbe thirty."

Fitch thanked them for the report and waved them on. He mounted Bob and rode back next to Sir Gerald. "That's twenty or thirty who won't be able to keep pace with the column," Fitch said with a grin, "and one officer who just lost his mount, plus about a hundred the archers hit."

"The horse," Sir Gerald asked, concerned, "is it lamed?"

"If they can catch the horse and remove the calcitrapae, the horse will heal in a week or so. If they don't and it gets infected, that horse will be miserable."

"For the ones who won't be able to keep up with the column," Sir Gerald asked, "should we leave a detachment behind to deal with them?"

"If I knew where the Skamorrans would stop for the evening and more about how that unit could rejoin the others, I'd suggest it," Fitch said. "But I don't know how much longer the Skamorrans will continue. It's going to be slow going for them on the old road, with the trees we dropped and with them thinking we'll have an ambush waiting at all of them. When Dame Kapiste predicted this morning that they'd only get as far as McGovern, I was pessimistic. Now, I'm thinking she was correct."

"How much further do you think they'll proceed after that?"

"If we sting them as hard at Oldcastle as we did this morning," Fitch reckoned, "I'd wager they will have seen enough."

Fitch and Sir Gerald followed the rest of the group through the now-empty town of McGovern, taking the opportunity to water their horses. When they reached the far edge of the town, they were the last of the column. Waiting for them was Willum Gergel.

"My compliments, Sir Gerald, Lieutenant Fitch," Gergel greeted them, "there is a hot meal and feed for the horses waiting in Oldcastle. Dame Kapiste would like to meet and discuss tomorrow's activities. I'm sorry to have missed out today, but I have been damned busy."

14

The three men picked up their pace. Fitch hadn't noticed until now, but the mention of a hot meal reminded him that he hadn't eaten since breakfast. Judging by the position of the sun, it was getting to be late afternoon. He hoped there would be some food left when he arrived, if not for him, at least for Bob.

About five miles out of McGovern, they reached the lake that Dame Kapiste had shown on the map the night before. The lake was large enough that Fitch could not see the shore on the other side. They trotted along the shore for another two miles when the ground to the left began to rise. Another thousand yards, and they reached the spot Kapiste had pointed out. The slope was gradual enough that the horses would have no difficulty, and the crest of the hill was only about two hundred yards away from the road. A group of lancers sweeping down would shove the Skamorran column right into the lake.

Two miles further on, they reached Oldcastle. The streets were filled with the men and women who had started out that morning at Baust, all eating. "Is this your doing, Willum?" Sir Gerald inquired.

"Yes, it is, sir," Willum answered proudly.

"Well done," Sir Gerald replied.

Willum led them to the inn on the town square. While everyone else was eating outside, with kettles of hot beef stew and fresh bread, Dame Kapiste had arranged for them to eat in the inn's common room. The food was the same, but they had a table where maps were already spread. There were two new people Fitch had not yet met: a tall black man introduced as Sir Jamel, and a red-haired woman introduced as Ma Oldham.

Sir Jamel was a cataphract, like Sir Gerald. Oldcastle would be adding a hundred riders to their force, most of them lancers. Ma Oldham was from the next town up the King's Road, Center Sands, and she brought forty more riders, half lancers, half archers. With Willum Gergel's help, Sir Jamel organized the meal for everyone. "Since we carted out most everything today," Sir Jamel stated, "it was easy to divert some to feed the soldiers. There was also enough that everyone will get a loaf of bread for tomorrow's breakfast."

Fitch was happy to see Mira in improved spirits. She whispered to him that she would like to talk later. Over dinner, the group recapped the events of the day so far. Fitch repeated what he had discussed with Sir Gerald, that he did not believe the Skamorrans would press on past McGovern this evening. Sir Gerald excused himself and went outside briefly. When he returned, he told the group that he sent some of his men back toward McGovern to keep a watchful eye on the Skamorrans in case that changed.

After they ate, they looked at the maps spread out on one of the tables. Sir Jamel suggested they plan on spending the night on the back side of the hill facing the King's Road next to the lake, Lake Dogtail. That was easily agreed to by all. Then they turned to the maps.

They discussed where to hit the Skamorran column when they arrived. "With just over three hundred lancers in the open like this, I think we stay at the front of the column."

"The Skamorrans have moved an archery unit near the head of the column," Fitch mentioned.

"A great target for the lancers," Sir Gerald remarked, "especially if we have our own archers in support."

"I agree," Sir Jamel confirmed.

They worked out the details of who would lead the attack and what the signals would be. Then they turned their attention to the next opportunity. Between Oldcastle and the next town, Center Sands, there was a set of four volcanic rock formations. The King's Road twisted around them. Sir Jamel spoke up.

"The gap between the third and fourth group of rocks is narrow, plus the fourth formation is the largest, and it's crescent-shaped. It's open ground—shared grazing land ordinarily. I suggest we take the lancers behind the fourth formation and wait until the Skamorran column emerges Due to the crescent shape of the rock formation we should be able to stay out of sight until roughly a thousand of the Skamorrans have come through the gap. We could also hide another hundred archers in the crescent and a hundred to a hundred and fifty behind the third rock pile."

"Hitting the archers, if they move another unit up, makes the most sense here too," Fitch commented.

Again, they worked out the details and the signals. After the town of Center Sands, there weren't any topographic features that suggested themselves as places where the terrain would give the Austerians an advantage. That's when Ma Oldham made a suggestion.

"After Center Sands, it's grazing land. The grass is high and dry right now. The wind generally blows from the east. What's to stop us from setting the fields on fire?"

"Nothing," replied Dame Kapiste, "but let's hope it doesn't come to that."

"It would be damned effective," Fitch commented, "but I hope they give up before that."

"What are the chances of that happening?" Ma Oldham asked.

"We eliminated at least six hundred of them this morning. We likely killed or wounded another hundred or more at Carter's Creek," Fitch recounted. "Most importantly, we showed them that the countryside is mobilized against them. They know that we will grow stronger the further they proceed and that their chance of reaching Austeria is nil. I think tomorrow morning will see them returning to Chartage."

"Good," Sir Gerald commented.

"Which begs the question," Fitch asked, "are there any routes by which we could pass them by and meet them on their return?"

The Austerians shook their heads. "Especially not at the speed with which they move," Dame Kapiste stated.

"We do have the advantage of being mounted," Fitch offered. "We can harass them all the way back. Another reason I believe they will turn back tomorrow."

"Harassing them all the way back to Chartage will be a very great pleasure," Sir Gerald commented.

"If that is the case," Fitch warned, "I'm afraid I cannot accompany you. I was sent on an urgent matter of state and need to get to Austeria and the Court as quickly as I can."

"I promised my father that I would be his guide," Mira stated, "so I must leave as well."

"That being so," Sir Jamel said, "having a letter of introduction signed by Dame Kapiste, Sir Gerald, and myself would certainly speed things up for you in Austeria. If we're finished here, let's repair to my office across the square and draft that for you quickly."

"One more thing," Fitch requested. "Mira Grimble and I were not able, before we left the coast, to obtain bedrolls or other equipment that would enable us to sleep in the open. Would any of you be able to help provide us with—"

Sir Jamel laughed. "We're having dinner in an inn," he said. "Take what you need, and I'll repay the innkeeper."

"Thank you, Sir Jamel."

"No, thank you, Lieutenant Fitch," Sir Gerald replied. "Without you and Mira Grimble, the Skamorrans would have caught us much less prepared. We, and our countrymen, owe you a much bigger debt than a few blankets will offset."

They went across the square to Sir Jamel's offices. He, Sir Gerald, and Dame Kapiste shooed Fitch and Mira outside and quickly wrote a letter. When they gave Fitch the letter, it was sealed and addressed to the Lord Chamberlain. Their names and titles were affixed on the outside, which they said would enable Fitch to put the letter directly into the Lord Chamberlain's hands, and the contents of the letter would grant them a speedy audience with the King.

Fitch and Mira went back to the inn. They found a linen cupboard where spare blankets were stored. Fitch showed Mira how to make a bedroll.

"This may end up being the only night we sleep outside," Fitch commented, "but at least we can, if we need to, for the rest of the trip.'

As they left Oldcastle, twilight was deepening. They rode back down the road, and where the ground began to rise, they followed the bent and broken grass where others had split off from the King's Road. There were at least a thousand riders and their horses scattered on the back side of the rise. Fitch and

Mira hobbled the horses, then found an open spot and spread their blankets in the tall grass.

"You seem much better than you were earlier," Fitch commented.

"I had a nice talk with Ma Ratledge," Mira said. "She helped calm me down. It still bothers me that I killed three people, but, just like you, she reminded me that they wouldn't have hesitated if situations were reversed. So … if I have to do it again, I'll be able to. I'd rather not, though. Do you really think the Skamorrans will turn back?"

"If I were in command," Fitch stated, "I'd turn back. Their only hope was that the countryside would not be ready for them and they would be able to sweep through, plunder food stocks to help their supply situation through the winter, and possibly make it near Austeria without resistance. Instead, they found we knew they were coming. We mounted a small attack, and they found Baust and McGovern stripped of food before they arrived. There's no point to them continuing. They aren't stupid—quite the opposite. They'll turn back."

"Then we ride for Austeria," Mira commented.

"Mhm."

"I've never been further away from the coast than I am right now," Mira remarked. "Austeria is another eleven- or twelve-day ride further south. Not only that, but we're going to go to the Palace, and you're hoping to see the King. That's pretty exciting to me."

"What's exciting?" Fitch teased, "The spending another eleven or twelve days with me, or maybe seeing the King?"

"The one I have to endure," she teased back, "the other I'm looking forward to."

After they had fallen asleep, Fitch woke when Mira joined him on his blanket. When he turned his head, she whispered her excuse, "It got chilly." She snuggled up to his back and threw her arm over his chest.

It was the dim light of false dawn when Fitch woke again, hearing the noise of others rising. He and Mira had switched positions in the night, and she was now tucked into his front, with his arm over her and his hand clasped by hers. Fitch pulled himself away gently, making Mira murmur in her sleep. He went to see if there was any news. He saw Dame Kapiste, Sir Gerald and Sir Jamel in the dim light and went to talk with them.

After whispered greetings, Sir Jamel said, "We're waiting to hear from the scouts. It'll be another hour or so."

Fitch nodded and returned to where Mira and the horses were. He stretched out on his back next to Mira. She rolled over and threw her arm and leg over him, along with some of the blanket. She put her head on his shoulder and went back to sleep.

Fitch stared at the brightening sky, pondering how much and how quickly his life had changed. He didn't hold out much hope of finding Prince John. Dame Kapiste and Sir Jamel had no recollection of any sort of retinue traveling south on the King's Road. Though Fitch knew the prince was not much for pomp and fuss, there would have been at least a handful of others accompanying him and a group of foreigners would have been sure to draw attention.

Without the prince, he couldn't return home. He would need to stay in Auster. Thanks to Mira, that was beginning to seem like an attractive alternative. Plus, he reasoned, the Austerians could use someone with his skills and training in the conflict with Skamorra. He idly stroked Mira's hair as he thought about these things.

As false dawn gave way to real dawn, Fitch rose again and returned to Dame Kapiste. As he drew closer, he could hear those nearby chatting happily. He figured they'd received good news.

"Lieutenant Fitch," Sir Jamel called, "you were correct. We just heard from the scouts that the Skamorrans have already begun to march back to Chartage. Sir Gerald is already forming a group of riders to hurry them on their way."

"That is good news," Fitch smiled, "but also means I must take my leave."

"Not before breakfast," Sir Jamel suggested. "The innkeeper is already preparing one for us. Go collect your horses and Mira Grimble and meet us at the inn."

15

Fitch went back and found Mira had already risen. He rolled up the blankets and untied the horses. He told her about breakfast. They saddled Shasta and Bob and set off to Oldcastle. After breakfast, they headed south down the King's Road. The towns they passed were abuzz with activity. Since they came from the north, they were asked for news. Mira usually told them what she knew. They would stop at whatever town they reached in the late afternoon or early twilight.

Fitch would always groom Bob while Mira went to get the room. She always claimed they had only one room left and that they would need to share. On the third night after leaving Oldcastle, Fitch noticed there were only four other guests.

"Only one room left?" he teased.

Mira's face flushed as a blush spread from her neck upwards. "Yes," she lied, "the other rooms are closed off for the winter."

Fitch did not press the issue until later. As they lay in bed, with Mira tucked as close to him as she could be, he asked quietly, "Mira, do you want there to be more between us than this—just sleeping in the same bed every night?"

"Do you?"

"I asked you first," Fitch replied with a smile as he propped himself up on an elbow to look at her, "but I will tell you that any man would find it impossible not to think about it while sharing a bed with a woman as beautiful as you are."

"Then why haven't you done anything about it?" Mira asked.

"Because I'm not that way," Fitch replied. "I know we've been flirting and teasing each other, but I don't want to do anything you don't want as well. So, I'll ask you again. Do you want there to be more between us?"

Mira's response was to twine her arms around Fitch's neck and pull him to her for a kiss. She put all the feelings that had been growing inside her into the kiss. When they broke to catch their breath, she whispered, "Yes. I want there to be more."

The next day, as they rode, Fitch brought up the future. He explained once again that he must look for Prince John. Only when he had exhausted all possibilities and was convinced that the prince was dead would he be able to commit to staying in Auster.

"What would I do?" he asked. "I'm a soldier. Auster doesn't keep a regular army like Boreas does. I know farming, but I turned my back on farming twelve years ago. I'm not cut out for life on the sea—I get seasick. About the only thing I'm sure of is that I would like to know if there's a future for the two of us."

"That's enough for now," she replied. "The rest will sort itself out in time."

"How can you be so sure?"

"Because Ma Ratledge told me," Mira said smugly. "You are a good bit of what I was talking with her about after that morning outside of Baust. She'd seen the way I was looking at you, and she saw the way you were looking at me when you thought no one was watching. She told me not to worry about the future but to enjoy whatever each day brought. She didn't mean that I should act like an irresponsible child. I wish the future were more certain for both of us, but it's not. I know you're a soldier and that Auster has a need for soldiers right now. I also know it's dangerous, and it's probably not the life for me. But if I worry about the bad things that might happen, I ruin my enjoyment of today. That's not to say I shouldn't prepare myself. Does that make sense? It did to me."

"I'll have to think about it," Fitch replied. "It makes sense in some ways, but it's not how I've lived my life."

On the sixth night after leaving Oldcastle, Mira returned while Fitch was still grooming Bob. She announced, "They were expecting us."

"What do you mean?"

"Word was sent by the Palace to be on the lookout for us and to extend us every courtesy, with the Palace picking up the bill," she answered.

"I'm guessing Sir Jamel or Dame Kapiste sent a dispatch rider to Austeria to inform them of what was happening," Fitch suggested. "It was nice of them to mention us."

"We're having dinner with Dame Polk in less than an hour," Mira added, "and there will be a hot bath waiting for us in the room. Do you have any other clothes?"

"I have another uniform in my bag," Fitch answered. "It's clean."

"Wear that," Mira suggested, "since the innkeeper will also wash our clothes.

It was the first chance they'd had to bathe since the first evening after Fitch arrived. It felt good to both of them to wash away the dust from their travels. Mira went first again. She no longer asked Fitch to turn around when she disrobed. Instead, he stared with hungry eyes. She did the same to him when he took off his clothes. Later, when she dressed, she wore the blue skirt she had worn while running.

"You don't have any other clothes, do you?" Fitch inquired.

Mira shook her head. "Why?"

"When we reach Austeria, I'll have to buy you a proper gown and slippers so you can meet the King and Queen in style."

"So you won't be embarrassed by me," she remarked sourly.

"So I can show them the most beautiful lady in Auster," Fitch replied, "and leave them with their mouths hanging open and their tongues out. If you're dressed like they are, they'll see how beautiful you are. If you're dressed differently, they'll only see the clothes."

"Good comeback, Ralph," she said, sticking her tongue out at him.

"Mira, do not doubt your attractiveness," he said with a shrug. "By my reckoning, my growing relationship with a woman as beautiful in her nature as she is in appearance more than balances the unfortunate circumstances that drove me here."

The next two days it rained unceasingly with buffeting winds. Mira commented that it was likely the fringe of a larger storm that likely was centered in the north. Each town they passed was larger than the last. The head of every town was now a Sir or Dame. At each stop, they dined with these nobles and told the story of turning the Skamorrans back. The last town (really a small city) was Austinton. They dined that evening at the home of Dame Gruber, who was damned attractive for her age ("fifty-six, dear, and I'll admit to every minute of it—I've had too much fun not to"), charming, witty, and elegantly dressed. Fitch mentioned her dress and his plans to buy some court clothing for Mira.

"Good heavens!" Gruber exclaimed. "I have the most marvelous seamstress here in Austinton. First thing in the morning, Mira, you and I will go visit her and create your outfit."

"Won't that take some time?" Fitch asked.

"Two–three days, tops," Gruber responded. "I'll send a message to Teddy and let him know Mira and I will be delayed and also that he is buying Mira appropriate clothing for court."

"Teddy?" Mira asked.

"Theodosius III," Gruber replied, "the King. My cousin. Bring the better of your uniforms as well, Lieutenant Fitch. You're looking a bit careworn, and she should be able to spruce you up a bit. You'll set off a day or two before us. It would not be acceptable for Mira to travel into the capital without a chaperone. It would create an unnecessary bit of scandalous gossip. That's not what we need right now."

"Why would the king pay for her clothing?" Fitch asked.

"It's the least he can do for a hero who helped rouse the countryside," Gruber said.

The next day, Fitch accompanied Mira to the home of the seamstress. Dame Gruber was already waiting. Dame Gruber took his uniform and dismissed him until dinner.

When he returned for dinner that evening, he could hardly believe his eyes. Mira was in a beautiful dress with a square-cut bodice that showed a hint of décolletage. The green of the dress brought out the flecks of green in Mira's hazel eyes. Her hair had been artfully arranged in a set of braids that wrapped her head before dropping to her shoulders. The combination of the dress and hairstyle showed how long and graceful Mira's neck was. She had on earrings and a necklace, both of pearls. While the style of what she was wearing was different from what Fitch was accustomed to at the Borean court, it was elegant and quite fetching.

Dame Gruber laughed and clapped her hands in pleasure when she saw Fitch's reaction. "Lieutenant, do close your mouth," she teased. "You were quite right in what you told Mira, you know. Dressed in a similar fashion to what others are wearing at Court, they won't notice the dress as much as they will her beauty and how the dress enhances it."

Over dinner, Dame Gruber and Mira explained to Fitch what they had done that day. The dress Mira had on was one that had come from Dame Gruber's closet and had been quickly altered. Mira had been almost overwhelmed with the luxuriousness of the fabrics and the richness of the colors at the seamstress. She had never worn such fine jewelry before—lent to her by the Dame. She began to thank Dame Gruber profusely.

"Mira, dear," the Dame responded, "I always wanted a daughter but the gods saw fit to only give me two sons. They're grown and married with families of their own now. My husband left me a widow five years ago. This has been as much fun for me as it has for you."

"I feel like I'm in a fairy tale," Mira admitted, "like the poor step-daughter whose fairy godmother helps her go to the ball."

"I don't know about a ball, dear," the Dame teased, "but I do like the idea of being a fairy godmother."

Dame Gruber confirmed over dinner that the clothing they had selected would not be ready for another day. Fitch would leave in the morning and Mira and Dame Gruber would follow in her carriage when the rest of the outfits had been finished. This, of course, prompted Fitch to ask what, exactly, they had purchased.

"Five dresses, so Mira won't wear the same one twice in a row, an evening dress, since Teddy may invite you to a state dinner at some point—though with the current troubles, that might not happen. It's still better to be prepared, though—and two riding outfits. Mira will go back to the inn tonight, pack her clothes, and spend the night here. You'll leave tomorrow. Time it right, and you'll arrive in Austeria too late tomorrow for any sort of fuss," the Dame explained.

"Dame Gruber," Fitch inquired, "would you have heard if Prince John had arrived recently."

"Yes, I would have," she replied, "and I can tell you I've heard nothing of the sort. Nor was he expected. Mira explained your whole purpose in traveling at this time of year was in hopes of finding him. Unless Teddy is playing a trick on all of us, I'm afraid you will not find your prince in Austeria. It does sound like your problems in Boreas and our problems in Auster are related and I am certain that Teddy will want to discuss this with you at great length. There is more going on than what you've been a part of. Also, now that we have begun to know one another, please call me Vicki in private. I much prefer it."

She continued, "After you deliver your news, Ralph, what do you plan to do?"

Fitch grimaced slightly. "D— Vicki," he began, catching himself. Gruber smiled. "I'm a soldier. If Mira told you my story, then you know I cannot return to Boreas without the prince. If the king wants me, I'll join Auster in the fight against Skamorra."

"She did," Gruber confirmed. "And from what I understand, Auster would be foolish not to offer you a position. And what will you do, dear? You told me you didn't exactly enjoy your experience." Gruber asked Mira.

"I'd prefer not to fight, that's true," Mira admitted. "But I don't want to return home. There's nothing for me there except an arranged marriage to a fisherman. If I could figure out a way—"

"Vicki," Fitch interrupted, "we haven't had the opportunity to discuss this with each other very much yet."

Gruber laughed. "Well, you ought to. I've seen the way you look at one another. One minute, you're awestruck, as though all the gods revealed themselves to you. The next minute, you look at each other the way lions look at meat. Mira, does it bother you that Ralph is a soldier, and if he swears fealty to the king, he's off to war? You might never see him again."

"I will wait. I want to see if what I've felt so far is real," Mira said evenly, "but I can't return home. If I do, my father will marry me off."

"I understand, dear," Gruber said comfortingly. "What about you, Ralph?"

Looking at Mira and clasping her hand, he replied, "I've never met anyone like you. I wish we had more time to spend together because I think there could be a future for the two of us, and I hope there is. But I can't marry you—not yet.

We don't know one another well enough, and, well, I'm a soldier, and there are risks that go along with that."

"I will wait for you," Mira stated calmly.

"How will you live?" Fitch asked. "You said you can't go home."

"Ahem," Vicki cleared her throat. Ralph and Mira both blushed and sat back. "What were you thinking of doing?" Vicki inquired.

"When I was married before, I worked for a seamstress in Chartage. I thought I told you that."

"You did."

"I was hoping I could find a similar position," Mira said with a shrug. "Getting by will be difficult, but with Ralph's help, I should be able to afford lodgings."

"Mm," Vicki mused. "I might have a better idea, but you'll have to allow me to sleep on it. If worse comes to worse, you can live here with me."

With that, Vicki changed the subject and began talking about the dresses and clothing they had ordered for Mira that day. After dinner, Dame Gruber's servant gave Fitch a bundle containing his "spruced up" uniform. Gruber's carriage took them back to the inn and waited while Mira packed her few belongings.

16

The next morning, Fitch rose. He left the wrapped bundle alone and put on his more careworn uniform. He rode at an unhurried pace, keeping Dame Gruber's advice in mind, planning to arrive in the early evening. He reached the gate in the walls of Austeria as afternoon was giving way. A guard, noticing Fitch's uniform, stopped him, inquiring if he were Lieutenant Fitch. When he confirmed this, the guard asked him to follow.

Fitch followed him through the busy streets of the city. At the gate of the palace, the guard handed him over to a woman he addressed as "Captain." The captain explained that Fitch was expected. Fitch mentioned he had a letter for the Lord Chamberlain. The captain smiled. "To whom I am taking you," she said.

The captain clicked her fingers, and a page took his bag while a groom led away his horse. Fitch would not allow them to take his weapons. The captain led him inside the palace to an office. "Please wait here," she told him, then disappeared through a side door.

The page was waiting silently behind him. After a short wait, a stocky man entered, elegantly dressed in velvet and lace with a fringe of gray hair around a bald head. "Lieutenant Fitch," he said with warmth and enthusiasm that did not seem quite sincere but instead felt somewhat oily to Fitch. "Welcome. I apologize for not being here to greet you, but I was dining with their Royal Highnesses just now. I'm afraid it is too late in the evening for you to join us but I will have dinner sent to your room shortly."

The lord chamberlain clicked his fingers and another page appeared bearing a candelabra. The lord chamberlain told him to follow the pages to the room. The page with the light led them out to a corridor, then up two flights of stairs. There were sconces in the corridor, providing illumination. The page reached a door and opened it. The room was dark. Fitch stayed in the corridor. The page began to light candles around the room. Once he could see inside, Fitch stepped inside.

The page continued to light candles in other rooms from the candelabra. When she finished, she explained the layout. "This is a guest apartment, and we are in the sitting room." Pointing, she said, "That is the bedroom. In this room," she pointed, "you will find a privy chamber with running water. Would you like us to draw you a bath?"

"Yes, please," Fitch confirmed.

"We will bring your dinner shortly and then draw your bath. If you wish to leave the apartment, please pull this rope. It rings a bell, and one of the pages will come and take you wherever you need to go."

In the bath, Fitch found shaving gear. He could hardly wait to remove the beard that had grown since Mira last shaved him. It had been irritating him more every day.

The next morning, Fitch rose and dressed. He wore the uniform that Dame Gruber had her seamstress freshen up. He pulled the rope to summon a page. When she appeared, he asked about breakfast, and the page led him downstairs to a dining room. There were a number of people there eating. Halfway through, the lord chamberlain appeared. Spotting him, he came straight for Fitch.

"Lieutenant Fitch, good morning. I trust you slept well?" he said in what Fitch thought was an overly pleasant tone. Again, Fitch thought, "oily" in terms of the lord chancellor's manner.

Fitch nodded.

"The king would very much like to see you this morning," the lord chamberlain continued. "He will finish his audience at the tenth hour and requests that you join him then."

Fitch agreed, and the lord chamberlain left him to finish. Fitch thought to himself, *There's something about him. He says all the right things, but he doesn't feel them.*

After breakfast, a page led him back to his room. Fitch sat quietly, trying to puzzle through what the lord chamberlain's off-putting behavior might mean. A knock at the door let him know the page was there to take him to the king.

The page led them into the residential area, not to a formal reception room. The lord chamberlain met them and took Fitch the rest of the way. King Theodosius was in a fairly humble office, looking at some papers on his desk when they arrived. Behind him stood two of the Palace Guard. The lord chamberlain announced Fitch, then backed out of the room and shut the door.

Fitch bowed at the waist and said, "Your Majesty."

"Please sit," the king said, waving at some armchairs opposite the desk. He picked up a piece of paper, came around the desk, and sat down.

"We understand we owe you great thanks," the king commenced. "It was you who spread the word from Dostin to Baust. Sir Gerald, Sir Jamel, and Dame Kapiste speak quite highly of you and the young lady who was your guide. I've also heard from my cousin Vicki about you—well, mostly about the young lady, but she did mention you, Lieutenant. I understand you have quite a story to tell."

"Yes, Your Majesty," Fitch replied. He then began to tell the story of what had happened in Boreas—the death of King Philip, his suspicion of the chancellor, the problems with succession to the throne in the absence of Prince John, and his decision to try to find the prince. At this, the king interrupted.

"Prince John did not come to Austeria on a state visit," he replied. "There was no reason for him to come, especially at such a dangerous time to sail."

"The chancellor claimed it had something to do with our continued alliance against the Skamorrans," Fitch recounted. "I was not present in the meetings, but I heard that there was a letter to Prince John in your name, bearing your seal. The chancellor urged Prince John to leave immediately based on the urgent tone of your letter."

"Hmm," the king replied. "That is troubling. There was no letter from me. And Prince John has not arrived, as I told you. What will you do now?"

"Your Majesty, I cannot return to Boreas without the prince. I must either find him or—"

"Where could he be, Lieutenant? He is not here. The ocean is so vast you could spend your entire life searching the coasts and cover only the tiniest fraction."

"There is a possibility," Fitch said heavily, "that he is a prisoner of the Skamorrans."

"If that is the case," the king stated, "we will learn about it when they choose to trumpet that news far and wide. There is nothing you can do if that's true."

"I suppose," Fitch answered glumly.

"In the meantime, we have the problem of several thousand Skamorrans in our country," the king said. "Since you cannot return to Boreas without your prince, would you consider granting us your allegiance temporarily? Sir Gerald, in particular, feels strongly that you would be of great assistance. From what he tells me, you have far more knowledge and experience than any lieutenant he's ever known. Is there a story there?"

Fitch explained his career and how he had taken a step back in rank when he joined the Border Wardens and another step back when he joined the Palace Guard. The king asked pointed questions of him at different times in Fitch's narrative. When Fitch reached the end of his summary, the king nodded gravely.

"We are prepared to offer you a position in our army," the king stated. "You may know that Auster does not keep a large standing army, as Boreas does. Most of the time, our army serves as a training cadre for the local militias. People like Sir Gerald and Dame Kapiste and some others you met have spent time in our small regular army in their younger days. During times like these, when we are called to war, the standing army serves as the backbone, with the militia units added and the army's officers in overall command. I would like to appoint you as a colonel in our army. Ordinarily, you would be in command of a troop of a hundred army soldiers of mixed arms supplemented by between six and seven hundred members of the militia—almost all mounted. In the current circumstances, I will appoint you to the staff of General Gladstone and not a regiment. His brigade will spearhead our siege of Chartage and, I hope, its quick recapture. He will arrive this evening, and you will meet him tomorrow and depart with him.

"Once the war is over, if there is still no hope for you to return home, you would be based here in Austeria. You would take regular tours of the kingdom, making sure that militia training is regular, rigorous, and ongoing. If you find it deficient in an area, you would report back to me.

"We know such a decision would not be easy to make for a man such as you. We would like you to think about it overnight and return to us tomorrow at this same time. If you are willing to bend the knee to us, we would gladly accept you into our service."

"Thank you, Your Majesty," Fitch replied humbly. "I will consider it carefully and tell you my decision tomorrow.

The meeting with the king was over. His Majesty rose and began to return behind his desk. Fitch got up and went to the door. The lord chamberlain was waiting for him. Before he said anything, the king called out, "Lord Chamberlain, a few minutes of your time, please."

The lord chamberlain signaled for a page to take Fitch back to his room. The lord chamberlain entered, closing the door behind him. "Please sit," the king said politely. At the same time, the king flashed the hand signal to the palace guardsmen to "stand ready." The king was busy writing a brief note. He signed it, then used a candle to melt some sealing wax below his signature and pressed his seal into it.

"Lieutenant Fitch has done us a very great service," the king stated as he looked up from what he had just written, "though he does not yet know how great a service he has performed."

"What do you mean, Your Majesty?" the lord chamberlain asked.

"He told us the most fantastic story," the king continued, "about the assassination of King Philip and about how Prince John has gone missing. Have you heard the story?"

The lord chamberlain was feeling a bit uncomfortable but refused to show it. Pretending interest, he leaned forward. "No, Your Majesty. I have not heard."

"We would have thought you had," the king muttered.

"I'm afraid, given the current crisis," the lord chamberlain said smoothly, "I haven't had the chance to stay abreast of the latest rumors."

"Yes, the current crisis," the king said. "So many things that went awry. Corsairs reported to appear at Bergin in force and attack the city—we sent the fleet to respond, and in the fleet's absence—the Skamorrans invaded and captured Chartage. Thank the gods for Lieutenant Fitch's timely arrival and able assistance or we might be looking out at a Skamorran army right now."

"His arrival was quite fortuitous," the lord chamberlain agreed.

"Quite," the king stated. "You will be disappointed, no doubt, to hear that the news from Bergin is not good."

"News from Bergin?" the lord chamberlain questioned, feeling uneasy.

"Yes, from Bergin. Did you know we sent Captain Morganthaler to Bergin?" the king asked.

"No, I did not, Your Majesty."

"Well, we did. We just received a dispatch from him. Very troubling. There were no Skamorran corsairs at Bergin. We sent our fleet to pursue a ghost and left Chartage Harbor undefended. Perfect for the Skamorrans who happened to sail in a few days later. It gets even worse, you know."

The lord chamberlain shook his head, pretending to be dismayed by the news.

"Our fleet was caught by a typhoon with a lee shore," the king continued. "Thirty-one of our fifty galleys wrecked. Almost one-third of our Navy was destroyed, chasing ghosts. Captain Morganthaler planned to speak with Dame Wisenhut but learned that Dame Wisenhut died just before he arrived, supposedly by her own hand."

"That's horrible," the lord chamberlain emoted, feeling a bit less threatened.

"She apparently left a note in her own hand, claiming she had lied about the Skamorran corsairs in order to draw the fleet away from Chartage and admitted working on behalf of Skamorra. Her guilty conscience forced her to kill herself."

"Immortal gods!" the lord chamberlain exclaimed, trying to mimic surprise.

"Yes, who would have believed it?" the king said. "Certainly not us. We've known the good Dame for almost our entire life. Fortunately, Captain Morganthaler was there to figure things out for us. And then, today, we see this Borean and hear his incredible tale. The most unbelievable part of his story was when he told us that Prince John left Boreas at the beginning of the stormy season, responding to an urgent letter from us—a letter marked with our seal. Of course, we didn't believe him."

From behind his desk the king gave a hand signal to the guards which meant "seize him on my signal."

"Of course," the lord chamberlain said with some relief.

"But then it occurred to me that the Borean Palace Guard would certainly have heard if an official letter with the seal of the king had been received. Our own guards see and hear everything that is discussed in our meetings. The only problem is that we did not write the letter and there is only one other person who has access to my official seal, Lord Chamberlain. Then we recalled who was so adamant that we send the fleet to Bergin when we received the urgent message from Dame Wisenhut. Come to think of it, we never got a look at that urgent message, did we, Lord Chamberlain?"

The king flashed the signal to the guards to move. They advanced and pinned the lord chamberlain in his seat with their swords drawn. The lord chamberlain began to sputter in protest.

"Spare us your denials, you traitor," the king spat. "Since you've been in this post, we've had our doubts about you. For two years, your fake smiles and false sentiments have irritated us. Captain Morganthaler's letter and Lieutenant Fitch's tale have combined to shed light on your dark doings. Before this day is over, we will have the truth from you."

17

In Boreas, Captain of the Palace Guard Stan Barthlemy stared at the ceiling in a quiet state of despair. He had returned from the Skamorran border four days ago, having, of course, found no trace of Lieutenant Fitch. After the first day, when they had nearly captured him, they lost all trace of his trail. Barthlemy's men were aware of his frustration and could attest that his search had been thorough. None of them had the slightest inkling that it was all a hoax. Two days after their return, the chancellor had promoted Stan to Captain of the Guard.

Stan found it easy to play the part of the betrayed friend since it was what everyone expected. The first night, after they had almost caught up to Fitch before their horses faltered, Barthlemy cursed his friend when the other members of the guards questioned what was going on. None of them could believe the Fitch had anything to do with the king's death, but after Stan's performance by the campfire that night, they never questioned it again.

Barthlemy knew the chancellor had a low opinion of soldiers, thinking them sluggish and stupid, only capable of carrying out simple orders. To think that Fitch, who served under Prince John for six years, would have anything to do with the king's assassination was completely ridiculous to any human being with a smidgen of common sense. Since the chancellor believed soldiers were dullards, Barthlemy would pretend that he would believe whatever the chancellor told him.

Barthlemy had already learned that the chancellor had sent another group riding south, looking for Fitch in the ports on the southern peninsula. They had returned without sighting him. The chancellor seemed unconcerned by Fitch's clean escape, and so Barthlemy would appear unconcerned as well. Reading between the lines, though, the chancellor's lack of concern indicated to Barthlemy that it was unlikely the prince was still alive.

This afternoon, Barthlemy had stood guard behind the chancellor as he reassured different members of the nobility that they would summon Prince John from Auster as soon as typhoon season ended. The slick way in which the chancellor had dismissed their worries grated on Stan. He wished he could draw the different nobles aside and share what he knew but it was not the right time for that.

While he stared at the ceiling, Barthlemy wondered whether he should bother trying to tell the nobles at all. It might be easier to simply kill the chancellor at the appropriate time. When that time would be, he had no idea. He hoped at some point in the future to get word from Fitch whether there was any hope the prince still lived.

That afternoon, there was an undercurrent of energy in the palace. Fitch could feel it. When he took lunch, there were many whispered conversations that died as he drew near. He felt the pressure of many eyes making surreptitious glances at him. He hurried to finish the meal and left. He found his way to a garden and paced, pondering what he would do. That evening he dined alone once more, again feeling the eyes of everyone on him. The next morning's breakfast was similarly uncomfortable.

A page came to his room later and took him to the king's chambers. Upon entering, Fitch bowed. The king rose and came around the desk, sitting and gesturing for Fitch to do the same.

"Are you willing to accept our offer?" the king asked.

"Your Majesty," Fitch answered carefully, "I am extremely flattered by your offer. I am willing to swear allegiance to you with one condition—that if Prince John still lives, my allegiance must return to him. I hope you can understand."

"Colonel Fitch," the king said with a smile, "we understand and approve. Further, if there is any news of the possible whereabouts of the prince, alive or not, the Crown of Auster will lend you any aid you need to pursue it."

Fitch let out a sigh of relief. "Thank you, Your Majesty. Then I am prepared to swear my allegiance to you."

Late that afternoon Dame Gruber arrived at the palace with all the subtlety of a thunderstorm. She sent a note telling Fitch that he would be dining with her that evening, but he did not see her or Mira. A page knocked quietly on the door of the apartment just before the nineteenth hour and asked Fitch to accompany him. He followed the young man through the corridors. He led Fitch to a dining room. Dame Gruber and Mira were waiting for them.

"Well, Lieutenant," Dame Gruber said immediately, "you certainly kicked over a hornet's nest. Or should I say, Colonel?"

Mira's eyebrows raised. Gruber explained, "Teddy offered him a colonelcy based on his experience and competence. It's enough rank that people will be forced to listen to him and take him seriously, even though he's Borean. He will be on the staff of General Gladstone, who is due to arrive momentarily."

"What do you mean about a hornet's nest, ma'am?" Ralph replied when she finished her explanation.

"I'm no more 'ma'am' than I am Dame Gruber to you here in private, Ralph," she admonished, wagging her finger at him. "I was just chatting with Teddy, getting caught up," she explained. "Your story yesterday was apparently the missing piece of a puzzle that makes all the others fit properly. Teddy had not been happy with the lord chamberlain since he was thrust upon him two years ago or so. There was a group of the nobility that pushed very hard for Jeremy, the now-deceased lord chamberlain—"

"Now-deceased?" Mira asked.

"Yes, dear, now-deceased," Dame Gruber stated. "Teddy never liked him—felt he was slimy and untrustworthy—but trying to keep the barons happy is important. Since Jeremy has been in the position a number of small things have been happening that bothered Teddy—not the least of which was his being the most insincere person I've ever met. The most recent thing that troubled Teddy before you arrived was the 'urgent' message from Dame Wisenhut that resulted in sending the Western Squadron of the fleet to Bergin. The lord chamberlain had urged that we respond to her emergency in the strongest way possible by sending the entire squadron.

"This, of course, left Chartage Harbor empty for the Skamorrans to sail in. With corsairs in Chartage Harbor and the Skamorrans holding the city, the fleet would not be able to dislodge them. A bonus for the Skamorrans was that our ships were caught by the typhoon that you sailed through, Ralph. It hit our fleet with a lee shore and over half the Western Squadron was wrecked. Teddy had already smelled a rat before any of the bad news arrived and had already sent one of his palace guards to Bergin to investigate. The whole thing was a hoax. There had likely never been any corsairs off Bergin, and the letter the lord chamberlain claimed he received from Dame Wisenhut probably never existed. Captain Morganthaler of the guard reported that Dame Wisenhut was dead, and it had been arranged to look like a suicide. The captain did not think it was—he called it a hasty and clumsy attempt at making a murder seem self-inflicted.

"Then you arrived and told Teddy the story of what happened to your king and Prince John, and that, along with the sack of Chartage and the ruse to pull the fleet away, made everything fit into place for Teddy. He had the lord chamberlain arrested and spent the rest of yesterday extracting information from the weasel. It appears the Skamorrans have wormed their way deep into the governments of both Auster and Boreas. Teddy now has a problem with the nobles who pushed so hard for Jeremy to be named lord chamberlain and also with his ambassador to Boreas, who was certainly part of whatever scheme was going on, not to mention needing to push the damned Skamorrans out of Chartage. So, quite a hornet's nest," she concluded. "There is usually always something sinister going on behind the scenes concerning the crown. Teddy told me he's had enough and will be taking steps to put an end to it. I would imagine it's not far different in Boreas."

Ralph thought a moment before responding. "I suppose it is, Vicki," he said, forcing her first name out despite his instincts. "But in Boreas, I knew who was untrustworthy, and here—"

"It's all new," Vicki finished. "New to you, perhaps, but to those of us more familiar... What about Boreas? Did you have a feeling about your chancellor?"

"Yes."

"Why didn't King Philip or Prince John?"

"I think they knew, in their hearts, that Mark was not a good person," Ralph explained, "but their mother defended him so vigorously while she was alive. I think Philip and John intentionally disregarded his flaws because of that. From what I understand, he was always careful around them, but he treated everyone else like dirt when they weren't around. I'm sure they had heard about some incidents but made allowances because of their mother."

"Interesting," Vicki commented. "Are you certain he killed King Philip?"

"I don't know whether he did or one of the Skamorrans," Ralph replied, "but it doesn't really matter."

"Are you surprised by his actions?"

Ralph paused and thought. "A bit," he said at length. "I didn't think he had the guts. I'm sure he was jealous enough. The more I've thought about it, the more I think he'd been planning this for some time, but I certainly saw no signs that something was brewing. That said, I tended to avoid the chancellor. We all did."

"Mm," Vicki murmured in response. "Does he have any support among the nobility?"

"Not that I'm aware of," Fitch said with a shrug, "but then again, I wouldn't be the best person to know. I was unaware of any dissatisfaction among the nobles, but that doesn't mean there wasn't any."

"I never had the impression that Boreas had the same level of palace intrigue that we do in Auster," Gruber commented, "so there might not have been any. In Auster, our line of succession was broken four generations ago. Teddy's family did not have the strongest claim in terms of kinship, but did have the most support. There's another family, led by the Duke of Volplane, that feels they should have been granted the throne, and they've been unhappy since, sometimes openly, sometimes not. They have a group that follows them. It was that group that put the late lord chamberlain in place. Teddy went along with it to appease them and try to keep them happy. Now Teddy finds he has two kinds of conflict to deal with—one with the Skamorrans and the other with some of the nobility."

"If Prince John is dead," Fitch explained, "our line of succession gets murky. The closest claim is a childless old man whose mind is gone. Behind him are a couple of second and third cousins who have roughly equal weight in terms of kinship and presumably support from their region. Without proof that the prince is dead, like a body or an eyewitness, Borean law requires a three-year period before the courts will make a ruling. During that time, the government is in the hands of an interregnum, headed by the chancellor, who is himself a distant cousin on the old queen's side."

"Hmm," Gruber mused, steepling her fingers. "If any of the cousins moves before the three years is up, then it makes them look complicit in the murder of the king. If the cousins don't make a move before three years, the chancellor will have that time to consolidate his grip on power. Clever. Mira, are you following all this?"

"Yes," Mira replied with a sad shake of her head, "though I must say it's disappointing."

"You would expect the nobility to behave better?" Gruber asked.

"Yes."

"They don't. Often, they are more petty, selfish, and childish. But enough of this dreadful business. After you left, Mira and I had the chance to discuss her future at some length," Vicki continued. "The two of you are quite famous in a small way. The story of how you rode to raise the alarm had already made it to Austinton before we left. I was absolutely correct in separating you two—tongues would wag this close to the capital. While I was meeting with Teddy this afternoon, I asked him to add her to the Royal Courier Service. She'll be a dispatch rider. That way, she won't have to be in the army, will get to enjoy her marvelous horse, and see you from time to time. Sadly, it means she won't get to wear those wonderful gowns we made, but I will keep them for a better time. Speaking of clothing, Ralph, what are you doing for uniforms? You can't wear your Borean ones."

"A man came by this afternoon and took measurements," Fitch explained. "He said my uniforms would be ready the day after tomorrow and sent ahead to meet up with me. Tomorrow, I meet General Gladstone and leave with his unit. We will gather various militia groups along the way, including those I fought with already."

"I'm to be fitted for my courier uniforms tomorrow and will leave for my posting as soon as they're finished," Mira commented with a small frown. "I am going to join the Chartage Road barracks for now."

"That means she will be riding up and down the road between Austeria and Chartage, carrying government dispatches," Gruber explained. "They run dispatches in relays, with each rider only carrying them a couple of towns down the road, then handing them off to a fresh horse and rider."

"We have a similar system in Boreas," Fitch commented. "Each leg is ten to twelve miles. It keeps the horses sound and has proven to be the quickest way."

After dinner, Ralph escorted Mira and Vicki back to the rooms in the palace allotted to the Dame. Vicki excused herself after entering what looked to be a small apartment, giving Fitch a chance to say goodbye properly. Suddenly shy, Mira leaned forward tentatively. Fitch read her cue and grasped her shoulders and kissed her. He led her to a settee.

"Mira, I don't know what the future holds for us, but I'd like to find out. When this war is over, if there is any chance of my finding Prince John, I must pursue it. That's the only thing I can think of that stands in the way of my having a life with you."

"But what if you find him?" Mira asked.

Fitch smiled ruefully, shaking his head slightly. "That would change things as far as my obligations, but I would still want you in my life somehow. Honestly, though, I don't think I'll ever find him. I suspect he's dead—drowned from the storm that caught him—or somehow a prisoner of the Skamorrans. I would imagine I'll learn if that's the case when I get through with the business at Chartage."

18

The next morning, a page woke Fitch at daybreak. After washing up briefly and shaving, he put on the better of his two uniforms, packed the small remainder of his belongings, and followed the page down to the dining hall. A group of men were seated there. Near the center of the group, a stocky, broad-shouldered man with a swarthy complexion stood as Fitch neared.

"Colonel Fitch," he said, extending his hand in greeting.

"Sir," Fitch replied noncommittally as he shook hands.

"Bert Gladstone," the man informed him. "Have a seat and dig in. They're bringing our mounts around, and we leave in a few minutes."

Gladstone introduced Ralph to the other men and women in the group. Some looked at him with curiosity, others with a bit of a challenge written on their faces. Food was brought to him and Ralph wasted no time in eating, dropping into a habit that he developed over his years of military service. There was something vaguely familiar about General Gladstone that caused Fitch to look at him several times. When Gladstone laughed, Ralph was convinced he had heard that deep rolling guffaw before.

"Sir," he asked, when he had the opportunity to break in, "have you ever been to Boreas?"

"Yes," Gladstone replied. "About seven years ago, the king sent me to get some experience with your Border Wardens. I was there for about ten months. You were in Prince John's regiment, if I recall correctly."

"Yes, sir, I was. I thought you looked familiar, but our paths didn't cross much. It was when I heard you laugh that—"

Gladstone laughed again, interrupting. "It gives me away, it does. Gentlemen, I can tell you from experience that Colonel Fitch has more experience fighting the Skamorrans than the rest of the table added together, including me. From the reports I've read, he was instrumental in calling out the militia and working with them to convince the Skamorrans to turn back to Chartage when they first ventured out. As far as your units go, rest easy. He's here to work with me, not to take any of your commands."

One of the men who had been giving Fitch a guarded look earlier spoke up. "We thought he was taking one of the regiments, General."

"Nope," Gladstone replied. "He will be an advisor. And I'll be leaning on his advice heavily."

Fitch could see, out of the corner of his eye, that several at the table relaxed slightly upon hearing this. "Now that they know you're not here to take their posts, maybe they'll treat you decent, eh?" Gladstone commented to Fitch, ending with another guffaw.

"Looks like everyone's finished," Gladstone added. "Time we left."

He stood and everyone else followed suit. Fitch grabbed his bag and trailed the group. When they reached a door to the outside, he found grooms waiting with horses. Fitch hadn't seen his horse for two days and took time to greet him before slinging his bag behind the saddle. He then checked the girth and the rest of the tack and found all was in order. He mounted and waited for the group to start.

As they headed out of the palace and then out of the city, Fitch found himself near the rear of the group. Gladstone was chatting amiably with the men and women in the group but gradually drifting further and further back. When the group was entering the rolling farms outside the city, he and Fitch were the last of the group.

"Don't mind them," Gladstone muttered quietly. "They were all worried that a new guy, and a foreigner at that, would take over one of their units. They're good commanders—have a strong bond with their people. It helps because we're set up differently from Boreas. We spread half the regular troops around and seed the militia units with them, keeping the other half as our reserve. Knowing that you have a backbone in every unit that is comprised of soldiers you trust helps everything work—at least in exercises. We haven't had a ground war in generations, but this is the system we used the last time, and it worked well then.

"That's why having you here is what I consider to be a piece of damned good luck," Gladstone continued. "You have recent and extensive experience in fighting the Skamorrans. We don't—not on land. We skirmish with them fairly often at sea, but it's not the same."

"Speaking of the sea," Fitch responded, "if we hope to lay a siege on Chartage, we have to prevent them from getting supplies shipped in. Who is in charge of the navy and how do we coordinate with them?"

Gladstone grimaced. "That's going to be a bit of a pickle, I'm afraid. We recently lost thirty-one of the fifty galleys in the Western Squadron, including the admiral. I don't know who the new admiral is yet."

"I heard about that," Fitch admitted.

"Yeah," Gladstone said glumly. "And of the nineteen left, five are banged up pretty good and the rest all have some storm damage. So, we have only fourteen galleys we can count on to enforce a blockade. That's plenty to keep them bottled up in the harbor but not nearly enough if they decide to force the issue from the open ocean. I don't expect them to try anything until the spring, and we might have the other five galleys repaired by then, but we'll still be too few. We'll have to pull some from the Eastern Squadron and that will have to wait until spring.

"The other issue we have is that we're besieging our own city. The remaining residents are hostages to the Skamorrans. In a normal siege, we'd try to starve the Skamorrans out, but in this case, it's our own people who'd suffer first and the most. I've been wracking my brain trying to come up with better answers, but nothing has come to me yet. If you develop any ideas, throw 'em out there."

As they journeyed north towards Chartage, Ralph had the chance to meet the others in the group. Knowing that he was not going to replace any of them, they relaxed and were curious about his background and experience. Along the way they rode through two storms, each lasting for two miserable days of driving rains and howling winds. One of the group, Major Newagen, lent Ralph an oilskin from her pack. Though it was too small for him to button up front, it did help keep the wind and rain off most of him.

When they reached Oldcastle, a dispatch rider caught up with them, bringing Ralph his new Austerian uniforms. He changed into one of them before dinner. The rest of the group whistled at him when he entered the dining room. Ralph had to admit the uniform was attractive: dark blue and buff.

The next day they rode past McGovern and to the place where Fitch had helped stop the Skamorran advance. The bridge over the creek had already been rebuilt. As he was explaining to Gladstone the different actions they had taken that day, the rest of the group closed in to hear. They were curious about the calcitrapae. Ralph headed down the bank to near the ford and found several, which he passed out. They passed what was left of the town of Baust, which the Skamorrans had put to the torch. Fitch was pleased to see people rebuilding already.

Another day and a half of riding brought them to the main encampment near Chartage. The regular army units had only arrived the day before and a small city of tents had sprung up. That afternoon, Fitch had a chance to look at detailed maps of Chartage and its defenses.

The city was on the western side of a large, egg-shaped bay. The narrow end of the egg opened to the ocean, with a small fort built on the western headland. The eastern side of the bay rose steeply about two hundred feet to the eastern headland. This eastern side gradually lost elevation to the east and south. Near the bottom of the egg, the ground was only about twenty feet above the tide line, and it was here that the city walls began. The city walls ran from there in a fish-hook shape up to the fort on the western headland.

The area outside the walls had buildings indicated on the map where the city had spread. General Gladstone informed him that most of the outer buildings had been destroyed by the Skamorrans. About half a mile south of the walls, there was a tree line, the beginning of a forest. Fitch asked the general if he knew of any weaknesses in the defensive walls.

"We'll have to ask someone who has more local knowledge," Gladstone answered. "They're old—more than three hundred years. We didn't build them."

"Who did?"

"The Skamorrans," Gladstone replied with a shrug. "Way back when, the Skamorrans controlled Chartage for a couple of centuries. Auster wasn't unified when they came—we were a bunch of separate kingdoms. They built the walls to help hang onto it."

"How did Auster recapture the city?"

"Siege and blockade. We never breached the walls, if that's what you're asking."

"Which we should try to avoid," Fitch commented, "since the Austerians still in the city will be the first to suffer. If you don't mind, tomorrow I'd like to ride over and take a look at the layout myself."

"Hell, I'll come with you," Gladstone agreed.

They set off the next morning. When they reached where the road came out of the trees, with Chartage in sight ahead, they were stopped by a group of soldiers. Fitch was pleased to see Sir Gerald among them. Ralph and the general dismounted. Sir Gerald broke into a grin, seeing Ralph in his new Austerian uniform.

"I'm delighted they took my recommendation to heart," he said, smiling. "How are you, Bert?" he said to Gladstone.

"I'm well, Gerry," he replied, shaking hands. "How are things?"

"Fairly stable," Sir Gerald shrugged. "Occasionally, they send out a patrol in the middle of the night, but thanks to Fitch's dirty little tricks, they don't have much luck."

"The bent nails?" Gladstone inquired.

"Precisely. We've spread them quite heavily in certain areas. Impossible to spot them in the dark but we sure know when they step on one," he chuckled. "Come to take a look at things?"

"Fitch and I were going over the maps but there's no substitute for seeing it for yourself."

"Let's ride up to the head," Sir Gerald suggested. "That's the best view."

They remounted, waiting for Sir Gerald to get his horse. He led them back up the road and then along a trail recently cut through the woods. They exited the trees suddenly, and the ground began to climb. They reached the top of the eastern headland, and Ralph could see the entire bay.

The bay was filled with Skamorran corsairs. Fitch counted quickly and came up with a rough estimate of a hundred and sixty of the sleek vessels. They rested at anchor, just far enough away from one another that they would not touch as the wind or tide moved them about. Compared to the Borean galleons, the corsairs were much lower in the sides and, from the cocked spars, seemed to employ triangular sails instead of square ones.

"Is this all their ships?" he asked.

"No," Sir Gerald responded. "A dozen and a half left a few days ago and looked to be sailing back to Skamorra. Our lookouts watched them disappear over the horizon."

"How many troops have we assembled?" Gladstone asked.

"Last count, just shy of eight thousand," Sir Gerald replied.

"Not enough to storm the city," Gladstone remarked glumly.

Turning his attention to the town and its defenses, Ralph could see that the Skamorrans had razed all the buildings outside of the walls. While this made it easy to see the layout of the defenses it also would make it near-impossible to get close to the walls without being seen. The map he had studied had been accurate but seeing it in person was sobering.

The defensive wall, built by the Skamorrans hundreds of years earlier, was stout and tall. The lowest part was in the east but the Skamorrans had been busy and dug a broad and deep ditch in front of that section. In addition, when the wall was built, they had hewn away the rock, cutting a notch in the upward-sloping ground, effectively ending the wall in a cliff face that rose fifty feet straight up.

Ralph asked if they could ride along the coast. Sir Gerald and General Gladstone shrugged their shoulders in silent agreement, and they mounted and followed a trail along the heights overlooking the ocean, leaving the bay behind. "What's down there—under the water?" Ralph asked.

Sir Gerald looked at him, puzzled.

"How deep is it? Are there shoals or reefs?" Ralph clarified.

"I have no idea," Sir Gerald responded.

"Do you have anyone in camp who is familiar with this coast?"

"I don't know. We'll check," Sir Gerald replied.

"What are you thinking, son?" General Gladstone asked.

"From looking at the wall," Ralph explained, "even if it's weak in spots, we'd need some catapults or trebuchets to pound on it in the hope of making a breach. That might take a long time. It occurs to me that the only easy way into Chartage is the same way the Skamorrans came—by water.”

“But you saw those corsairs in the harbor,” Gladstone pointed out. “And with our fleet depleted the way it is…”

“We wouldn’t stand a chance in a fair fight,” Ralph admitted. Then, grinning, he added, “I’m not thinking about a fair fight. Let’s go back to camp and find some sailors. I have an idea, but I need to talk it over with some people who know these waters first.”

19

John's memory still eluded him. From time to time, he would remember snippets of things but had no way of summoning these moments. His head healed, and his headaches went away. He became restless. The feeling that there was something he was supposed to be doing nagged at him.

When the weather permitted, he took longer and longer walks around the island. On one of his walks, he came across a man whose light-brown hair was twisted into long, ropey tendrils. Instinctively, John reached for where his sword would be if he carried one. He stopped in his tracks.

"Hold there, brother," the man said, noticing John's reactions. He held up his hands in a sign of peace. "That's not necessary."

John eyed him warily. The man made no move. They stared at one another for a few minutes.

"Who are you?" John asked, finally.

"Isaiah," the man replied. "Isaiah, son of Levi, though God only knows if he's still above the earth or below."

"You're from—"

"Skamorra," Isaiah answered. "Originally. Now I live on the island, just like you."

"Skamorra," John whispered to himself. The word meant something to him. It had to, since he remembered grabbing for his weapon that wasn't there.

"You're the fella that washed up a couple of moons ago, ain't ya?" Isaiah asked. "Lost your memory, I heard."

John nodded guardedly.

Isaiah laughed. "Not all of it since you were reaching for a sword when you saw me. I heard tell you're Borean, and that proved it."

John was genuinely puzzled. "Our countries—at war. Why?"

"Religion," Isaiah answered. "We don't believe the same as you. You don't believe the same as us. We fight about it. Only back in the world, though—not here."

"Not here?"

"On the island. There's a handful of us, some even in Town, but those in Town go along to get along, so to speak. They gave up Skamorran ways. They cut their hair, for instance."

"You don't," John countered.

"A handful of us, here on the eastern end, keep to it," Isaiah answered with a shrug of his shoulders. "To honor our God, mostly, so that when we come to be judged, he finds favor with us for keeping faith. He saw fit to cast us here when he could have drowned us, so we owe him something, I reckon. We keeps to ourselves mostly. Nobody wants trouble here. Not like the world."

"Back where we come from," John clarified, "we fight about religion? This feels like something I should know, but—so many of my memories are still not returning."

"Well," Isaiah said, stroking his chin, "it's important enough to both sides that our countries have been fighting each other for hundreds of years. Not important enough to fight about here. We just keeps to ourselves except for them that doesn't. Them what's missing being people decided to cut their hair and move to Town. Whatever gods you want to worship, you go on and do it. I'll worship my God."

When John returned from meeting Isaiah, he had many questions he wanted to ask. Cia was hanging laundry to dry when he walked up. She saw him and smiled, then noticed the quizzical look on his face.

"Hi, John. Did something happen on your walk?"

"Hi, Cia. I guess you could say that. I went to the eastern end of the island and met a Skamorran," he explained.

She heard what he said. After a moment, her hand flew to her face when she realized how unusual that would have been for John. She hadn't experienced it the way.

"Caleb," John asked when Cia's father returned, "today I encountered Isaiah, a Skamorran. As soon as I saw him, my hand went to where my sword would have been. We talked, and he explained our two countries have fought for centuries over religion. Could you explain more?"

"Let's sit down," Caleb suggested. "This might take some time."

"Why?" John asked.

"Because it involves religion, and religion takes time to explain, Caleb said. "We need to start with the idea of the divine—that there are powers greater than ourselves that control and manipulate the world and influence our lives. Does any of that seem familiar to you?"

John paused and thought. Nothing came to him. He shook his head.

"Hmm. Let me try it this way," Caleb said. "You were on a ship. It was caught in a storm. You were injured—perhaps you fell, or the boom of the sail hit you in the head, or something else happened. Somehow, you ended up drifting here, to Daubmer Island. You were likely unconscious for most of the trip. How long it took, I can't guess. Why didn't your ship sink? It was clearly quite damaged. Why did you survive? You could have been washed overboard or died of thirst, or died from your injuries. How do you explain this?"

"I can't," John said

"Religion is the idea that your being here is not the result of blind chance," Caleb said. "Religion is an attempt to understand what forces or powers might have decided to save you. If you believe that much, then you might wonder what their purpose was in doing so."

"Caleb, I have been troubled recently that there is something I am meant to be doing—that I have a responsibility I am shirking," John said. "I don't know what it is—I can't remember. The storm prevented me from attending to this obligation. I was on my way to do something or meet someone, and I still feel the urge to get on with it, even though I have no idea what *it* was."

"If you believe you were saved so you could complete that assignment, then who or what acted on your behalf?" Caleb asked.

"I have no idea," John said, shaking his head.

"Well, you are Borean," Caleb said, "as I am. We believe there are fourteen major Gods and Goddesses and a host of minor ones. The Gods are supposed to work together for the betterment of humanity. For the most part, they do—in subtle ways that often we only perceive well after the fact. Occasionally, some of the Gods work at cross purposes, causing chaos and unrest in the world of man. Believing in this divine structure helps us men understand things that cannot be easily explained otherwise—like your particular situation.

"In order to maintain the favor of the Gods, they also prescribe certain behaviors that men should follow. Some of the qualities they demand are honesty, fidelity, respect for them and for one's fellow man, doing one's duty to his family, his ancestors, his country, and the Gods, of course. Certain behaviors are to be avoided. Some of these are greed, lust for another's property, or excesses in living, such as gluttony or drunkenness."

"Isaiah, the Skamorran, said they have different beliefs," John said.

"The Skamorrans believe there is only one God. Their God commands them to behave in a similar fashion to what our Gods demand. The difference is that they think the rest of us are wrong—so wrong, that their God wants them to convert us to their thinking or kill us," Caleb said. "For hundreds of years, they have been at war with Boreas and the country that possesses the continent to the south of the Midland Sea, Auster. Boreas and Auster share the same beliefs. The countries on the other side of the Solortus Ocean also believe as we do, though they use other names since their languages differ."

"And the Skamorrans have been fighting the rest of the world because of this?" John asked.

"Since before written history began," Caleb confirmed.

"Seems silly," John said.

"I think most non-Skamorrans feel the same way," Caleb agreed. "For the Skamorrans, it is something they are deadly serious about."

"Caleb, do you believe the Gods saved me for a reason?" John asked.

"I'm certain they did," Caleb replied. "Why? They might provide us with an indication of their purpose in the future. We might never know. For that matter, why are any of us here? Daubmer Island is a small speck in the middle of a vast ocean. Why were any of us sent here instead of drowning? Men have spent their entire lives pondering questions like these."

"That seems to be a waste of time," John commented.

"I don't disagree with you—most of the time," Caleb said. "It is enough for me to believe that there are divine forces that shape the world and guide our actions—not always, but in important moments. Sometimes, though, I am struck dumb, wondering what the meaning of all of it is."

"Are there consequences for people who choose not to follow the dictates of the Gods?" John asked.

"We believe that everyone possesses a soul—a spirit inside of us that is our essence. That spirit lives on—in a different plane of existence—after our physical body dies. If we have lived good lives, our spirits enjoy a pleasant existence. If not, our spirits are consigned to one of the known hells, where our spirit is tortured by the knowledge of our misdeeds and failings or by the victims of our crimes. The Skamorrans believe in the soul as well. For them, the soul of someone who has lived a good life goes to be with their God. Those who transgress are confined to a place of eternal punishment. I don't know that much about it, but I always sensed their hell was much more harsh than ours."

"Isaiah said there are Skamorrans who live in Town, but they have turned their backs on their religion," John commented.

"I don't think it is that they have turned their backs on it," Caleb said, "as much as they have no desire to cause disquiet with anyone. There is no temple on the island. We have no priests. I would venture a guess that everyone here believes in the divine and is grateful for their safe passage to the island, but our worship is private. Just because the Skamorrans here in Town no longer keep their hair in ropey tendrils does not mean their beliefs have changed. Isaiah leads a solitary existence. His appearance is not as troublesome as someone we might see every day."

"Thank you, Caleb," John said. "Some of what you mentioned seems vaguely familiar—as though I knew it at one point. Perhaps it will rise to the surface of my mind, and I will remember more clearly."

That night, John woke from a terrible dream. Men with their hair in long, ropey tendrils were approaching Caleb's house. They were armed with swords and carried torches and were clearly planning on burning the house down with everyone inside.

John sprang from bed, grabbed his sword, and dashed outside. There was no one there. He saw no men with swords or carrying torches. He realized, standing barefoot in the dirt road, that it had only been a dream—but a vivid, frightening one. The Skamorrans were enemies, though, and would kill him given the chance. Not on the island, perhaps, but in the world from which he came he knew he had fought them many times. John understood better why he reached for his sword when he encountered Isaiah.

Now, as the adrenalin wore off, he felt sheepish. He was standing in the dark, sword drawn against a phantom threat. He turned to head back inside but sensed someone in the doorway.

"Is everything alright?" Cia asked in a whisper.

"I—I had a frightening dream," John said. "It was only a dream and nothing to worry about now."

"Would you like some company?" she asked.

What a horrible question for you to ask, Cia, John thought. *I would like nothing better than your company in my bed this evening, but I cannot. For all I know, I have a wife wherever I came from. It would not be fair to you or to her for me to enjoy your company in the way that I think you mean.*

"No, thank you, Cia," John said. "I'll be fine. I'm sorry to have disturbed you."

20

When they returned to camp, Fitch waited for Gladstone to have his people gather sailors who knew the local waters. Some of the first people to wander over to the general's tent were Paul Escamil, Hector Grimble, and Sven Gunnar. Fitch jumped up to greet them.

"What are you doing here?" Fitch exclaimed.

"There are Skamorrans to fight," Sven replied. "Couldn't pass on the opportunity. What uniform is that?"

Fitch quickly shared the story. He told them of how Mira and he raised the alarm and helped turn the Skamorrans back. When he finished, he asked for a moment alone with Grimble.

"Sir, there is more to the story than the others need to hear," Fitch said. "After spending this time with your daughter, I must confess I have feelings for her. My situation is complicated. I'm a soldier, and my first duty is to find my prince if he still lives. It now seems unlikely that he does. I have sworn allegiance to King Theodosius, and he had made me a colonel in the army. I hope that—"

"Good Gods, man," Grimble interrupted. "Just spit it out. You want to marry my daughter?"

"Yes, but not right away. We are still getting to know one another. And not until after we send the Skamorrans home," I said.

"Good. Then I won't need to skin you alive for the things you haven't told me," Grimble said. "That's the insignia of a colonel on your uniform, sure enough. That means to me that you'll be able to provide for her. Go on and marry her."

In all the conversations, Fitch never asked about pay. If Auster paid at roughly the same rates as Boreas, he would indeed be able to support Mira—and in some style and comfort. Fitch wanted to laugh at himself for never inquiring.

"Where is she?" Grimble asked.

"Dame Gruber from Austinton secured Mira a position with the Royal Courier service," Fitch said. "Right now, she is probably somewhere between where we are and Austeria."

"Good for her," Grimble said. "Dame Gruber, eh? How do you know such fancy folk?"

"I don't, sir," Fitch admitted. "She heard about us and took us under her wing when we arrived in Austinton."

"Sounds like a good friend to have," Grimble said.

"She is, sir. The king is her cousin," Fitch said.

"Even better," Grimble agreed. "Now, if you're going to be marrying Mira, you need to stop calling me 'sir.' My name is Hector. Use it. Now, tell me why they want to talk to sailors?"

"I will, in the meeting, Hector," Fitch said. "I don't want to repeat myself. It looks like they have a fair number gathered, so let's rejoin them."

There were a dozen and a half men. Hector knew all of them. Paul Escamil and Sven knew some. They introduced Fitch. General Gladstone called for their attention.

"Colonel Fitch and I were scouting the harbor," Gladstone said, "and he came up with an idea but wanted to talk to those who knew more about wind and tides. I will turn things over to him."

Fitch stood, remembering what he saw earlier. The Skamorrans controlled the bay from the fort on the western headland to where the wall ends on the eastern side of the city, before the ground begins to climb up to the cliffs of the eastern point. The prevailing wind blew from west to east. The location of the fort was the problem.

"Gentlemen, thank you for coming," Fitch said. "The idea I have is simple, but I don't know whether it can be done. I would like to get rafts past the fort into the harbor and then to the western side. The rafts would be piled high with combustibles. If we set them on fire and let them go, they should drift into the Skamorran ships. Is something like this possible?"

The sailors began talking among themselves in different groups. Fitch was heartened to see that they seemed to be discussing ways to make his plan work rather than dismissing it quickly. After a few minutes, the men who were the leaders of the small groups separated. With the other leaders, they put their heads together. When they reached a consensus, one of them stepped forward.

"What you suggest can be done," he said, "but not right away. We need to bring some of our boats up, out of sight of the fort. That will take a couple of days. We need to construct the rafts—again, out of sight from the fort. The moon is currently waning crescent. The new moon is in five days. Low tide will occur in the middle of the night, then. Those conditions will give us the best chance of success."

"I'm not much of a sailor," Fitch said. "Paul Escamil and Sven Gunnar will attest to that. I understand the reason for the new moon—it will make it harder for the Skamorrans to spot what we are doing. Please explain why the other things matter."

"The best way to get these fire rafts into the harbor will be to tow them and release them at the mouth. Then, we let the rising tide carry them in. We will need some men to guide them as much as they can toward the western side and to ignite them," the man explained. "Once that is done, the men will swim to the foot of the eastern point. There is a small shelf of ground exposed for an hour or two until the tide rises to cover it. We might want to position someone there with a torch to guide them. He can ignite the torch once the rafts are lit. When the men have swum over, we can row and collect them."

"Do you think this is something that will be successful?" Fitch asked. "Remember, I'm no sailor."

"Oh, we think it will be devilish," the man said. "Depending on the breeze that night, you might get half or more of them corsairs. They have only a couple of people on each ship—if that. Not enough to fight a fire."

"What if it rains?" Fitch asked.

"Then we hold off to the next night," the man shrugged.

"Let's proceed," General Gladstone said. "Do I need to name someone to be in charge, or will you work it out amongst yourselves?"

"We can take it from here, general," the one said.

Two days later, Fitch saw Mira ride into camp, bearing dispatches from Austeria. He was waiting when she emerged from General Gladstone's tent. When she saw him, she took two running steps toward him, then slowed, looking around to see who was watching.

When she and Fitch reached one another, they clasped hands. An embrace in the middle of the camp would draw too much attention of the wrong sort. Fitch led Mira away from the center of things.

"I spoke to your father," he said. "He has given me permission to marry you if we decide that is what we want."

"Is that what you want?" she asked.

"Mira, being away from you the last few days—I missed you so much it was almost a physical pain," Fitch said. "I think I love you. I've never felt this way about anyone else before, but my feelings are so strong they scare me. Everything has happened so fast—we're in the middle of a war—it's all so confusing to me. Can we slow things down and make sure the way we feel is real?"

Mira threw her arms around Fitch and buried her face in his shoulder. He could feel her sobbing. He tried to soothe her as best he could.

"I wanted to say the same things," she said through her tears. "I think—I hope—what we have is real. I've been praying to the Gods for answers."

"What have they said?" Fitch asked with a cheeky smile.

"They are letting me figure it out on my own," she replied with a wry smile. "In the meantime, even though it is hard to be apart, can we continue as we are? You in the military, and me a courier?"

"As long as I get to see you every few days," Fitch responded.

"If I couldn't see you, I think I'd go crazy," she admitted.

"When do you need to return?" Fitch asked.

"Not until tomorrow morning, at the earliest," Mira said with a sly smile. "But before we can think about that, I need to attend to Shasta."

"Colonel Fitch?" General Gladstone called from inside his tent.

"I have responsibilities, too, it seems," he said.

Fitch looked both ways quickly. He tugged Mira by her hands closer to him. He pecked her lips quickly, then turned to attend to the general.

"Interesting news, Colonel," Gladstone remarked, handing the dispatch to him. "This is a report from the king. The noble families who put the late Lord Chamberlain in place are unrepentant. As soon as we finish dealing with these damned Skamorrans, we may find ourselves in the midst of a civil war."

"Sir, we haven't even dislodged the Skamorrans from Chartage yet," Fitch protested.

"I know," Gladstone said with a sigh. "Speaking of which, what happens after we burn their ships?"

"Well, how much of the Skamorran fleet is in the harbor?" Fitch asked.

"Roughly two-thirds of their total number of ships," Gladstone answered. "The last I heard, they had over two hundred corsairs."

"Auster uses galleys, don't they?" Fitch asked.

"Yes," Gladstone answered. "Two squadrons, fifty galleys in each."

"And the Western Squadron was just hit by the typhon and lost thirty-one ships. Is that right?" Fitch asked.

"Yes, with five badly damaged," Gladstone added.

"With fourteen lightly damaged galleys, how many corsairs could we expect them to take on?"

"It depends," Gladstone said. "On the open sea, or in—"

"In Chartage Harbor," Fitch replied.

"If we manage to eliminate half the corsairs in the harbor, the galleys should be able to handle the remainder," Gladstone said. "Being in an enclosed space, with little room to move, takes away the best advantage the corsairs have—speed. Our galleys will be more nimble in the tight space and should be able to sink the rest."

"Then you need to request that they order those ships here right away," Fitch said. "I think we will be successful. Then the question will become, what do we do with the prisoners?"

"Let's not get too far ahead of ourselves," Gladstone cautioned.

"We will need to be prepared," Fitch said. "If we destroy those corsairs, we can prevent the Skamorrans from resupplying their soldiers. They will have the choice to surrender or starve."

"Let's not too far ahead of ourselves," Gladstone repeated.

"Fine," Fitch said.

"Come with me," Cia said to John.

"Where are we going?"

"To watch someone depart on an attempt to reach the mainland," she said.

"Who is it?" John asked.

"His name is Peter Rathbun," she replied. "I've known him my whole life."

"What makes him think he will be successful when others have failed?"

"He thinks his boat will be able to sail against the prevailing winds," Cia said. "He says it's not like the fishing skiffs. He has been building it for over a year. He is waiting for the turn of the tide, so we must get moving."

John left with Cia. As they left town, Cia reached down and clasped his hand. John enjoyed holding her hand, though it did remind him that he had no idea what sort of life he left behind. He hoped there was no wife waiting for him.

"Why is he leaving now?" John asked. "I thought sailors avoided sailing in the winter."

"I thought so, too. Typhoon season is probably over," Cia said, "so that eliminates the worst weather. He is probably impatient, though, and willing to risk the usual winter storms."

They reached a spot near the western point of the island. John saw the boat. It was longer and thinner than the fishing skiffs. Like them, it had a single mast just forward of midships. Unlike them, there was a long, curved board sticking in the air not far behind the mast, pointing to the rear.

They could see a number of water barrels in the front and back. There was a sail attached to the mast, waiting for him to raise it. A small crowd of a dozen or so gathered to watch.

Just after Cia and John arrived, Rathbun must have judged that the tide was now going out. He climbed into the boat and sat down to the oars. Some of the onlookers helped shove him into the waves. Rathbun extended the oars and dipped them into the water and began pulling himself away.

When he reached a point over a hundred yards away, he stopped rowing and shipped the oars. He stood and did something with the curved board. It slid down, and then Rathbun bent over to attend to it in some way. When he finished, he moved to the rear and pulled on a rope. The sail raised and filled, and Rathbun took the tiller. With a last wave at the group on the shore, he sailed off. It appeared Rathbun was heading at a diagonal heading, in the direction from which the wind was blowing.

"Son of a bitch," one of the onlookers muttered. "He might just have figured it out."

21

Stan Barthlemy had settled into a life of quiet despair. The chancellor solidified his grip on power every day. No one dared oppose him.

Stan did not know to whom he could speak about this. His opportunities to leave the palace grounds were few. He did not know who he could trust with any sort of message.

In the meantime, he played dumb. He allowed the chancellor to insult him on a daily basis. Fortunately, Stan was away on his "search" for Fitch while poor Dougie and then Gilchrist were tortured into false confessions and then publicly executed. He did not think he could have stood by and kept his mouth shut.

"Chancellor wants you, Cap'n!" a page called as he came running down the corridor.

"Thank you," Stan replied, then hurried toward the chancellor's office.

The chancellor had not yet moved in and taken the king's quarters. Stan wondered how long it would be before he did. That would be a sign that the chancellor was confident no one could interfere with his plans.

"Who is it?" came from inside the office when Stan knocked on the door.

"Captain Barthlemy, Lord Chancellor," Stan replied.

"Enter."

Stan came inside, shutting the door behind himself. The chancellor was pretending to examine some papers on his desk, but Stan knew he was just playing a game, making Stan stand at attention. When the chancellor felt the point was made, he cleared his throat and looked up.

"Captain—all the members of the Regency Council are arriving at the palace shortly. The seneschal and pages will send them to the reception room where we will meet," the chancellor said.

"Yes, Lord Chancellor," Stan affirmed.

"Once they gather, I will delay my arrival in order to give them the opportunity to chat among themselves. I want you to station yourself in the room and listen carefully to what they say between themselves. When the meeting ends, I will summon you to provide me with a full report. Do you understand?" the chancellor asked in a critical tone. "A full report."

"Yes, Lord Chancellor. A full report of whatever they talk about among themselves," Stan answered firmly.

"Show me that you are a man I can count on," the chancellor said. "You are dismissed."

Stan backed out of the room. He learned this early on. The chancellor insisted on being treated as royalty.

He left and walked calmly away. Once he knew he was out of earshot, he picked up his pace. This might provide his best and only opportunity to inform someone of what he knew. Stan returned to his quarters.

He had some paper but no ink. He needed to write at least two brief notes. Getting his hands on ink without drawing attention to himself would be impossible. He hit upon a solution as he walked.

There were two men on the Regency Council that Stan felt he could trust. One was Lord Wexler, a second or third cousin of the late king and Prince John. The other was the Duke of Roundel. He was not related to the royal family but had served in the Border Wardens. While the duke was no longer in uniform when Stan was with the Wardens, Stan felt he could trust anyone who had been a Warden.

Back in his quarters, Stan found the piece of paper he knew he had. After tearing it into two small pieces, he then retrieved a needle and stabbed himself in the middle finger of his left hand. Squeezing his fingertip, he forced a drop of blood out. Using the thicker end of the needle, where the eye was, he dipped it into the blood and wrote two quick notes:

> The chancellor killed the king. Trust nothing he says. Do not confront
> him yet.

He waited for the blood to dry, then folded the pieces of paper. He wrote Wexler on the outside of one and Roundel on the other. Then he continued folding the papers as small as he could. One lick of his finger removed the remaining blood. Though tender, no one would know anything.

Now Stan needed to figure out how to pass the messages without anyone seeing anything suspicious. That would be a challenge. The chancellor had replaced half the palace staff with his own people, putting long-time employees out on the street. Stan was certain the new hires reported everything they saw and heard to the chancellor. He had also put two dozen of his stooges in the Palace Guards. They were not liked at all by the other men and women in the guards. No one trusted them.

He hurried to the courtyard where the visitors would arrive. No visitors were there. He then went to the reception room to see if anyone was already seated. Seeing no one, he decided to wait in the courtyard for the first arrivals.

General Gladstone was atop the peak of the eastern headland, along with his officers. The night was dark, with no moon. To guide the ships carrying the fire rafts, they were tending a signal fire Away from the fire, Gladstone could see lines of faint blue light in the water of the ocean, where the waves met the shore. It was remarkable—he had never seen anything like it. He reckoned the sailors knew all about it and would use it to guide themselves.

The signal fire on the eastern height was all the guidance Hector Grimble needed. He guided his boat to the mouth of the harbor. Paul Escamil was following them, and another Austerian boat was behind him.

Fitch was aboard Hector's boat. He was one of fifteen men on each vessel who volunteered to guide the rafts into the harbor and set them alight. Like the others, he was stripped naked. They just finished covering themselves with animal grease to protect them from the cold of the water. With whispers, they started lowering the rafts over the side. Each raft was accompanied by a man who would attempt to guide it to the proper position before using his flint to ignite the combustible materials loaded onto it. When it was Fitch's turn, he slipped into the water.

It was cold enough, even with the grease coating him, that he gasped. He took hold of the raft and, using the signal fire as a guide, began kicking his way to the harbor. The others told him to aim for the area where the luminescence of the waves breaking on the western headland stopped.

The tide helped carry him into the harbor. Fighting against the slight breeze and staying toward the western edge was the challenge. When he entered the harbor, he could see dark shapes ahead in the dim light spilling from the town.

The exercise of guiding the raft helped him fight off the cold of the water. He concentrated on staying to the right—the western side—as he progressed further in. Suddenly, his raft bumped into something. Fitch looked up and saw he swam into the hull of one of the corsairs. Kicking powerfully, he guided his raft past.

Far ahead, Fitch saw someone striking a spark from his flint. It quickly caught the frayed rope that was soaked with pine pitch. The first raft was ablaze quickly. It was the signal for everyone else to ignite his.

Fitch pulled his sword around in front of himself and withdrew it. Then, fishing the flint from the pouch, he held it next to the combustibles. He struggled a moment, trying to figure out the best way to use his sword to strike sparks from it. He cursed silently as he suddenly realized that a knife would have been far less cumbersome. He ended up needing to pull his upper body up on the raft and rest on his elbows before he could manage to strike sparks into the material. As with the first raft, the material on his caught fire quickly. Before the heat grew too much, Fitch pushed it in the direction of the nearest corsair.

He waited until his eyes adjusted to the dark again. He swam to the anchor cable of the corsair his raft lay alongside. Using his sword, he began sawing through the thick rope. It was difficult. By the time he finished, the corsair was ablaze. Freed from its anchor, it would now drift into other ships in the harbor and spread the rapidly growing flames. There were now more than twenty ships burning, but he did not look at them. In the light those fires cast, he could see his next objective—the northernmost dock on the western side of the harbor.

Fitch and the other swimmers were meeting there. It was the dock that was closest to one of the gates in the walls. When all forty-five of the swimmers gathered, they would emerge from the water and fight their way through the gate.

Eventually, Gladstone grew tired of standing and found a place to sit where he thought he might still have a view. When the ground proved to be uncomfortable, he stood again. As he did, he saw sparks flashing on the far side of the harbor. Seconds later, those sparks became flames. More sparks followed, then more flames, and Gladstone could see them moving slowly from west to east. He could also start to discern the silhouettes of some of the Skamorran corsairs.

The flames floated along in total silence. He watched as two, three, then five stopped when they drifted into the hull of a corsair. Within a minute, orange flames were licking up the sides of the ships. Still, no alarm was raised.

Flames reached the decks of the first five corsairs before Gladstone heard yelling and shouting from the harbor. By now, another ten corsairs were beginning to burn while the remainder of the flaming rafts drifted into the rest of the anchored ships. The light from the flames was bright enough that Gladstone could now see the docks. There were people standing, watching. None of them were making a move to try to save the ships in the harbor.

Gladstone watched as sparks and flaming bits of sail lifted into the air and floated onto new victims. The burning ships themselves drifted into others. He tried to count how many ships were affected but lost track at thirty when the rising smoke forced him to move. It was time to begin the next phase of the assault. Gladstone and the others started climbing back down the path, hurrying to find breathable air.

They reached a spot where they could breathe without coughing. Gladstone noticed that it did not take long for the hull of a ship to catch fire. If one of the flaming rafts stayed in place for a minute, the pine tar coating the wood of the ship ignited. The drifting, flaming hulks loosed from their anchors were causing fires to spread even more widely as fiery ashes drifted on the breeze to other corsairs nearby. As quickly as the hulls caught fire, the rigging took far less time.

"Great Gods!" Gladstone gasped. "Great Gods!"

At least fifty ships were blazing. Flaming hot ashes were swirling through the air, finding new food for the hungry flames. The shouting from the docks died down. Gladstone could see the Skamorrans standing in stunned silence as their fleet was destroyed before their eyes.

Tomorrow would bring the Skamorrans no relief. The ten least-damaged Austerian galleys were anchored just out of sight of the fort on the eastern headland. They would row into the harbor after dawn broke and destroy any corsairs that managed to survive the fires. From what he witnessed, Gladstone reckoned there would not be many.

Once that was done, the galleys would lay a heavy cable across the harbor mouth. They would anchor one end just off the eastern headland and extend it to the western point. No ship would be able to sail past. The Skamorran army would be stranded in Chartage.

Fitch and the other swimmers were assembled. They climbed from the water quietly, weapons at the ready. Following the others, Fitch headed for the nearest gate.

Faced with forty-five naked, armed men, screaming and yelling, and with the harbor beyond them ablaze, the guards at the gate ran away. As Fitch ran through, he realized this was a missed opportunity. If the army had been massed on the other side, they would have gained the city that very night.

22

Stan knew he was putting his life at risk by passing his notes to the Duke of Roundel. Nor did he wish to jeopardize them. Whatever he did needed to be something that would not draw attention to them. He reckoned an encounter that reinforced the chancellor's opinion of him as a stupid oaf might be the best option.

With that in mind, he determined how he would accomplish the handover. Stan left the courtyard and took a position just inside the doors of the reception room. He could see the guests approach out of the corner of his eye. When the Duke of Roundel came through the door, Stan walked into him as though he did not see the nobleman.

The impact nearly caused the duke to fall, but Stan quickly caught his hand to prevent it. Of course, he pressed the two pieces of folded paper into the duke's hand as he did. Stan stepped back quickly in embarrassment.

"Oh! Your Grace!" Stan stuttered as he bowed. "I did not see you coming. My most humble apologies."

The duke said nothing. He merely glared at the clumsy Captain of the Guard before proceeding inside and finding a seat at the large table. Stan was too scared to look, so he did not see when the duke surreptitiously unfolded one of the notes underneath the table and read it. Stan did observe one of the pages recently brought on by the chancellor sneering at him. He had no doubt the chancellor would hear of his clumsiness before lunchtime.

When the council was fully assembled, the chancellor made them wait, just as he told Stan he would. Stan did try to listen to their conversations. The subjects were generally innocuous, other than the few who expressed irritation at the chancellor's tardiness. Stan decided he would not pass those comments along.

The chancellor finally swooped in, making insincere apologies for the delay. He claimed he was caught up in reports regarding the grain harvest and lost track of time. He welcomed the group and formally opened the meeting.

"With the approval of the council," he said, "I propose that we declare that an interregnum has begun."

"Is Prince John dead, then?" Lord Wexler asked pointedly.

"I have no idea," the chancellor replied smoothly. "He left for Auster and will probably not return for several months, when sailing season resumes. In the meantime, with the king assassinated, I need the authority to manage the affairs of the kingdom—as I have been doing since the king's death."

"An interregnum can only be declared when the king has died and there is no clear successor," the Earl of Courtenay stated. "Since Prince John is still alive, to the best of our knowledge, we cannot institute an interregnum. Tell me, Lord Chancellor, have you taken any steps to inform the prince of his brother's death?"

"No, milord," the chancellor replied. "Typhoon season has just come to a close and there are still several months before the winter weather clears and it is safe to sail."

"You certainly had no qualms about sending the prince onto the sea at the beginning of typhoon season, did you, Lord Chancellor?" Courtenay replied. "Surely, there are sea captains willing to undertake the journey to Auster at this time of year. I know for a fact that many smugglers enjoy a brisk trade during these months."

"Milord, the decision to send Prince John to Auster was not mine alone," the chancellor objected. "The council agreed the situation was urgent."

"Some of you did," Courtenay said, "but it was not a unanimous decision by any means. And no voice was more strident than yours in urging that we act immediately. And yet you have yet to send anyone to Auster in search of the prince. I find that … inconsistent."

"Are you suggesting that I engage smugglers and or other law-breakers to contact the prince?" the chancellor replied indignantly.

"I'm not suggesting anything," Courtenay replied calmly. "I am merely commenting on the difference between the zeal with which you championed sending Prince John to Auster at a dangerous time of year, and your current lack of urgency in responding to a far graver crisis here at home."

While Stan was pleased to hear someone challenging the chancellor like this, he also worried. He suspected that the Earl of Courtenay would have a fatal accident, or find himself mired in some disgraceful scandal soon. Stan also noticed that none of the other members of the council were speaking up, though several were listening intently.

"There can be no interregnum declared," Viscount Huntington interrupted. "As far as we know, Prince John is still alive. Until proven otherwise, Lord Chancellor, you may continue to fulfill your duties—as chancellor. Any decisions that would normally be the responsibility of the monarch will need to be put off. If there are any that cannot be delayed, then the Regency Council should gather and discuss what to do. This is the only legally defensible solution."

Several days later, Stan Barthlemy watched as another group of nobles gathered at the palace. This group had no official role like the Regency Council. Though Stan was not extremely well-versed in politics, he did recognize some of the names by reputation. Two he had heard were profligate gamblers. One was suspected of killing his own father in order to gain his title. At least three were second sons who were rumored to be insanely jealous of their older siblings who inherited the family lands and titles.

At the meeting of the Regency Council, the chancellor directed Stan to listen in on the guests' private conversations. For this meeting, the chancellor ordered him to stay away. The only staff allowed anywhere near the meeting were those whom the chancellor had brought on after the king's death.

Stan suspected the topic of this meeting concerned displacing the members of the Regency Council. From what he knew of the chancellor, it would be through subterfuge. Some of the members of the Regency Council would meet with various ends—accidents, poisonings, or robberies turned to murders. Though some of this group he assembled were not known for their discretion, Stan was sure the chancellor would arrange things so that nothing would lead back to him. Though they did not know it, the men he invited to this meeting were only pawns in the chancellor's game.

In the morning, Fitch went with General Gladstone and some of the other officers to see the results of their attack. Smoke was still rising from several hulks. The group climbed to the top of the eastern headland and could see the whole bay.

"Great Gods!" Gladstone exclaimed when he stopped and looked.

Fitch did a quick count. Three-quarters of the Skamorran corsairs were charred wrecks or sunk. Thirty-seven intact ships were all that remained.

While they stood there, they watched as the ten Austerian galleys nosed around the point and entered the harbor. Fitch had learned just enough about sailing to know that they timed their entrance for the change of the tide when the channel would be at its calmest. As the Skamorrans spotted the galleys, crews that had returned to the surviving ships after daybreak sprang into action.

Fitch heard orders shouted and saw men running for the anchor cables. Using axes, they were hacking away at the thick ropes. Apparently, cutting the anchor cable would be quicker than trying to raise it from the bottom of the harbor. It was of no use for the corsairs nearest the galleys. The Austerians were on them in hardly any time at all.

Fitch watched as the galleys crashed into the sides of the corsairs. Below the waterline, the bronze-clad ram punched a massive hole in the belly of its target. The crunch of the impact was followed by cheering from the Austerian crews. Backing their oars, the Austerian ships quickly freed themselves and began looking for their next victims. With great skill, the captains guided their vessels through the charred corsairs, found other victims, and smashed into them.

Three of the ten galleys now turned and headed back to the harbor mouth. The remaining intact Skamorran ships had now cut their anchors loose and raised sails. They were hampered in their attempt to escape by the profusion of wrecks. The Austerians, not dependent on the wind, were able to maneuver and chase the Skamorrans down. The three galleys at the mouth were there in case any of the Skamorrans evaded destruction. None of the corsairs made it that far.

"Have you given any thought to the matter of prisoners, general?" Fitch asked as they were returning to camp.

"By the fourteen major Gods and all the minor ones," Gladstone replied, "I've never seen or heard of anything like what we just witnessed these last few hours. I'll even forgive you for your cheek, Colonel, seeing that this was all your idea. To answer your question, I have not been thinking about prisoners, but I suppose I should, eh?"

When he returned to camp, Fitch sought out the sailors who had taken his idea and made it happen. He found them sitting in a boisterous group, talking about the events of a few hours before. When they spotted him, they called him over genially and began clapping him on the back.

Fitch extricated himself after a few minutes and returned to where General Gladstone was. Gladstone pulled Fitch aside and asked him to sit. The other high-ranking officers were wandering over and sitting down as well.

"Here's the problem," Gladstone said. "To regain Chartage quickly, launching fireballs over the walls will force the Skamorrans to surrender. Unfortunately, we would destroy the city and put any of our citizens still inside at risk."

"Sir, with all due respect, none of our citizens remain alive," Colonel Gillies stated. "We've been looking from the eastern headland down into the city and have yet to see anyone who was not a Skamorran soldier. If we put the city to the torch, none of our people will be harmed."

Fitch liked Gillies. She was one of two women in the group of regimental commanders. Outspoken and blunt, Gillies was as direct a person as Fitch ever met.

"But there is the cost to rebuild," Gladstone countered, "which also delays repopulation. We will be at war with Skamorra for the foreseeable future. Chartage has always been the home port for the Western Squadron. I think it is in our best interests to reestablish the squadron here as soon as feasible."

"Sir?" Fitch asked tentatively.

Having been the author of the idea that resulted in the destruction of the Skamorran ships did not embolden Fitch. On the contrary, he was acutely aware of his outsider status. He did not want to seem like the teacher's pet, especially as a foreigner. Still, he thought they were overlooking the obvious.

"Yes, colonel?" Gladstone acknowledged.

"In Boreas, I was taught that most walled cities—like Chartage—were brought down by someone inside opening one of the gates," Fitch said.

"You're right, Fitch," Gillies agreed. "Absolutely right."

"I mean no offense, but we missed an opportunity last night," Fitch said. "We had forty-five men inside the walls, and all we did was break out, back to our army. If we had been prepared to exploit—"

"By all the known hells, you're right, Fitch," Gladstone exclaimed. "And no offense taken. I was entirely focused on the destruction of the corsairs."

"It seems apparent that following the same general plan seems the smartest and easiest way to get a squad of soldiers into the city," Colonel Gillies remarked.

"We'll need a diversion to draw their attention away from the harbor," Fitch said. "Have you made any forays against the walls?"

"No," Colonel Reubens replied.

"When you spread the calcitrapae, did you leave alleys clear of them where we could approach without stepping on the damned things?" Fitch asked.

"We did," Reubens said, pleased because he had thought to do so. "They are marked by stakes. From any of the stakes, if you take a direct path to the wall, you should have no problems. Each lane is roughly ten feet wide."

"Excellent," Fitch commented. "If you were going to make a legitimate attack on the wall, where would it be?"

The group murmured in discussion before Colonel Nadeau said, "On the eastern portion."

"Let's get a map," Fitch said. "It will help."

"The most likely place to get over the wall is here," Nadeau said, pointing to a spot on the map once it was spread out in front of them.

"And the next best?" Fitch asked.

"Over here," Nadeau pointed to another place about fifty yards from the first."

"Tonight, about a half hour after the change of the tide, we need to mount attacks against both these spots," Fitch said. "They need to be legitimate attempts to scale the walls. We need ladders, archers—everything you would normally use to get up and over."

"And the people we drop in the water will go to this gate here," Colonel Gillies said.

"Let's target two gates," Fitch suggested. "That one, and—"

"This one," Reubens said, pointing to another gate. "On either side of the quay on the western side since we will mount the outside attacks on the eastern side."

"How many do you think we will need to pull this off, Colonel Fitch?" Nadeau asked.

"At least two dozen," Fitch replied. "They should have a slightly easier time of it than those who brought the rafts in a few hours ago. The wind blows west to east. They needed to drag the rafts against the breeze. Tonight, we won't need to worry about rafts."

"We?" Gladstone asked.

"Sir, by now you should have realized that I'm not accustomed to ordering my men to undertake a task I would be unwilling to tackle myself," Fitch said. "I helped with the rafts last night. Another night in the water seems to be called for. You will need to order me to stay behind, sir."

"Any of the rest of you want to go with Colonel Fitch?" Gladstone asked.

"Hell yes," Colonel Gillies responded, just slightly ahead of the others.

Fitch was pleased that all his fellow officers answered in the affirmative. Gillies was just a little quicker and louder. The others looked slightly disappointed.

"From listening in," General Gladstone said, "it seems you plan to have a couple of dozen armed swimmers cross into the harbor at the change of the tide. After giving them the opportunity to reach shore, you plan to assault the wall at two points opposite—on the eastern side. Once that attack is mounted, I presume the swimmers will try to overwhelm the guards at the two gates on the western side. When the gates are open, the rest of us—except for those mounting the demonstration attacks—need to pour into the city. Does that cover everything?"

"You'll need to send every soldier we can through the gates once they're open," Fitch said. "And the normal watchfires need to be maintained. Silence will be our ally. The noise of everyone moving will cause failure."

"Colonel Fitch and Colonel Gillies, you need to get with the sailors and arrange your transportation for tonight. You also need to select the soldiers who will join you. Colonel Nadeau, I'm putting you in charge of the attacks on the eastern wall. Two companies will be enough to make it look serious. The rest of you, prepare your soldiers to move silently after nightfall to be in position in the early morning when our people open the gates."

23

The meeting broke up. Fitch took Gillies with him and returned to the group of sailors he chatted with earlier. When they explained what they planned to do, the group greeted the idea with broad grins. They told Fitch to return just after dinner with the soldiers, and they would take them to the boat. The fishing boats they used in the first attack were anchored a couple of miles to the east in a small cove.

"I don't have a command of my own, Colonel," Fitch said, "so I will rely on your judgment regarding the volunteers for the mission."

"Fair enough," Gillies said. "And you can call me Allison since we're in this together."

"My name's Ralph," Fitch replied.

"Glad to know you, Ralph," she said as she stuck her hand out to shake.

"Pleasure's mine, Allison," he said as they shook hands.

When they reached the spot where her regiment was camped, she called her second-in-command over. Major Venning was one of the tallest men Fitch had met, standing a good six inches above his own six-foot height. Allison explained the plan to Venning. When she finished, they called the regiment to order.

"Following up on the success of early this morning," Allison announced to her soldiers, "we are planning another bold stroke to cripple the enemy. We need two dozen strong swimmers who are good with a blade. Who wants to come with me?"

Fitch was impressed when over a hundred men and a few women stepped forward from the ranks. Gillies swept her eyes over the group. She shook her head.

"Strong swimmers, I said. Johnson, I know you can't swim a lick. If you're not a strong, experienced swimmer, step back."

Over a dozen retreated back into the ranks with sheepish expressions. Gillies looked up and down the group again. She shook her head once more.

"Good with a blade, I said. Not good with a bow. Step back, McEachern," Gillies said.

A sturdy blonde woman went back into the larger group. Another fifteen or so joined her. There were still nearly a hundred.

Gillies started at one end and walked along. Occasionally, she pointed at one of the soldiers with her right hand, then jabbed with her left thumb over toward where she left Fitch. When she finished, a group of nineteen men and five women were standing around Fitch.

"Let me tell you something important," Gillies stated to the remainder of the regiment. "You make me proud to the point where my heart feels like bursting. To have so many of you step forward like you did shows your quality. If you were not chosen, do not despair. We will be opening the gates for you tonight. Follow Major Venning's commands, and I promise you all that you will have the opportunity to meet the Skamorrans face-to-face in the wee hours of the morning. I hope that is enough to soothe your disappointment. Dismissed!"

There were hours and hours to wait before Fitch and the others needed to begin the march to where the fishing boats were anchored. It had been four days since he last saw Mira. He reckoned it would be at least another four until she returned again.

Fitch debated with himself whether he should write a note to Mira in case he fell that night. When he thought of what he might say, words failed him. Never before did he feel such attraction for a woman beyond only the physical dimension.

He certainly thought Mira was attractive in appearance, but there was so much more that appealed to him. Her quick wit, her sense of humor, her intelligence, her way with her horse, the ways she treated those around her—all of these distilled into a heady brew for Fitch. The suddenness with which he was overwhelmed was truly his only cause of concern. He decided not to write anything. If the Gods wished for him to marry Mira, they would see him through the night safely.

It was rare for Stan Barthlemy to take a night off away from his duties in the palace. With Ralph Fitch gone, there was no one for him to go drinking with. Tonight, though, Stan needed a change of scenery. He headed for the inn he and Fitch used to frequent.

He hoped Fitch was safe. Stan had no idea whether Fitch had sailed south and reached Auster or was still waiting for winter to pass. He missed his friend and hated the charade that surrounded him now.

Snow was falling as Stan handed his horse Hammer to the groom behind the inn. Making his way inside, the innkeeper teased him about the lengthy delay between visits. Stan confirmed he was alone and took a stool at the counter.

He asked for dinner, not wanting to drink on an empty stomach. The innkeeper returned with a shepherd's pie and set it in front of Stan, along with a mug of ale. Stan had just taken his first mouthful when a man occupied the stool next to him. The man was turned slightly away, so Stan could not see his face.

"Captain Barthlemy, don't move a muscle except to keep chewing," his neighbor said. "There is someone watching you and I have no wish for you to face questions about this evening."

The voice sounded vaguely familiar to Stan. Being told not to look made him want to do that much more. Stan followed instructions though, and continued to chew, then swallow.

"I work for the duke," the man said. "Your note was a bold move. How did you know the duke would be receptive?"

"He was a Border Warden," Stan whispered back without moving his head and keeping his lips as still as possible. "That counts for something with me."

"As it does for him," the man replied, "and for me."

"Sergeant Varnes?" Stan asked.

"The same, Cap'n. I knew you would recognize my voice eventually," Varnes said. "Where is Fitch?"

"Interesting," Stan commented. "You assumed I would know. He's a wanted criminal, you know."

"If you make me laugh, you'll draw unwanted attention to us," Varnes replied, as the innkeeper brought him a serving of shepherd's pie.

"Ralph is no more capable of working with the Skamorrans to kill King Philip than you are, or me, or the duke," Varnes continued, speaking quietly around the food in his mouth. "Besides, if you wanted to catch Ralph, you would have. Instead you put on a show to make it look as though you gave it your best effort."

"He was going to try to reach Auster to look for Prince John," Stan replied. "I don't know whether he found someone to take him or is still stuck here waiting for better weather."

"He didn't go to one of our southern ports, or the chancellor's men would have him by now," Varnes commented. "I'm guessing he headed down the goat track near Hanville. Sven Gunnar is working with someone there—a small-time smuggler. If he told Sven the reason he was there, I would wager they took off for Auster immediately."

"Good," Stan grunted quietly.

"Not necessarily," Varnes warned. "The prince never reached Auster."

"How do you know?"

"The duke is like a spider. He builds webs and when something hits one of the strands, he knows," Varnes explained. "King Philip, and King Seamus before him, made good use of the duke's webs."

"So the prince is dead."

"Probably. It gets worse, though. The Skamorrans attacked Auster. They took Chartage, the Austerian port nearest to Skamorra," Varnes added.

"How does the duke know all this?" Stan asked.

"On the coast of his duchy, he has people like Sven Gunnar's partner," Varnes explained. "They have an arrangement. The duke allows them to do their smuggling without interference and protects them from the revenue cutters. They give him ten percent of the profits and any information they pick up. The intelligence they provide is often more valuable. Apparently, one of them was traveling to Chartage after the last typhoon passed and saw the harbor full of corsairs, so he turned right around. On the trip before that, the same person was able to confirm that Prince John never arrived in Chartage, which would have been where they would have headed."

"How did he know whether the prince arrived?" Stan asked.

"Because people tend to make a fuss when a foreigner of such elevated status arrives," Varnes said. "No fuss means no prince."

"Crap," Stan muttered.

"I've shared what I know. It's your turn, Cap'n," Varnes said.

Stan told him about the meeting of what he termed the Degeneracy Council. Varnes reminded Stan not to make him laugh but agreed with the name. Stan provided a complete list of the attendees. Varnes asked him to repeat several names so he could remember them and write them down after he left the inn.

"That's how he plans to do it, then," Varnes commented. "The Earl of Courtenay ruined the chancellor's hope of being installed as the regent during an interregnum, so he will target the Regency Council."

"How? None of the people in the second meeting control anything," Stan whispered.

"The duke explained it to me. It might take a year or two," Varnes said, "but even working through the Regency Council would have taken time. The fathers and older brothers of the second group will begin to have accidents, eat bad mushrooms, or fall victim to highwaymen. By the end of two years, enough of the chancellor's people will be in place so that he can move forward. Not only would they be in control of the Regency Council, they also muster more than half the men-at-arms in the kingdom."

"Speaking of which," Stan commented, "is someone looking out for the Earl of Courtenay?

"Yes," Varnes replied. "The duke is trying to determine whether the earl is very brave, or very stupid. Now, you've finished your meal, Cap'n. I suspect you came to get drunk tonight but I would not advise it. Head back to the palace. I'll come back here for three days centered on the first and the fifteenth of the month if you need to speak with me about anything."

Stan settled with the innkeeper for dinner and the mug of ale. He pushed away, having only looked at the man next to him with the casual interest one might give any stranger at an inn. Heading to the stable, he retrieved Hammer and flipped a copper to the groom.

24

Finally, it was time to set sail. Hours before, Fitch and the others reached the spot where the fishing boats were anchored. During the hours of waiting to depart they spent the time chatting with the sailors. The sailors advised them all to create a lanyard for their swords. Binding a line around the hilt and guard of the sword, with a lanyard to go around their necks would enable them to keep their hands free for swimming.

"Strip," one of the sailors ordered, "and smear this all over. It will keep you from freezing in the water."

There were some buckets filled with the same animal grease Fitch slathered on the night before. It was slimy and thick. After he stripped off his uniform, Fitch scooped up a handful and began rubbing it onto his legs.

When he finished every part he could reach, he asked Colonel Gillies, "Would you do my back?"

"If you do mine," she replied.

They traded favors. When they finished, they sat on the deck waiting. The other members of their group joined them.

"In a minute or two," came a quiet voice, "you'll climb over the side using the nets like a ladder. When you reach the water, ease yourself in—don't splash. Let the tide carry you into the harbor. You'll be able to sense when you're through the inlet as the strength of the current will lessen. Once that happens, head toward the right. There won't be much light—probably from a few torches in the city—but find something you can aim for. There are dozens of burned ships, and you will run into them and need to work your way around them. If you have an aiming point, you should be able to stay on course. Eventually, you should see the quay."

"Once we hear the commotion from Colonel Nadeau's units on the other side of the harbor, we move," Fitch said. "My group to the right, Colonel Gillies' group to the left. We kill the guards quickly and quietly, then throw the gates open for our people. Any questions?"

"What do we do for clothes, sir?" asked one of the women.

"Fight naked," Gillies replied. "The damned Skamorrans will be thunderstruck seeing such an incredible example of Austerian womanhood. Once the battle is over, you can go change—or not. If you want to prance around in the altogether to let folks know you were with us tonight, I'll allow it for a day."

Some quiet chuckles greeted the colonel's crack. Everyone was mindful of the need for silence, though, so the response was restrained. Fitch was looking over the side of the boat, watching the waves with their eerie blue light. When the light came to an end, he knew they had reached the harbor mouth.

Sure enough, the sailors whispered, and guided the soldiers to the nets hanging over the side of the boat. Fitch and Gillies went last. They climbed down into the water, their swords dangling from their necks, then let go.

Fitch was now thankful the sailors had them coat themselves with whatever that jelly was. He could tell the water was cold, but the animal grease kept most of the chill at bay. The tide gushing into the harbor pushed him along. When he felt the pull of it lessen, he set off at an angle to his right. There were three torches he could see. He aimed for the one in the middle.

He did not get far before something in his way blocked the light. Fitch worked his way around and found the three torches again with his eyes. Before he reached the edge of the harbor, he encountered five more wrecks.

The swimming was not too difficult, but it was frustrating to continue to encounter obstacles. Fitch heard only a couple of softly muttered curses along the way. When he reached the shore, he spotted what he guessed was the quay since all he could see was a looming shadow.

Sure enough, when he arrived, he found the rest of the group. All were down on one knee. They waited while they caught their breath after the swim.

It was quite evident when Colonel Nadeau made his assault on the eastern side opposite where they were. The Skamorrans were shouting and lighting torches. Ralph and Allison tapped their people on the shoulder one by one. With swords in hand, they headed for the wall and the gates they hoped to open. Fitch led his dozen down the middle of a street, then hesitated at the first intersection.

"Sir," came a whisper, "I've been here many times. I know where to go."

"Lead on," Fitch said.

They followed the soldier at a trot down the dark streets. When they reached the last buildings before the wall, they stopped outside the range of the torchlight from the guard post above the gate. Fitch could understand a soldier not wanting to be left in the dark, but having a torch nearby ruined your ability to see in the night.

Fitch could only see one soldier at the post. He suspected there were more—as many as five or six—but they were probably sitting where he could not see them. The post itself was a platform over the gate, connected to a walkway that carried along the entire wall. A set of stairs on either side of the gate provided access to the platform. The rear of the platform was open. From his earlier views of the city, Fitch knew the outside wall was crenellated, to give defenders opportunities to fire arrows, and to take cover from incoming weapons.

Fitch had already planned with this group who would do which tasks. He would lead four up the stairs on the right. Four would ascend the stairs on the left. The remaining four would open the gate.

After getting everyone's attention, Fitch counted down with his fingers: three-two-one. After one, he padded off on bare feet to the stairs. Reaching the platform, there was the one guard he saw from below, and five others sitting with their backs against the wall.

Fitch skewered two of those sitting down before his presence even registered to them. He then whirled and stabbed the guard who was standing, but not before the man screamed for help. The other guards were now dead.

"Down to the gate," Fitch ordered.

When he reached the ground, the group wrestling with the gate nearly had it open. They were slowed because the massive beam holding the gate shut was not only resting on sturdy iron angles, but hinged angles also came from above and were padlocked to the lower. Not having the key, the soldiers improvised.

The Skamorrans kept a sledgehammer handy to loosen the wooden bean from the angles on which it rested. Fitch's men used the sledgehammer to destroy the two padlocks, but it took time.

They were just lifting the wooden beam out of the way. Skamorran soldiers arrived, responding to the scream the one guard made. Sword in hand, Fitch turned to face the threat.

"On me," he called to his soldiers.

The Skamorrans wore helmets, breastplates, and greaves. Fitch and his people wore only a thin coating of the grease they smeared on before they entered the water. The Skamorrans carried shields and spears with sharp-bladed tips. Fitch and his soldiers carried swords. The numbers were even or would be, once Fitch's four soldiers lifted the beam out of the way. Until then, Fitch was outnumbered and outmatched in terms of weaponry.

Fitch did not hesitate for an instant. He had faced Skamorrans many times before. Their armor, shields, and spears did not frighten him. Fitch had learned that the best chance of success lay in closing the distance, where his sword would be effective and their longer spear would not.

He picked the one in the center of the enemy group and rushed at him. It was easy to block the soldier's spear thrust to one side. Fitch could also twist and dodge the attack by the soldier on his target's left. Unfortunately, Fitch could only contort his body in so many different directions at once, and the sharp-edged spear tip from the right struck his ribs, then grazed off, slicing into his side.

Fitch had been wounded before. While he didn't enjoy it, he knew sometimes it was inevitable, as it was now. The cut to his side stung but he knew it was not a serious injury. It certainly did not slow him down as he stepped right up to the Skamorran and thrust the tip of his sword up into the man's skull.

His victim was already crumpling to the ground as Fitch shuffled backward. He was readying himself to take on the next Skamorran when his enemy's eyes grew wide. Rather than fight, the Skamorran turned and ran. Fitch wondered why for only the briefest moment. He was almost knocked to the ground by Austerian troops charging through the gate.

Behind him, Fitch heard Colonel Newagen holler, "This way!"

Fitch turned around. That was the direction where the bulk of the city was, and presumably, the majority of the Skamorrans. Ahead he could hear the sounds of conflict increasing. He joined a group that was heading closer to the harborfront.

"Fitch!" he heard someone bellow.

Fitch stopped, looking for who was calling him. He was turning around to his right when the arrow buried itself in his left buttock. Fitch later decided he was glad he turned, or the arrow would have hit a place far worse.

"Son of a bitch!" Fitch yelped.

General Gladstone, who yelled for Fitch, was distracted by what happened. He forgot what he was planning to tell Fitch. Instead, he was clutching his sides as he laughed.

"I was—I was going to tell you—tell you to fall back—" Gladstone choked out between guffaws. "Wasn't quick enough!" he blurted, then could no longer continue.

Fitch, still naked, still coated with slimy goo, now bleeding from the grazed ribs on his right side, and with a Skamorran arrow in his left buttock, tried to summon whatever dignity the Gods might grant him and began limping for the nearest gate. He would get someone to pull the arrow. Then he would try to wipe the jelly off. He would have his ribs bandaged and get dressed. Then he would hide from General Gladstone for the rest of his life.

He found the medics as dawn was breaking. It also had begun to rain heavily. They withdrew the arrow, then gave him soap and told him to use the rain to wash up and get the jelly off. When he finished, they cleaned up a couple of spots that Fitch missed, then dried him. They poured alcohol into the puncture in his buttock and the cut on his chest. Fitch yelped when they did. Then they stitched up the slice on his ribs.

Fitch limped to his tent and dressed, then began hobbling back to the city. He met many wounded soldiers on his way. They told him the battle was still raging. Fitch continued walking until he saw an officer he recognized.

"How are things in the city?" Fitch asked.

"The Skamorrans are fighting to the death," she said. "The fighting is street-by-street and house-by-house. They're giving as they're getting, but we are slowly forcing them back. Our casualties are heavy, but theirs are worse."

Fitch continued heading into the city. He saw Colonel Gillies jogging back to the camp, still naked and covered with the jelly. She waved but did not stop. He saw others from their group also returning.

When he reached the city wall, soldiers directed him to the first safe gate. Fitch walked down and entered the city. It took only a couple of minutes before he found General Gladstone.

"Welcome back, Colonel," Gladstone said.

"I've heard the fighting is brutal," Fitch said.

"You heard correctly," Gladstone sighed. "I'm beginning to be tempted to smoke them out. We've protected the western half of the city. Even though it is the less densely built portion, it would give us a base from which to rebuild."

"What casualties have we suffered?" Fitch asked.

"I don't have a firm count," Gladstone said. "I think we've lost five hundred killed and another thousand wounded."

"So, if we keep going, we may lose as many as four thousand?" Fitch asked. "General, has King Theodosius kept you informed regarding the political climate?"

"What about it?"

"As we left Austeria, you shared with me that the noble families who put the chamberlain in place were still expressing open opposition to the king, and there was a possibility of civil war," Fitch said. "Knowing that, can we afford to lose that many soldiers?"

"Damn it!" Gladstone muttered. "You're right."

Gladstone hollered for a messenger. After telling the messenger what he wanted, the youth ran off. Gladstone came back to Fitch.

"I got swept along by our success in breaching the walls," Gladstone said. "Thank you for helping me put my feet back on the ground. Time is our friend, not our enemy. The Skamorrans have no escape and no hope of resupply."

"What do you plan to do from here?" Fitch asked.

"I just gave orders to have the commanding officers report to me," Gladstone said. "We will build a barricade behind our current position. Once it is complete, we will pull back. After that, we will begin rotating the troops out to eat."

25

For the next three days, it rained. The Austerian soldiers maintained a careful vigil over the trapped Skamorrans. Gladstone's army and militia kept a constant watch on the barricade, the harbor, and the outer walls in the section where the Skamorrans were hemmed in. There was no activity during this time.

Mira returned to camp on the fourth day after they opened the gates. She arrived late in the day bearing letters just as the rain stopped. Fitch's heart soared to see her. After she delivered her dispatches, she threw herself into Fitch's arms, heedless of onlookers. With her arms around his neck, her legs around his waist, and her lips firmly fastened to his, they drew curious stares at first before the watchers turned their gazes away. Fitch needed to set her down after a minute.

"What's wrong?" she asked breathlessly, noticing his grimace of pain.

Fitch's face turned red.

"I was hit by an arrow four days ago," he said.

"Where?" Mira asked with concern.

Fitch put his hand over his face and snorted with an embarrassed laugh, "In the butt."

"Are you alright?"

"I'm fine," Fitch responded. "It's still quite sore. I'm more embarrassed than anything."

"You will need to show me later," Mira said with a wink. "Right now, I need to tend to Shasta and see my father if he is still here—"

"He is."

"Then we can eat whatever they're serving, and you can show me your battle scar," she said with a giggle.

No sooner did Mira walk away than a messenger showed up.

"The general wants to see you and the other colonels," the lad said.

Fitch headed for the tent Gladstone used for meetings. As he neared, he saw some of the other eight colonels approaching. Two were on duty. One was inside the city. The other outside, watching the walls and gates in the section that Skamorrans still controlled. Those officers would be the last to arrive.

"We'll wait for Reubens and Strait," Gladstone announced. "I don't want to share the news more than once.

Reubens and Strait arrived a few minutes later. Gladstone ushered them into the tent. He bade them all sit.

"The dispatches I received today bear ill news," he said. "The king reports that the noble families of the south and west have presented him with a list of real and imagined grievances, demanding satisfaction. If their demands are not met, they intend to remove the king by force and replace him with his cousin, the Duke of Volplane. Apparently, they are already mustering their forces. As soon as we finish our business here, we will need to march to Austeria. The king is very pleased with our progress to this point but asks us to conclude things 'expeditiously.' That means quickly. I need you to figure out the quickest way to force the Skamorrans into submission with the least loss of life on our side. Meanwhile, I need to meet with all the mayors and mas and pas to inform them of this news and to confirm their support."

"Do we still want to try to save the city?" Colonel Gillies asked.

"If you are asking whether to burn it all down," Gladstone responded, "I hope to avoid that. If you are asking to destroy the portion the Skamorrans now hold, I am willing to consider it. Anything else? No? Very well. Let's reconvene after dinner."

Fitch walked out with the other colonels. For the first time since they arrived at Chartage, he felt like an outsider. The others were talking among themselves, discussing the political implications of the news Gladstone shared. None of them were addressing the problem of removing the Skamorrans.

While the two ideas Fitch had brought forward proved to be entirely successful, they did not endear him to the other officers. They resented being shown up by a foreigner. Fitch felt his best relationship was with Allison Gillies. He tried to catch her attention. It took a few minutes before she noticed him looking at her. She left the group and crossed to him.

"What do you need, Ralph?"

"We need to concentrate on Chartage," he said. "I understand enough to know that the political situation is dire, but we cannot influence things until we deal with the Skamorrans."

"You're correct, of course," she replied.

Gillies stuck the ends of her index and smallest finger in the corners of her mouth. She then let loose an ear-piercing whistle. The discussion stopped instantly.

"Ralph just reminded me that we need to do as the general asked," she said. "Let's figure out how to get rid of the Skamorrans, then worry about the political landscape."

The group displayed mixed reactions. A couple wore sheepish looks. The rest glared at Fitch.

"Does anyone have an idea they would like to share?" Gillies asked.

Fitch had an idea, but he was unwilling to share it given how some of his fellow officers were treating him. He supposed if situations were reversed, he would resent a foreigner coming in the way he had. Still, he thought, none of them offered anything.

"Yes," Reubens said. "Burn them out. Bring the galleys into the harbor and use their catapults to set that end of the city on fire."

Fitch was relieved to see Reubens make that suggestion. It was what Fitch was considering. It would bring matters to a head in the quickest and most decisive way possible now that waiting for the Skamorrans to run out of food was no longer an option.

The group started to discuss the idea Reubens brought forward. The biggest worry was keeping the Skamorrans hemmed in. With everything burning behind them, they would rush the barricade and burst from the gates they still controlled.

"You have two watchers tonight. Did you know?" the man at the bar asked quietly, without moving his head or his lips.

"They weren't subtle," Stan Barthlemy said. "They also shadow me in the palace now."

"Is it you? Or is this general?"

"I think it's because the chancellor did not put me in the Guard to begin with," Stan replied. "He only trusts his own weasels, and them not too much."

"I told you before that if you make me laugh, we'll both end up dead," Varnes said.

"Do you have more information?" Stan asked. "Because I have nothing new to report."

"I do," Varnes answered. "Lieutenant Fitch is now Colonel Fitch in the Austerian army. He was instrumental in raising the alarm and helping stop the Skamorran advance well short of the capital. Since then, he has also played a significant role in the fight to regain Chartage."

"Colonel, eh? Good for Ralph," Stan said. "I would wager he is having more fun than I am."

"I wouldn't be so sure," Varnes replied. "The duke's sources say that Auster is on the brink of civil war. It's difficult to determine at the moment, but indications are that the Skamorran attack is tied in somehow."

"What?"

"You need to understand Austerian politics," Varnes said. "The duke explained it all to me, but we don't have time. Things have begun to happen with the Regency Council. Lord Pacquie was killed by highwaymen."

"And you feel the chancellor is involved?" Stan asked.

"There were no other reports of banditry in the area. Just Lord Pacquie," Varnes said. "The Earl of Turris just suffered a riding accident. Fell off his horse and broke his neck. That explanation does not fit with the many other bruises found on his corpse."

"Who killed him?"

"His son," Varnes whispered, "though that's not proven—just strongly suspected by those who know what else is going on."

"Why the bruises?" Stan asked.

"The earl changed his will two days before his body was found," Varnes said. "The son was the one who delivered it to the magistrate. Apparently, the handwriting on the new document was not the same as on the previous versions.

When questioned, the son admitted he wrote it out for his father. The father's signature, although written with a trembling hand, matched closely enough that the magistrate accepted it."

"How many more before the chancellor obtains a majority on the Regency Council?" Stan asked.

"Five," Varnes replied.

"And Courtenay?

"Still alive," Varnes said as he pushed away from the bar. "See you again the next time."

Captain Barthlemy stayed in his seat since he was still waiting for his dinner. When it arrived, he ate in a leisurely fashion. He paid the innkeeper, put on his cloak, and then went to retrieve his horse from the groom.

Stan sensed movement from both right and left. He noticed the groom was nowhere to be seen. He stopped, making sure his hands were outside the cloak. He took a step back to put the closed door at his back. He guessed the two men who followed him were the ones waiting for him.

Stan sensed the man on his right was making his move. He darted forward, away from the door, and into the dim light from the sconce on the wall of the stable. As he moved, Stan unsheathed his sword. Both his would-be attackers stepped into the light to follow up. They were carrying knives, only half as long as Stan's blade.

The two separated and began moving to get on either side of Stan. The sight of Stan's sword did not seem to deter either of them. In fact, they were both grinning.

Stan was not going to allow them to put him in the middle. He jab-stepped to the right, feinting a strike to the man's face. When his opponent lifted his knife to block Stan's blade, Stan quickly changed the direction of his strike and slashed down on the man's left thigh.

As the man gasped in pain, Stan spun to his right and away from the man's right hand, which held the dagger. When he stopped his turn, the other man was almost upon him, knife outthrust. Stan stepped forward and dipped down so the man's blade went past his ear. He drove his blade up under his assailant's chin and saw his body collapse.

"Stop right there, or join your partner in death," Stan said as his first victim was trying to stagger away. "Drop the knife."

The man dropped his weapon and turned slowly towards Stan, favoring his wounded leg. Stan looked the man up and down in the dim light. He recognized him as one of the chancellor's recent additions to the palace staff. The dead man probably was, as well.

"Who set you on me?" Stan asked as he kicked the knife away.

"Who do you think?" the man snarled.

"What was all this about?" Stan asked. "You two were supposed to kill me? Why?"

"Damned if I know why. Boss tells me to do somethin' I do it. Askin' questions ain't exactly encouraged."

"I already knew that," Stan said.

"Prolly don't want you around no more," the man sneered.

Stan knew he could not return to the palace. He had no idea where he could go. Sergeant Varnes knew where to find him, but the reverse was not true. Frustrated, Stan plunged his sword through the man's chest. The man dropped to his knees, clutching the wound.

"Thanks, *friend*," Stan said as he wiped his blade clean on the man's coat before walking away.

He watched the man topple forward. Stan turned and sheathed his sword. He knocked on the closed stable door.

"You can come out now," he called to the groom.

There was no answer. Stan opened the door. The frightened groom was sitting in the corner.

"C'mon. I want my horse. Give it a minute or two, then start hollering. Tell people you were in the loft and heard a ruckus outside. By the time you came down and looked out, it was all over, and you didn't see the other man or men," Stan instructed.

The groom nodded nervously, still clutching himself in a ball on the floor. Stan shook his head and retrieved Hammer. He opened the large door wider and took the horse outside.

"Remember, you didn't see anything," Stan reminded the groom. "By the time you came down, it was all over and you never saw who else was here."

As Stan rode away, he headed to the inn where he and Fitch used to stay when they visited the city before joining the Palace Guard. If Varnes were in the city, Stan hoped he would hear of the incident and come find him. The question was whether the chancellor's people found him first.

After watching Rathbun sail away, the feeling John had that he was neglecting something important plagued him even more. His sleep was troubled. That sense of anxiety would not leave him. Cia tried to help him figure out what was bothering him, but it was no use. It was even more frustrating since he could not explain what was causing this feeling.

His dreams were disturbing. He could not remember most of them. One, however, was detailed.

He was on a large ship with square sails. Three smaller ships with triangular sails intercepted the ship he was on. Men with long ropey hair, like he saw on the man Isaiah, clambered over the sides.

He fought them using his sword. The other men on his ship fell to the attackers. Three of the men with the hair cornered him and forced him backward. He fell through a square hole in the deck. Fortunately, he landed on two bodies which broke his fall. He scrambled and found a place to hide in the front of the ship, burrowing into coils of rope.

The men came to look for him, but did not find him. He could hear them calling to one another. Hours after he last heard their voices, he ventured out.

Cautiously, he climbed to the main deck. The ship was tossing side to side, its sails flapping in the stiff wind. The three smaller ships were gone. He was the only survivor. John knew nothing about sailing. That thought disturbed him enough that he woke from his dream.

As soon as he woke, he was irritated. He wanted to learn what happened next. If what he saw in his dream was a memory, it would explain how he came to the island.

He shared the dream with Cia. She insisted he tell her father. John then recounted everything to Caleb.

"Huh," Caleb grunted. "That explains the tar all over your clothes."

"It does?"

"Ropes are covered with tar to keep them from fraying and stretching. If you were hiding in the rope locker, the tar would have gotten all over you. You say the sails were square?" Caleb asked.

"Not exactly square," John explained. "Rectangular."

"How many masts did it have?"

"Two tall ones, in the middle and front," John said. "A shorter one in the rear."

"A galleon then," Caleb said, "The smaller ships you describe sound like Skamorran corsairs. They are faster and more maneuverable than galleons. They would have been able to intercept your ship easily. You mentioned the wind was strong when you came up on deck. How strong?"

"Strong like when the last typhoon approached," John said.

"And you know little about sailing, you say. What is the little you know?" Caleb asked.

"The wind pushes the sails, and the sails push the ship," John replied. "Oh, and you steer the ship with a big wooden wheel up at the back."

"I think what you experienced is a memory more than a dream, John," Caleb said after he thought for a few moments. "Though you woke before you remembered what happened next, I think I can imagine it pretty well. I reckon you went up to the wheel and managed to turn the ship so the wind filled the sails. It sounds as though you were in the way of the typhoon that landed you here."

"What would have happened?" John asked.

"As one person, with no knowledge of sailing or navigation, you ran before the wind until the typhoon caught up to you," Caleb explained. "It might have taken a day or two before the storm reached you, and you would have covered a tremendous distance in that time. When the typhoon finally did hit you, it would have ripped the sails apart and probably broken the masts. That's probably when you were cracked on the head—by something falling from above. After that, the storm would have continued to push the ship along until you hit the shoals on the eastern side of the island. The wind and waves would have slammed your ship against the rocks. They also pushed your body ashore."

"Thank you, Caleb," John said. "It's very interesting. The important thing is still missing. Where was I headed, and why was I going there?"

"Indeed," Caleb agreed. "No sailor with any sense would take a galleon into the open ocean during typhoon season without a compelling reason. It's simply too dangerous, as you apparently learned the hard way."

26

Fitch watched from the harbor front as the Austerian galleys rowed into the harbor. They lined up in two lines of five, overlapping one another, broadside to the city. When they reached the spots they chose, they dropped their anchors.

Within minutes, Fitch watched as the catapults launched clay pots filled with oil. As they flew, the pots left a smoky trail from the lit rags stuffed into their necks. When the pots landed, they burst into pieces, spraying the flammable oil they carried, which quickly ignited.

The oarsmen shifted the position of the galleys slightly, so the next shots would hit fresh targets. Though Fitch could not see what the Skamorrans were doing behind the buildings, he imagined they would be forming ranks in preparation for an attack. General Gladstone had stationed men atop the western height with flags. There were four gates in the part of the city the Skamorrans still controlled. With signals already agreed upon, the men on the heights would communicate which gates the Skamorrans intended to use.

A second volley of oil pots flew from the galleys. Fitch could now see smoke rising from where the first group landed. He left his vantage point, mounted Bob, and rode out the nearest gate and around, behind where two-thirds of the Austerian soldiers were waiting outside the city walls.

General Gladstone had taken precautions to ensure his forces had the greatest advantage possible. He had off-loaded the catapults from the four galleys judged too damaged to join this fight. They were now lined up facing the gates through which they expected the Skamorrans to rush. Like the galleys, they would be firing oil pots. Unlike the galleys, they would be aiming for soldiers, not buildings.

Fitch saw a flurry of flag movement from the heights opposite. He could hear the Austerian officers begin to encourage their soldiers for the imminent attack. Suddenly, all four of the gates swung open. With shields up, the Skamorrans came rushing out. As soon as the gates opened, the catapults fired.

One shot sailed too high, missing the onrushing enemies and sailing over the wall. Two hit the wall just above the gate, shattering and spraying the soldiers underneath with the flammable liquid. The fourth pot took a man's head off, striking him squarely in the helmet. It, too, splattered everyone nearby with oil.

Austerian archers sent flaming arrows into the midst of their enemies, and their success was marked by the screams of the Skamorrans who found themselves on fire. The flames jumped from soldier to soldier, and also found the oil on the ground. Any Skamorran wanting to exit through that gate would need to pass through a gauntlet of flame.

The Austerian lancers rode in from the side quickly. Weapons lowered, they smashed into the side of the Skamorrans who made it through the gates untouched. The Skamorrans remaining inside the walls did not brave the flaming opening.

Fitch could hear the Skamorrans shouting. He reckoned they would shift their forces to assault the barricade. Seeing the flags signaling from the western height, Colonels Nadeau and Reubens ordered the reserves to reinforce General Gladstone inside the city.

The galleys would move as well and shift their aim to drop their oil pots on the places where the Skamorrans would try to stage their troops. Using fire pots against soldiers bothered Fitch, but he reminded himself that the Skamorrans would not hesitate to do the same if they had the ability. They chose to attack Auster without warning. Even worse, they had killed an entire city full of people. In the face of such cruelty, the concept of "fairness" did not apply.

Fitch rode back into the city, wanting to witness the Skamorran assault on the barricade. He could hear the Skamorran attack before he arrived. When he rode up, he watched the Austerian archers cutting down the Skamorrans as they tried to climb over the obstacles. The attack faltered.

On the other side of the barricade, Fitch could see the city ablaze. Suddenly, he heard whistles. This was the signal that the Skamorrans surrendered. Someone was waving a white cloth on a pole that stuck above the top of the barricade.

Skamorran soldiers, their armor and weapons left behind, began climbing over. When they reached the ground, they lifted their hands in the air. Officers directed them into a column, and sent them outside the walls. Waiting for them was an open space surrounded by Austerian soldiers with weapons at the ready.

Fitch left this location and rode back out and around to see what was happening at the gates. The fires from the oil pots that blocked three of the gates had died down, and Skamorrans were exiting the city with their hands up. Fitch started to wonder how many survived.

Of course, that brought to his mind a problem for which they had not yet developed an answer—what to do with the prisoners? With a civil war waiting for them, leaving soldiers behind to guard prisoners presented a problem. Fitch hoped they could figure out a way to make use of the Skamorrans. Otherwise, the only remaining option was repugnant to him. Slaughtering unarmed prisoners was something the Skamorrans did. Boreas never did such a thing, and he hoped the Austerians would not consider it either.

Certainly, they could leave a small group behind to clean up the mess here in Chartage. Bodies must be buried, and rubble would need to be cleared away. That made Fitch wonder what the Skamorrans did with the bodies of the residents of the city. Since he had not yet smelled rotting corpses, Fitch reckoned the Skamorrans burned them, probably using the materials from the buildings outside the walls which they razed.

The rest of the Skamorrans could accompany the army to Austeria. Fitch would never allow them to bear arms, but they could dig trenches and build fortifications. It would make the logistical problem of feeding everyone more difficult, though. It was General Gladstone's decision to make, and for that, Fitch was glad.

Colonel Newagen arrived and barked in Skamorran. A man stepped forward from the group. From the markings on his uniform, Fitch could tell he was an officer.

Newagen issued instructions. The Skamorran then spoke to his soldiers. A group of twenty stepped forward. Newagen led them back inside the city.

Fitch, curious, followed. Newagen took them to where a wagon with a two-handled pump stood. Coiled at the rear were canvas hoses with brass fittings on the ends. The Skamorrans pushed the pump forward, in the direction of the fire. Then they turned toward the water's edge.

Newagen barked some orders as she dismounted. She took one of the canvas hoses and attached it to an opening on the side of the pump housing. Then, the Skamorrans dragged the other end of the hose to the water and dropped it in. Newagen then fastened a length of hose to the other port on the housing, ordering the Skamorrans to unroll it in the direction of the fire. It did not reach.

Newagen took a brass coupling and attached it to the end of that hose, and connected another length to it. That brought them close enough to the fire to feel the heat. Newagen then attached a brass nozzle to the end of the joined length of hose.

Upon her instructions, the other Skamorrans began pushing the handles on opposite sides of the pump mechanism up and down in turn. At first, they moved easily. As the hose from the harbor filled with water, then the hose leading toward the fire did the same, and the resistance grew.

After a minute, a powerful stream of water gushed out of the brass nozzle. The hose began whipping on the ground like a frenzied snake. Newagen issued more orders, and two of the prisoners grabbed the hose and aimed the stream of water at the base of the fire.

"Fitch! Keep them working," Newagen called. "There's another pump I found and I'm going to get more prisoners."

Fitch dismounted and tied Bob to a post. He strode forward to where the hose was spurting water. The stream of water was knocking the flames down quickly.

Newagen returned and said, "In a few minutes, stop. Add another length of hose to the one in the water, then move toward the wall as far as it will let you."

"I'm curious, Colonel," Fitch said before she moved on. "Did the Skamorrans not know how to use these pumps?"

"They didn't even know what they were," Newagen laughed.

When Fitch judged that the area they could reach with the water was under control, he got them to stop. He didn't speak Skamorran, but with hand gestures, he was able to get his message across. He uncoupled the one hose that led to the harbor from the pump and added another, then fastened the two hoses together with a coupling. When that was finished, the Skamorrans pushed the wagon forward to where the fire was still blazing. Fitch got them to stop, and they started pumping again.

Newagen kept riding back and forth, directing the pumps. When the fires were knocked out in one area, she moved them to another. She rotated different groups of Skamorrans to do the hard work of operating the pumps.

As the sun was about to set, the fires were under control. Spots were still smoldering, and Newagen was directing the pumps to go back and pour water on those places until no more smoke could be seen. It was then that she realized Fitch had been there the whole day.

"Immortal Gods, Fitch!" she exclaimed. "I didn't mean to have you stuck here all day."

"I didn't see anyone relieving you, Colonel," he replied.

"Well, I'm the only one who speaks their language," she said. "I'm really sorry. You're wounded, after all, and none of the others are. It's not fair."

"Again, Colonel, no one offered to give you a breather," Fitch said.

"Let me grab a couple of other officers, and then you and I can go eat," Newagen said.

She rode out. A few minutes later, she returned with two officers wearing captain's insignia. Newagen explained what she wanted done, and told the officers where to take the prisoners once they judged all the smoldering coals were safely doused.

"C'mon, Fitch," she said. "Let's go."

"How did you come to speak Skamorran?" Fitch asked as he hoisted himself into the saddle.

"One of my family's servants was Skamorran," she explained. "His corsair wrecked on the coast to the west of here, where my father has his barony. He was the only survivor and in bad shape when we found him. We took him in and brought him back to health. Once he was back on his feet, he started doing odd jobs around our place and just sort of blended in with the rest of the staff."

"He was never a problem?" Fitch asked.

"Joshua—that was his name—told me he felt he owed us his life. He had no desire to return to Skamorra, and was happy with us."

"That's the first time I've ever heard of a Skamorran being willing to coexist with anyone other than another Skamorran," Fitch commented.

"Joshua told me he didn't know whether it was his god that decided to save him, or our Gods," Newagen said, "and he didn't care. He said that he was where he was, and it was where he was meant to be."

"I wish all Skamorrans were so level-headed," Fitch remarked. "The world would be a better place."

"It's their religion," Newagen said. "Joshua explained that their holy books and the priests all say that any non-believers must be converted or killed. Even worse, killing a non-believer is considered an act of godliness."

Newagen and Fitch reached the makeshift corral where the horses were kept. She handed her horse to a soldier on duty. Fitch did not—intending to groom Bob himself.

"You're not coming?" Newagen asked.

"I will, once I've taken care of Bob here," he responded.

"You groom your own horse?" she asked in mild disbelief.

"He lets me ride him," Fitch replied. "Why wouldn't I want to take care of his needs? Save me some of whatever they're serving."

27

It was the first clear day following four days of heavy rain. Cia begged John to go on a walk with her. John was ready to get out of the house as well and agreed quickly.

They set off for the western end of the island. As usual, once they were out of sight of Town, Cia clasped John's hand. After a few minutes, she shifted and entwined his arm with hers, drawing them close together.

John did not know how to respond. He was undeniably attracted to Cia. She was beautiful, intelligent, and kind. From the books he read since washing ashore on the island, he understood that he was in love with her. It was clear from her behavior that she was in love with him—at least, according to the authors' descriptions of love.

The problem he wrestled with was his lack of knowledge of the past. His feelings for Cia were unlike any other emotions he could remember experiencing. And that was the problem—the lack of memory. He did not know whether there was someone he left behind for whom he felt the same.

John accepted that he would remain on the island for the rest of his life. If he did leave someone behind, he would never see her again. But until he remembered his past, he felt unable to move forward.

His heart was trapped in the middle. He ached to deepen his relationship with Cia. Given the small population on the island, that meant marriage and a lifelong commitment. The idea of spending the rest of his life with Cia was an appealing prospect.

He also did not know how he fit in. The only skill that had come back to him was swordplay. There was no need for that on the island.

For her part, Cia understood John's dilemma, though she did not agree with his frozen position. To her way of thinking, the past was immaterial since they were never leaving the island. She felt that John should embrace the present and the future. She already felt a strong emotional and intellectual bond with John and was confident in his feelings for her. She wanted to escalate the physical part of their relationship to match.

Stan Barthlemy went to the door of his room with sword drawn. Although the voice on the other side sounded like Varnes, Stan wanted to be sure. He stood, listening to determine if there was more than one person outside.

"Sergeant? How many years did we serve together in the Border Wardens?" Stan asked.

If Varnes answered correctly, Stan would know he was alone. If the sergeant gave a wrong answer, he would be telling Stan that there were others. It was the best solution Stan could muster in the short time available.

"Eight."

With a sigh of relief, Stan unbolted and opened the door. Varnes was alone in the hall. Stan stepped aside and let him in, then bolted the door behind him.

"I'm glad you found me," Stan said.

"It was a hunch, that's all," Varnes said. "You can't stay here. The chancellor has people looking for you all over the city. They simply haven't come here yet, but they will."

"Where can I go?" Stan asked.

"We need to head to Roundel," Varnes said. "It's the only choice. I settled with the innkeeper for your stay and already asked the groom to saddle your horse. We need to leave *now*."

Stan put on his jacket and hat, then tied his heavy winter cloak around his neck. He nodded to Varnes, who unlocked the door and stepped into the hallway. Stan followed Varnes out.

Hammer was waiting alongside the sergeant's mount. They climbed into the saddle and set off for the west gate of the city in the late afternoon amid a heavy snowfall. Varnes advised Stan to pull his cloak tighter so his uniform would not show.

The guards at the west gate stopped them. With the portcullis down, there was no way to ride past. Stan saw one of the stooges the chancellor added to the Palace Guard.

"Middle left—one of the chancellor's men," Stan whispered to Varnes.

"Damn. I hope you're up for a fight, Cap'n," Varnes replied.

With that, Varnes spurred his horse right for the small group of men. Barthlemy did the same a moment later. The six men at the gate scattered out of the paths of the two horses.

Varnes and Barthlemy each guided his horse at the slowest man to move on their respective sides. They attacked from above, leaning out of the saddle. Before either of their targets had a chance to recover, both men dismounted quickly. Barthlemy executed a fleche, rushing inside the stunned man's guard and piercing his chest. Varnes' move was more of a flunge, but had the same effect. Barthlemy then performed a passata sotto, dropping down under the next guard's thrust and driving his blade up through the man's stomach. Varnes executed a balestra and a lunge, stabbing his target in the throat.

Now matched up man to man, both Barthlemy and Varnes needed to give ground to their attackers. Varnes utilized a ceding parry before sliding his sword along his opponent's in a coulé. When the two men were hilt-to-hilt, Varnes punched the man in the mouth with his left hand. As the man staggered back from the blow, Varnes whipped the tip of his blade across the man's throat. Barthlemy used a croisé against the chancellor's man, forcing both blades down in a prise de fer. Releasing quickly, Barthlemy then executed a colpo sottano, cleaving deep into the man's right side. As his enemy recoiled from the wound, Barthlemy rotated the tip of his blade upward, skewering his enemy's brain from under his chin.

Sheathing their blades, Varnes and Barthlemy quickly moved to the winch that controlled the portcullis. The two of them worked together to raise it quickly before the guards, already running along the walkway near the top of the city walls, could stop them. When they raised it high enough to ride underneath, they quickly mounted their horses and ducked under the portcullis.

Stan heard the twang of crossbow bolts firing. He felt a violent punch to his left shoulder, followed by a searing explosion of pain. Once he was able to focus on something else, he checked to make sure Hammer was untouched.

As he did, he noticed Varnes was slumped over his horse's neck. A crossbow bolt was sticking out of Varnes' back. As Stan watched, Varnes' body slid sideways from the saddle to the left. His horse continued to gallop. With Varnes being dragged by his foot caught in the stirrup.

Stan checked to see if anyone was pursuing him yet. With the heavy snow, he could see no one. He leaned over to grab the horse's reins. Because of how Varnes fell, Stan would need to use his left arm. Gritting his teeth against the pain, he moved Hammer closer. It took three attempts before Stan caught the reins and was able to bring Varnes and his horse to a stop.

Stan dismounted and checked on Varnes. Varnes was clearly dead. His face was a bloody mess from being dragged on the ground. Stan knew time was not his ally and quickly debated whether to leave the body or heave it over the saddle.

Deciding that leaving Varnes' body might give the chancellor confirmation of the Duke of Roundel's involvement, Stan untangled Varnes' foot from the stirrup. With great difficulty, he hoisted the body onto his right shoulder, then flopped it over the saddle. After adjusting it to center the weight as best he could, Stan directed Hammer to the left side of Varnes' horse. This way, he could hold the reins to Varnes' horse in his right hand.

He set off at a trot, the light failing. His shoulder was throbbing as the horse trotted, and he was beginning to feel winter's cold. While he rode, he tried to think of the route to Roundel. He knew it was generally east and south of the city, but he had never visited before. Stan also tried to recall if he knew anyone along the way.

He was much more familiar with the western portion of Boreas. The road from the capital to the border with the Skamorrans was one he had traveled many times. He believed he knew all the innkeepers by name. In this direction, he could not think of anyone he knew.

Stan was trying to decide if the increasing darkness was his friend or enemy. Traveling with a dead body and a crossbow quarrel in his shoulder made the darkness an ally. Feeling his strength failing and aware of the need to cover as much distance as possible made the night less welcome.

Stan needed help. He could not pull the bolt from his shoulder. His uniform made him a marked man. He hoped Varnes packed something he could wear that would fit.

His strength was failing when he saw lighted windows ahead. Whether he knew anyone, he could not continue without assistance. He rode into town and found the inn. The stable was in the back, and Stan headed for it.

"Hold there, friend," called a voice from the darkness. "You look in a bad way."

"You're not wrong, whoever you are," Stan replied. "And I need help from someone whose loyalty to king and country is strong."

An older man stepped into the dim light cast by the lone torch lit behind the inn. The man looked Stan over. He noticed the quarrel protruding from his shoulder, and Varnes' corpse.

"Why is loyalty to king and country so important?" the man asked.

"It's a long and unpleasant story that will put you in danger if you know the truth of it," Stan said.

"My life lacks much excitement these days," the old man said. "I'll take a chance you're not a criminal since criminals don't carry dead bodies around—they just leave them lie. Give me those reins, son."

The old man took the reins gently from Stan's hands and began leading them away from the inn. They walked for at least a quarter of an hour, to the edge of the village. Eventually, the man stopped.

"Wait a minute, he said.

Stan heard a door open and close, though he could see nothing in the snowy darkness. He heard the rasp of steel on flint, then saw the outline of the door. A moment later, and the stable door opened. Torch in hand, the old man collected the reins and guided both horses inside.

"I suggest you get out of the saddle before you fall off," the old man said.

He waited for Stan to slide off, then took the horses to the water trough. While the animals were drinking, he returned to Stan. He walked around him with the torch.

"Best get you in the house," the old man said, "and get that crossbow bolt out. I'll tend to the horses later."

The old man shut the stable door, then gestured for Stan to follow him out the smaller door through which he entered the building. They crossed to the door of a small house, which the man opened. He ushered Stan in and grabbed a candle which he lit from the torch. Once the candle was lit, he handed it to Stan. The man then inserted the torch into an iron bell that snuffed out the flame. He put the butt into a hole in a stone outside the door, then came in.

From the light of the candle, Stan could see he was in the kitchen. His host took the candle from him and lit two others. He then opened the firebox of the stove and from a rack next to it, added three logs.

"Sit down next to the stove before you collapse," the man said.

In the light of the three candles, Stan could see the man's features now. His host had a timeworn face with deep-set wrinkles. His hair was iron gray, glittering with water where the snow melted, and tied in a queue at the back of his neck. From what Stan could see, the man appeared fit—not skinny, not fat.

Stan was beginning to feel the warmth as the fire in the stove rekindled. His host took a wooden bucket and went back outside. When he returned. He took a large pot from a hook on the wall, set it on top of the stove, then poured water from the bucket into the pot.

"We're going to wait for the water to boil," the man said. "While we do, tell me what you think I need to know."

"Two men tried to murder me yesterday night," Stan said. "I killed them instead and went into hiding. A man who served under me in the Border Wardens found me and was going to take me to his employer. At the gate of the city, the guards tried to stop us. We defeated them, but others loosed their crossbows at us as we rode away. They killed my friend and, if not for the grace of an inch or two, would have gotten me, too. That's as much as I can tell you without putting you into much more danger than you are already in for helping me."

"If I'm in danger for helping you, from whom should I expect the threat?"

"The chancellor."

"Ah," the old man commented. "Stand up, Mr.—?"

"Barthlemy. Stan Barthlemy, until yesterday captain of the Palace Guard. And you?"

"Bernhardt. Scott. Stand up then, captain. I'm going to remove your cloak without ruining it any more than it is already. That means I'm going to pull it off while leaving the bolt in place. It will probably hurt a great deal. You should probably brace yourself against the wall."

Stan stood and moved to where he could put his hands against the wall. Bernhardt came around behind and untied the cloak from around Stan's neck. Stan could tell the man was trying to be gentle, but any movement of the quarrel in the meat of his shoulder made the wound throb anew.

"Ready?" Bernhardt asked.

Stan nodded.

"One—two—"

Before reaching three, Bernhardt pulled the cloak away. It tugged on the embedded weapon as he pulled the cloak over the fletching. Stan was caught by surprise. He thought Bernhardt would pull the garment from him on "three." The pain made his knees buckle, and he was glad he braced himself against the wall.

"Sit down when you're ready," Bernhardt suggested.

It took a moment before Stan felt his legs would not buckle. He moved cautiously back to the table and sat down carefully. Bernhardt had put his cloak off to the side and found a pair of shears.

"I'm going to ruin your jacket and shirt," Bernhardt explained. "Of course, they're soaked with blood, so pretty much ruined already, but this will complete the job. Once I get them off, I'll remove the bolt."

Bernhardt inserted the shears into the hole made by the quarrel and cut upward and then down. He was careful not to disturb the wound. The shears sliced Stan's jacket to the neck and then the hem. Bernhardt then slid the two halves down Stan's arms. He did the same with the shirt.

"Are you ready for me to pull it out?" Bernhardt asked.

"Go ahead, please."

Bernhardt grasped the bolt gently, trying not to move it. Even so, Stan winced. Without warning, Bernhardt yanked it out, then pressed part of Stan's ruined shirt over the wound to staunch the fresh flow of blood.

"Thank you," Stan gasped.

"Just wait a minute and we'll see if you're still grateful," Bernhardt warned.

He left Stan and went into another room. When Bernhardt returned, he held a bottle in one hand and a roll of gauze in the other. He walked behind Stan.

"What's in the bottle?" Stan asked.

"Alcohol," Bernhardt replied. "I'm going to put some on the wound to reduce the chance it gets infected. It will sting."

Bernhardt unrolled two lengths of the gauze and folded them into wads. One of the wads he soaked in alcohol. When he finished, he pressed it to the hole left by the quarrel.

"Immortal Gods!" Stan hissed through clenched teeth.

Bernhardt put the dry wad of gauze over the hole and then began to bind it in place. He wrapped the bandage over Stan's shoulder and around his chest. When he was satisfied it would hold the pad in place, he tied off the loose end.

28

Over five thousand Skamorrans surrendered. General Gladstone was planning on leaving four thousand of them behind to clear the rubble from the sections of Chartage they destroyed. The other fifteen hundred he would bring to the capital for the expected confrontation with the Duke of Volplane.

The large number of prisoners created problems. One was that Gladstone needed to leave at least two thousand of his own soldiers behind to guard them. The other issue was feeding the extra people. The Skamorrans were nearly out of food. They were expecting supplies to arrive soon.

Gladstone alerted the commander of the galleys to this. Ideally, the Austerian galleys would capture the Skamorran supply ships. That would ease Gladstone's logistical problems.

Gladstone's other concern was soldiers. Mira and other members of the Royal Courier Service had been sent to the Western Reaches of Auster to summon the militias and the small number of army soldiers stationed there. Gladstone had been busy, sitting with the mayors and head men and women of the towns and villages that supplied the militia currently encamped at Chartage.

It took little skill to persuade the militia to fight Skamorran invaders. Asking them to take sides in a civil war was more difficult. Fortunately, enough of the more influential local leaders were somewhat familiar with the Duke of Volplane. Sir Gerald, Sir Jamel, Dame Kapiste, and some others were able to share their own views of the rebellious duke.

Fitch was asked to share what he knew of Volplane's involvement. Ralph spoke with twenty-one different groups of militia. He shared with the people the ruse that drew the fleet away from Chartage to Bergin, and the suspected murder of Dame Wisenhut.

He told them what he knew and what he suspected. Though he did not have the evidence to prove it, he was certain that Volplane had worked with the Skamorrans. Volplane's scheme left Chartage undefended, allowing the Skamorrans to capture it easily. This, in turn, drew the army away from the capital, serving Volplane's purpose.

What Volplane and the Skamorrans did not expect was to lose Chartage so quickly. Fitch's inspiration to burn the corsairs, then to sneak in and open the gates the next night had been wildly successful. The Skamorrans not only lost Chartage, but more than half their fleet was destroyed. Volplane would not be getting much assistance from them in the future, Ralph guessed.

Ralph was also convinced that the scheming and plotting infected Boreas. His opinion was that the death of his king and the mission on which Prince John was sent were related to the invasion of Chartage. The Duke of Volplane was willing to give Chartage to the Skamorrans in order to overthrow the king. Ralph wondered what the chancellor was planning to sacrifice to gain the throne.

He wracked his brain. *When did the chancellor and the Duke of Volplane meet to discuss this? How did the two of them coordinate with the Skamorrans and each other?*

The assassins in the palace were Skamorran. With their distinctive hair, traveling in Boreas would have been impossible. The chancellor would have needed to sneak them into the country and then transport them in secret to the palace—no easy task. The timing of the king's murder, the prince's disappearance, and the attack on Chartage meant those events were linked and could not be the result of blind chance. Ralph hoped his friend Stan Barthlemy was finding answers.

Returning to the tent where Gladstone held meetings, Ralph was both pleased and troubled to see Mira's horse Shasta tethered outside. The flaps of the tent were closed. Ralph did not want to appear to be eavesdropping, but he was eager to see Mira. While he was shuffling his feet, wondering where to wait, she threw open the tent flap.

"Ralph! Good! We need you," she said, gesturing for him to enter.

Ralph ducked inside, giving Mira's arm a lingering touch in passing. General Gladstone was sitting on his camp stool. Hearing Mira's greeting to Ralph, he looked up.

"Mira and the other couriers are not having much success in convincing the people of the Western Reaches to join us," Gladstone said. "She made it only as far as Tarpot before encountering one of her colleagues returning bearing bad news. She believes it will be necessary for you to accompany her. Do you still have your Borean uniforms?"

"I do, though one is near to falling apart," Ralph said.

"Take it with you and wear it when you meet with them," Gladstone said. "The people of the Western Reach are concerned about the Skamorrans, based on history. No other part of Auster has suffered as many raids. They fear that if they send the militia to the capital, the Skamorrans will sweep down from the north and plunder and pillage to their hearts' content—especially since most of the navy's Western Squadron was destroyed not long ago."

"But we just burned up over half the Skamorran fleet," Ralph protested. "Did you tell them that?"

"Of course I did," Mira answered. "They did not believe me since I am not a soldier or sailor."

"You should also have our village leaders write letters to anyone they know," Fitch suggested.

"An excellent idea," Gladstone agreed. "That will lend even more veracity to the message. I will go speak with them now. Be prepared to leave at sun up."

Exhausted due to the loss of blood from his wound and lulled by the warmth of the stove, Stan fell asleep, slumped on the table. The smell of food roused him as his stomach reminded him that he had not eaten since breakfast. Disoriented and confused, he sat up quickly, which made his head spin.

"Easy there, captain," Bernhardt said.

"How long was I sleeping?" Stan asked anxiously.

"Just over an hour, I reckon. Long enough for me to feed your horses and relieve the one of the burden he was carrying. I hope you don't mind, but I took the purse from his body. It's on the table. I imagine you might need it."

Stan saw it and picked it up. Varnes' purse was as heavy as his own was light. Yes, he would need additional funds to complete his journey.

"I also brought in his saddlebags. You should change into fresh clothing and leave your uniform behind." Bernhardt advised.

"Sir, may I ask an impertinent question?" Stan inquired. "Why are you helping me?"

"I don't think that's an impertinent question at all," Bernhardt replied. "It's quite relevant. First of all, I'm a doctor. We are duty-bound to help the sick and injured. Even in the dim light, I could see you were injured. It's not often I encounter someone with a crossbow quarrel in his shoulder, leading a second horse with a dead man on it."

"But I could have been a criminal of some sort," Stan said.

"That doesn't release me from my oath as a doctor," Bernhardt said. "If I thought you were a criminal, though, there would be a constable with us now."

"And there is not," Stan said.

"Nor will there be. When I was able to see you in better light, I could tell you were probably not a criminal, unless you are of a better class of delinquent than any I have ever heard of. You even warned me that helping you would expose me to danger. Seeing your uniform, and you mentioning that the chancellor was the source of that danger convinced me you were not crooked."

"Again, why help me? You could turn me over to the authorities, and your hands would be clean," Stan inquired.

"Except, you see, I've met the chancellor," Bernhardt said. "And my first reaction was astonishment—having never seen a serpent in human form before. With a man such as he, handing you over to the authorities would not alleviate any danger to my person whatsoever, I fear. Rather than reward me, the chancellor seems to me to be the sort of person who would have me arrested for not leaving you in the cold to die."

"You sound as though you know him well," Stan said with a snort.

"No," Bernhardt said, shaking his head. "Only met him the one time, but he made a powerful and lasting impression. Enough talk for now—your food is ready. It's only salt pork stew, but I was not expecting a guest this evening. When I saw you, I was returning from eating at the inn."

Bernhardt placed a large bowl of the stew in front of Stan, along with a chunk of bread, a fork, and a cup of water. Stan was no stranger to salt pork stew, having eaten it many times while in the Border Wardens. He wasted no time and began shoveling it in his mouth.

"I plan to accompany you on your journey," Bernhardt announced.

"Doctor, I have no wish to mire you any deeper in my troubles."

"I'm already mired pretty deep, Captain," Bernhardt smiled. "Besides, you're wounded and will need someone to look after you. Without my help, I doubt you will make it more than another day before they reel you in."

"Won't you be missed?"

"Hardly," Bernhardt replied. "I'm seventy-two years old. Last year, I turned my practice over to a younger doctor. Since then, I have been rattling around with little to do. It will be days before someone notices I have not been around."

"What will we do with the body?" Stan asked.

"When we leave in a few minutes, we can abandon it outside of town," Bernhardt said. "I recommend we leave it on the side of town opposite the direction we intend to go."

"I hate leaving him unburied," Stan said.

"We don't have much choice," Bernhardt pointed out. "Someone will find him and bury him."

"I need to get to Roundel to see the duke," Stan said.

"East and south, then," Bernhardt confirmed. "We will leave him on the west road, as though you dumped him before entering the village. You and I should head north. Any pursuers will be heading east. I suggest we ride north for two days, then east. Eventually, we'll travel south, but I want to give the people looking for you the chance to become frustrated and lose hope. Is there anyone else other than the Duke of Roundel who could help?"

"The Earl of Courtenay," Stan answered, "but he is already viewed as a threat by the chancellor. I don't think Roundel is under the same degree of suspicion."

"Courtenay is north and west," Bernhardt said. "In order to avoid anyone searching for you, I think we should head north for two days. After that, east and then south. Finished?"

Stan was indeed finished with the stew. Barnhardt took the bowl, fork, and cup and washed them in a bucket of water. He then threw the water out the back door to the side. Bernhardt then pointed to the saddlebags.

Stan rose from the table wearily and went through Varnes' belongings. Retrieving a shirt and jacket, he put them on gingerly, favoring his wounded shoulder. Bernhardt took Stan's ruined uniform shirt and jacket and shoved them in the firebox of the stove.

"We should leave," Bernhardt said. "We need to put as many miles behind us tonight as possible. It will be especially hard on you, but we should not stop until tomorrow evening."

"Doctor, I've slept in the saddle more than I care to admit," Stan said. "I'll be fine."

Bernhardt used one of the candles to light the torch he left by the door, then made sure the rest of the candles were out. He carried Varnes' saddlebags out to the stable. The snow was now up over Stan's ankles.

Stan watched as the doctor saddled his own horse. He offered to help hoist the body back on Varnes' horse but Bernhardt waved him off. Bernhardt snuffed the torch, then climbed in the saddle of his horse, still holding the reins to Varnes' mount. Stan lifted himself onto Hammer's back, and they set off into the darkness.

29

Ralph and Mira set off at first light. They faced a three-day ride. Ralph felt slightly guilty about leaving the army, but his happiness at being able to spend time with Mira quickly overcame those negative thoughts.

The first two days would see them return to Dostin, the first village they warned about the Skamorrans. After riding past the little town, they would spend the night in the open at the foot of the pass of the western mountains. The third day would be spent negotiating the pass and reaching the first village in the Western Reaches, Badgerford.

They spent the first night in Alica. While Ralph groomed his horse, Mira arranged for the inn to prepare a bath for them. It was ready for them when they finished eating dinner.

Unlike the first time they shared a room, Mira undressed in front of Ralph. She slid into the hot water and beckoned him over. When he knelt by the side of the tub, she handed him a washcloth and leaned forward, indicating he should scrub her back. As he did, he tried to massage her shoulders, causing her to sigh with a sound nearing a purr.

When she was finished bathing, she stood boldly in front of him and stepped out. It was now his turn. This was the first chance Ralph had come across to bathe since his washing up in the rain. Mira assisted him with his hair and back, and her fingers worked on the sore muscles of his upper back. He did not purr, but it did feel heavenly.

When he finished, he dried himself, then quickly dragged the tub into the hall. Returning to the room, he locked the door behind him. Mira was already waiting for him. It was the first time in weeks they were able to sleep with one another in a proper bed.

Two days later, they arrived in Badgerford after dark. Mira obtained a room for them at the inn while Ralph groomed Bob. They decided to wait until morning to contact the head woman, Ma Ambrose.

After eating breakfast, they found Ma Ambrose. She was reluctant to talk with them, explaining that she had already told the first messenger she would not support General Gladstone. Mira merely asked her to read the letter which Pa Petten had written. The letter explained everything about the Skamorran attack and the subsequent destruction of their ships and the recapture of Chartage. Pa Petten also included the latest intelligence regarding the actions of the Duke of Volplane.

"You vouch for the contents of this letter?" Ambrose asked Mira.

"I don't know what the letter said," Mira explained, "but I imagine Pa Petten told you of what has happened and what challenges we face."

"And who are you?" Ambrose asked Ralph.

Ralph explained his role as briefly as he could. He recounted thwarting the Skamorran advance on the capital, the role of the Lord Chamberlain in the whole mess, the destruction of the Skamorran corsairs, and his role in breaching the gates of the city. Ma Ambrose listened with her hands on her hips.

"Damn," she muttered when he finished. "Double damn. What you've just told me is a different kettle of fish from the first fella. This sounds exactly like something Volplane would do. Badgerford will respond to the call from General Gladstone."

"Thank you, Ma Ambrose," Mira said. "Would you please write a quick note for Pa Thompson in Garrett, asking him to lend us an ear?"

"I'll be happy to," Ambrose replied. "And I'll also let him know that I support you."

After Garrett and the next town, Woolwich, Ralph and Mira would be calling upon titled nobles. This would slow them down since members of the aristocracy were usually not as readily available as mayors or heads of villages. It's not that they were busier, they just did not like to be too responsive.

After Woolwich, they had nearly a full-day ride to Jobson, where the Duke of Esser lived. Before stopping at the inn, Ralph suggested they call upon the duke. He did not think they would be allowed to see him that afternoon, but perhaps they might be given an appointment for the following morning. Ralph left the letter for the duke written by General Gladstone with the major domo.

"Colonel Fitch? Mira Grimble?" called a voice as the two were sitting down to eat.

"Yes?" Mira responded, looking to the common room.

"Oh, good. You haven't eaten yet," the man said with a look of relief. "The duke wishes to have you join him for dinner."

"We aren't exactly dressed properly—" Fitch started to say.

"Don't bother to change," the man said. "The duke is aware that you have ridden all day. You may come as you are. Bring your things. You will stay the night."

Ralph and Mira followed the man to a stately home not far away. Their guide left them with the majordomo they met earlier. He took them to the dining room. A thin man about their age rose when they entered.

"Milord," Ralph and Mira said, Ralph with a slight bow, Mira with a brief dip of her knees.

"Colonel Fitch," the man said, extending his hand. "Mira Grimble. Welcome. Please, let's dispense with formality. Call me Chet. I apologize for the lack of notice, but I just read the letter you left. We can discuss it over dinner."

Chet, the Duke of Esser, gestured to the seats on either side of his at the end of the table. Ralph helped Mira with her chair before moving to his own. He waited for the duke to sit before he did so himself. Almost as soon as the duke sat, a servant came, bringing out the first course.

"The first messenger the general sent did not do a good job of explaining the situation," the duke began. "The letter you left was far more informative. I understand Volplane has finally decided to act. Damn him for bringing the Skamorrans into it. How much do you know about our politics, colonel?"

"Only that there was a dispute over succession four generations ago. Volplane's family did not prevail despite having a stronger claim," Fitch said.

"Precisely," Chet agreed. "That entire family is a collection of supercilious snots—always has been. Theodosius' great-grandfather was able to garner much more support, though support is a relative term. A large part of it was more powerfully motivated by dislike of Volplane's family. Since taking the throne, however, Theodosius and his predecessors have done an admirable job."

"Then why does Volplane believe he will prevail?" Ralph asked. "Especially after bringing the Skamorrans into Chartage?"

"He will deny any involvement with the Skamorrans, of course," Chet responded. "And his people will believe him."

"But, even so, my understanding is that Volplane still does not have support from the majority of the aristocracy," Mira interjected.

"Sadly, he may not require it," Chet said. "The way Auster is organized, the northern tier and the western shore have more members of the titled nobility, and we support Theodosius. Volplane and his allies in the south and east are fewer in number but control larger territories with greater populations. Volplane will be able to muster an army of nearly twenty thousand—mostly infantry. General Gladstone said in his letter that he has eight thousand in arms outside Chartage, mostly cavalry. The rest of the north and west will be able to supply another seven thousand cavalry—if everyone responds."

"We will be outnumbered," Mira observed.

"And late, I'll wager," Chet added. "If Volplane does not already have the capital under siege, he is even more incompetent than I thought."

"You are not painting an attractive picture," Ralph commented.

"There is one more variable in this," Chet commented. "There are eight noble houses that control the area surrounding the capital. In the past, they have always been indecisive and unwilling to commit to one side or the other until they are sure of who will win. If they throw in with Volplane, he will gain an additional five thousand soldiers, including several hundred cataphracts. If they decide to join us, the numbers will become even, and I think Volplane will fail. They will be watching to see the results of the first skirmishes."

Stan and the doctor left Varnes' corpse by the side of the road on the east side of town. The snow was falling steadily enough that the body would be covered quickly. They then went back through the village and headed north.

Stan remembered little of the first day and a half of the journey. He spent most of it slumped in the saddle, asleep. The doctor took Hammer's reins and did not wake Stan until after daybreak when they stopped at an inn to eat. They rode through the day, reaching a town ten leagues north of where they started.

The doctor obtained a room for them at the inn. After dinner, he redressed Stan's wound and left him to sleep. The doctor was confident they were ahead of any pursuit but returned to the common room to listen for any indication of someone hunting them.

They rode north one more day, before heading east. By the fifth day, Stan was feeling more like his normal self. Sure, his shoulder still hurt, but the feeling of exhaustion was not as overwhelming.

It took eleven more days before they reached the Duchy of Roundel. Even then, they had a ride of one more day to arrive at the duke's manor. The light was fading as they approached the main entrance.

After debating how to approach the duke, Stan and the doctor agreed that the more direct, the better. Stan and the doctor dismounted and walked to the door. Before they knocked, a small panel opened.

"Yes?" a voice asked.

"Captain Stan Barthlemy, late of the Palace Guard, to see the duke," Stan announced.

"And you?"

"His personal physician," Bernhardt replied. "Captain Barthlemy is recovering from a wound."

The small panel slammed shut. Dr. Bernhardt and Stan looked at one another. The doctor shrugged his shoulders. They waited.

Less than ten minutes elapsed. The door opened, and two servants came to take the horses. Standing behind them was a finely dressed man.

"Welcome, Captain Barthlemy and Doctor—?"

"Bernhardt."

"Please come in. Let us not stand on formality. Please call me by my given name—Eric."

"Then I am Scott," the doctor said.

"And I already know from Sergeant Varnes that you go by Stan," the duke said. He is not with you."

"I'm afraid to say he is dead," Stan said.

"I suspected as much when you arrived without him. Come in out of the weather and tell me everything."

30

"You are fortunate to have found me," Eric said after Stan told him of his escape from the city and the death of Sergeant Varnes. "I plan to leave in the morning."

"Where were you headed?" Stan asked.

"As soon as I heard about Lord Pacquie and the Earl of Turris," Eric replied, "I sent letters to the other nobles who are suspicious of the chancellor. Your notes to me and Wexler confirmed to me that neither of their deaths was by coincidence. I warned my allies—our allies—to take every precaution with their lives. Courtenay feels we are on the brink of civil war. I agree. In the morning, I am planning on traveling through the duchy and meeting with the militias. We will need to be prepared to begin fighting when spring arrives."

"Do you really think it will come to that?" Scott asked.

"I am near-certain it will," Eric said.

"Can the chancellor muster enough troops to defend himself?" Stan asked.

"No, but he will not be the only one we will need to fight," Eric explained. "From what I know that happened in Auster, it seems logical that the Skamorrans will play a part."

"What exactly is going on in Auster?" Stan asked. "Sergeant Varnes told me that the Skamorrans seized Chartage."

"And have already lost it," Eric said. "Thanks in no small part to your friend Ralph Fitch. But their attack served its purpose—at least, the purposes of the Duke of Volplane."

"Who is he?"

Eric then summarized the political situation in Auster and provided more details about what happened in Chartage. He covered how Volplane's family had a stronger claim to the throne based on consanguinity. The Skamorran attack drew the army and militias away from the capital, and Volplane probably already had the city under siege.

"Volplane and his allies outnumber the loyalist forces," Eric said. "His soldiers are mostly infantry, while the loyalists are predominantly cavalry. That gives him a significant advantage in the type of fighting that will range around the walls of the capital. Volplane will dig in and construct siege works. It will be impossible for the loyalists to uproot him without infantry of their own. If they could meet him on open ground, it would be a different story, but whoever is advising Volplane is smart enough to avoid that, I fear."

"At least they don't need to worry about the Skamorrans any longer," Stan said.

"Don't be so sure," Eric countered. "I don't know for certain, but I suspect Volplane promised them Chartage. Similarly, I expect the chancellor has made his own arrangements with the Skamorrans."

"You mentioned that we would not only be fighting the chancellor and the forces he can muster," Scott said, entering the conversation. "The Skamorrans will also attack?"

"I believe so," Eric said. "Probably at Varenna and along the border. Our forces will then be split, and we will not be able to call upon the Border Wardens for assistance."

"Why would the chancellor, or this Volplane in Auster, make a deal with the Skamorrans?" Stan asked.

"They need the help of the Skamorrans to achieve the throne," Eric said. "Once they are firmly in place, both of them probably plan to oust the Skamorrans."

"Surely the Skamorrans see that as well," Scott commented.

"They would be idiots if they believed otherwise," Eric said. "In Auster and here in Boreas, the civil wars will probably last long enough for the Skamorrans to make Chartage and Varenna into impregnable strongholds. Volplane and the chancellor will not be able to dislodge them as easily as I believe they imagine."

"If Volplane and his soldiers are already at the capital," Fitch said, "they are probably building earthworks. It will be impossible for us to dislodge them with cavalry. We will need to force them into the open."

"How would you do that?" Chet asked.

"An army of twenty thousand needs food," Fitch explained. "Though we will not be able to evict them from whatever fortifications they construct, we can sever their supply lines with little difficulty. That has to be our focus. Assaulting their position will only get our people killed unnecessarily."

"Colonel Fitch, I believe the kingdom will best be served by you returning immediately to General Gladstone," Chet said. "Allow me to muster the other nobles here in the west. I promise I will not fail."

"Milord, I—" Fitch began.

"Chet," the duke reminded him.

"Chet, I mean no offense, but I was given orders," Fitch explained. "I cannot—"

"I understand, Colonel," the duke said with a wry smile. "Let me send one of me people to the general. We can write him and ask for your orders to be changed. When we finish, I will have my people prepare a bath for you and Mira Grimble. In the morning, the three of us will set out to summon the other lords."

Not quite an hour later, Ralph was relaxing in an enormous tub of hot water. Mira sat in front of him, and he was pretending to help her wash. In reality, he was using the opportunity to caress her entire body with his hands. She knew what he was doing and luxuriated in the feelings he was creating.

"I am afraid, my dear Ralph, that you have ruined my life," she sighed.

"Ruined it?"

"After the excitement I've had since your arrival, I would never be content to be a fisherman's wife," she said.

"I hope that our lives will not always be full of this sort of turmoil," Ralph stated.

"We must defeat Volplane," she said. "Then you must find your prince. Neither of those challenges will be easy. A peaceful existence for us is years away."

"And you are not unhappy about that."

"As long as we are together, I will be happy," she said, leaning back and twisting her head to kiss his cheek. "And I suspect that other predicaments will find you once those are resolved."

"You know I will not stop searching for the prince," Ralph said. "Not until I find him or know he is dead."

"I know. You've made that clear," she said. "I will help you find him. Your search will be my search."

Stan and the doctor joined the Duke of Roundel when he left to make the rounds of the duchy the following morning. The night before, the duke had his people prepare baths for both of them, which was a welcome bit of luxury. He also provided Stan with clothing and a new cloak of heavy wool, suitable for the winter weather.

"You don't need to join us, doctor," Stan said. "You've done enough already."

"And where would I go?" Scott replied. "Back home? Where I can count on being dragged in for unpleasant questioning regarding my sudden disappearance? No—let this old man play out the hand. Besides, if it comes to war, a doctor will be most useful, eh?"

A half dozen of the duke's armsmen rode with them. When they left the town of Arrun, where the duke's manor was located, they entered a stretch of dense woods. Less than a mile from town, they came upon six riders blocking the road.

Stan recognized them immediately. First of all, under their cloaks they were wearing the uniform of the Palace Guard. Secondly, he knew them as men the chancellor added to the Guard.

They recognized Stan. When they did, they unlimbered the crossbows attached to their saddles. They quickly cocked and loaded them.

"Oi, *Cap'n*," one of them said, putting a sarcastic sneer into his mention of Stan's rank. "An' you must be the duke. Our lucky day, lads. No more waitin' in the cold for 'em to finally show their faces."

"What do you want?" the duke asked.

"We're to take you to the chancellor," the man said.

"I don't think so," Stan sneered.

"He said, 'Dead or alive.' Seems t' me that dead'll be easier."

"Good luck with that," Stan snapped.

As he did, he touched his heels to Hammer's flanks and drew his sword. The horse surged forward as Stan dropped down to hug the horse's neck. The duke's armsmen joined the attack as soon as they saw what Stan did.

Stan heard the twang of the crossbows at the same time he felt bolts bury themselves in his right thigh and upper left arm. He heard a grunt from someone else who was hit and a scream from one of the horses. Straightening himself in the saddle, Stan readied himself to attack, ignoring the searing pain in his thigh and bicep.

It was not much of a fight. The men the chancellor added to the Palace Guard were little better than thugs. They had little skill with a blade. Stan quickly dispatched two of them. He wheeled to look for another foe, but there were none. The duke's armsmen killed the other four.

Looking back, Stan was dismayed to see the duke lying on the ground, with the doctor bent over him. The duke's horse had a quarrel buried deep in the center of his chest, with blood spurting from the wound. As Stan approached, the horse dropped to his knees, then toppled over.

The doctor was holding a piece of cloth to the side of the duke's neck. Stan could also see a bolt protruding from the duke's lower torso. He took heart from the doctor's calm, unworried expression.

"Just grazed him. And that one," Scott said, nodding at the quarrel in the duke's side, "doesn't look like it hit anything important."

Stan then turned to look at the armsmen. All were still mounted. None of them were touched. Stan realized their enemies aimed either at him or the duke.

"You can get up, Eric," Scott said. "Hold the cloth to the wound. It's not serious, but it will bleed profusely unless you keep pressure on it. I dare say your plan to tour your holding will need to wait for a few days."

"Aw, damnit! They got Arabelle," the duke cursed when he sat up. "Sons of bitches! How are the rest of you?"

"We'll live, milord," Stan replied.

"Stan! You're hurt again!" the duke noticed.

"Like he said, I'll live," Stan stated. "Can you ride? We should return to your manor. Who knows if there are others around."

"Right," the duke said, then gasped as he stood, the bolt in his side making its presence felt.

With the doctor's assistance, the duke mounted behind the doctor. It took a minute for them to adjust to riding double. They moved away, back to the manor.

"We'll need to collect Arabelle's body," the duke ordered his armsmen. "See to it."

"Aye, milord," one of the uninjured men said.

"Do you really think there are others nearby?" the duke asked Stan.

"The chancellor had placed two dozen of his own people in the Palace Guard," Stan explained. "Sergeant Varnes and I killed four on our way out of the city. Those were six of them. I have to figure that they guessed I would head either to you or to Courtenay. That suggests to me that there might be another group in the area and the rest near Courtenay."

"Have a group go looking for the others," the duke ordered his men. "If you find them, kill them. None of them will have any information that will be useful, and if any of them escapes, he will just inform the chancellor that his plan failed. Killing them gives us a few more days before he figures that out from the lack of news."

31

Ten days after the Duke of Esser sent a message to General Gladstone, new orders arrived for Fitch and Mira. Fitch was to return to the army. Mira needed to rejoin the courier service. The duke would continue mustering the other nobles in the western region.

"As I expected," the duke said. "Still, it has been pleasant sharing the road with the two of you."

"And with you, Chet," Ralph replied.

"That girl loves you, Ralph," the duke advised him quietly. "I hope you know that. And when my time comes to marry, I can only hope I find a woman half as good as Mira."

"I'm aware of how the Gods have blessed me, Chet," Ralph replied quietly. "But, in a sense, they have also cursed me. My duty—"

"Duty be damned, Ralph!" the duke hissed. "Life is uncertain. Nothing is promised for tomorrow. I'm not saying you should abandon your obligations. By the Gods, your sense of responsibility is an integral part of you. But there is a place for Mira in all that. Enjoy what happiness you can, while you can."

"Chet," Ralph whispered a few minutes later, "what are the customs regarding marriage in Auster?"

"What do you mean?"

"In Boreas, I would obtain permission from her father first," Ralph stated. "I think I've already done that. Then, I would buy her a beautiful ring as a symbol of my commitment to her. I would ask her to marry me when I presented her with the ring. At the wedding ceremony itself, I would give her another ring, much more plain, denoting our union."

"Our customs are not much different," the duke replied. "Since this is not an arranged marriage, but a love match, there is formal wording that we use as a verbal contract instead of a written one."

"Do you know the words?" Ralph asked.

"I think so," the duke replied. "Let's see. First, you get on one knee. Then you say, 'Though I am unworthy of your affection, I present this token of my love for you without obligation, desiring that you will agree to be my wife. How say you?' Pretty sure that's how it goes."

"And then?"

"If she accepts, she will ask you to stand up and she will state that she consents to accept your gift. Then you thank her for doing so."

"That's a bit more formal than Boreas," Ralph said.

"It might be more formal than what Mira expects," the duke said. "I'm going by what I know would be expected of me as the Duke of Esser."

"Well, more formal is better than too informal," Ralph mused.

"Exactly."

"Where do I obtain a ring? Ralph asked.

"That will be a challenge, given the current state of things," the duke acknowledged.

"Will it be possible that Austinton is not engulfed in the war?" Ralph asked.

"It should still be untouched," the duke replied. "Why?"

"I know someone there who might be able to help me."

"Who?"

"Dame Gruber," Ralph said.

"You know Vicki, do you?" the duke asked. "Yes. She would certainly be able to help you."

"And here you were going to send me away," Scott remarked as he cut Stan's breeches away from the crossbow quarrel embedded in his thigh.

"I'm exceedingly grateful you didn't listen to me," Stan admitted.

"I should think so," Scott sniffed.

As Scott pointed out, with a war looming, having a doctor on hand was a good thing. The doctor had already attended to the duke before coming to help Stan. He had pulled the bolt from Stan's arm a minute before. With a tug, he now yanked the quarrel from Stan's thigh. Stan grunted from the pain.

When Scott finished cleaning the wounds and bandaging him, Stan hobbled off in search of the duke. He found him in a study, dictating a letter to an assistant. The duke held up his finger, indicating Stan should wait.

"Write that out and send copies to the head men and women in every village. When you finish, come back. We need to send other letters outside the duchy," the duke ordered the man. "Captain, I'm afraid we're stuck here for the next few days. Neither of us is able to travel."

"Are the other letters you're planning to send going to your allies in the nobility?" Stan asked.

"I need to inform them that members of the Palace Guard attacked me," the duke stated. "With that, I would say that civil war has begun. We need to mobilize."

"The timing puzzles me," Stan said. "It is the wrong time of year if the chancellor hopes to pin the Border Wardens down. The winter snows will prevent the Skamorrans from attacking along the frontier for months. The success of the Austerians at Chartage devastated the Skamorran fleet, which will lessen their ability to attack Varenna."

The duke sighed heavily in response.

"What does that mean?" Stan asked.

"Did you ever stop to wonder why the chancellor suddenly turned on you? You thought you were doing a good job of playing dumb, and then those men tried to kill you."

"I never thought about it," Stan admitted. "From the time he killed the king, I worried he would discover my deception."

"When I returned from the meeting of the Regency Council, I sent Sergeant Varnes to find you," the duke said. "I also sent letters to those I thought were my allies, informing them that I thought the chancellor might know more about the king's death than he admitted. My guess is that someone I trusted fed the information to the chancellor. That put a target on your back."

"And yours and the Earl of Courtenay's," Stan added.

"The notes you passed to me and Wexler forced Mark to move before he was ready," Eric said. "He can expect no assistance from the Skamorrans for months. His plan to replace members of the Regency Council with, as you so aptly put it, the Degeneracy Council, is likely to fail."

"The chancellor still controls the army," Stan countered, "and has the advantage of a central position. You and the other nobles who oppose him are separated and will need time to gather your troops. In addition, some of your holdings are next to those of members of the Degeneracy Council. You may need to fight their men. The time it will take our side to prepare for war will be enough for the snows to melt in the passes and the Skamorrans to build more ships."

"There is one big difference, though," the duke pointed out. "He is not catching us unaware with his full strength at the ready. If you did not pass me that note, and three more months went by, think how unprepared we would be to resist."

"From what I overheard in the meeting of the Regency Council, I sensed there was suspicion of the chancellor," Stan said.

"Suspicion is not necessarily actionable," Eric said. "If the chancellor was patient enough, he could have waited out the three-year interregnum period and achieved what he wanted with any suspicion withering away as the time lapsed."

"I suppose that's why the law specifying an interregnum of three years was adopted," Stan said.

"You're probably right about that."

Mira and Ralph headed east to the Chartage road. Gladstone and the army were a day ahead of them. Mira planned to go to the first Royal Courier Service post and report for duty. Ralph hoped to catch up to the army before it reached Austinton.

Ralph wanted to be able to meet privately with Dame Gruber to discuss ideas for a ring that he would present to Mira. He was thinking of an emerald to bring out the green flecks in Mira's beautiful hazel eyes. His problem was that he did not know whether he had enough money for something suitable. For that matter, he never asked about his salary as a colonel in the Austerian army or when he would be paid.

When he reached the main body of the army, they welcomed him back warmly. He pondered the contrast between that and how they first greeted him. Then, his fellow officers were worried he would replace one of them. Now, they knew that was not the case.

In addition, they saw him provide the ideas that led to their success at Chartage and watched as he volunteered for the most dangerous assignments. They knew he was on their side in the upcoming civil war. In the short time, Ralph surpassed merely being "one of them." Ralph was now someone who had earned their respect and admiration, even though they teased him and often mocked his Borean accent. Instead of annoying him, it made Ralph feel as though he belonged.

When they reached Austinton the next day, Ralph excused himself to call upon Dame Gruber. The maid invited him in and went to find her mistress. Vicki came out, a broad smile on her face and hands extended. Ralph took them and offered her a kiss on each cheek.

"What brings you here, Colonel?" Vicki said. "I must admit I have been basking in your reflected glory, hearing of your exploits at Chartage."

"Thank you," Ralph said modestly, blushing. "We are headed to the capital, where we understand the Duke of Volplane has already begun putting the city under siege."

"He has," Vicki replied. "But why call upon me?"

"I have decided I wish to marry Mira," Ralph said.

"Marvelous!" Vicki exclaimed. "What fun news in the midst of all this unpleasantness with Volplane."

"Yes," Ralph said uncertainly, then changed the subject slightly. "In discussing Austerian customs with the Duke of Esser, I understand I need a ring to present to Mira as a demonstration of my commitment to her. I thought an emerald, to bring out the green in her hazel eyes—"

"An excellent idea," Vicki commented.

"I have not encountered a jeweler during my time in Auster thus far," Ralph said, "and my funds are—"

"By all the heavenly beings!" Vicki interrupted. "Do not trouble yourself. It happens that I believe I have just the thing. Wait here."

Ralph watched as Dame Gruber bustled away and charged up the stairs. He felt awkward. His intent in visiting was not to beg for a piece of jewelry from Vicki but to get information. As Vicki came floating down the stairs a few minutes later, he tried to tell her this, but she threw up her hand vigorously, indicating he should stop speaking.

"Ralph, I know you came seeking information, not charity," she said. "But if you remember, I told you I always wanted a daughter. My husband, before he died, gave me more jewelry than I will ever know what to do with. Mira compared me to a fairy godmother. Think of this in that regard."

With that, Vicki held out her hand. In her palm was a ring with a platinum band. Mounted upon it was a square-cut emerald as big as the entire nail on his middle finger. Small diamonds ringed the emerald all the way around. Ralph's breath caught in his throat. This was far beyond his means. He could not imagine ever being able to afford such a beautiful ring.

"Take it, Ralph," Vicki said. "Mira's fairy godmother wishes for her to wear it and enjoy it for the rest of her life."

"Milady," Ralph said, dropping to one knee. "It is too much. I—"

"Oh, get up, and don't be a fool," Vicki said, tugging Ralph by his hand. "And if it is too big or too small for her finger, have her come to see me, and we will visit the jeweler and have the band adjusted."

"Thank you, Vicki," Ralph said when he recovered the ability to speak.

32

After Ralph rejoined the army, he told the next rider from the Royal Courier Service that he saw to pass the word to Mira to come to see him. Ralph hoped the legs of her travel would bring her south, closer to him. If she started off riding north, it would take longer.

In the meantime, as they rode, Ralph explained his thinking regarding cutting off Volplane's supply line. General Gladstone convened the other officers that evening to discuss it. They immediately saw the merit in the idea.

"Though they are besieging the capital," Colonel Gillies commented, "we will besiege them, in a way."

"As long as they are entrenched, we do not have the forces to root them out," Ralph said. "If we succeed in severing their line of supply, they will be forced to emerge."

"Or starve," Colonel Newagen stated.

"Or starve," Ralph confirmed. "Where is their source of water?"

"The water table is close enough to the surface for them to dig a well," Gladstone said.

"Damn," Ralph muttered. "Well, hunger will force them out."

"Then what?" General Gladstone asked.

"It depends," Ralph said. "For instance, are Volplane's infantry soldiers equipped similarly to the Skamorran troops we fought?"

"Halberds instead of spears," Colonel Reubens stated.

"Eh," Ralph grunted with a frown. "That's not good. We will need cataphracts."

"If we are successful in cutting Volplane's supply lines, it might be enough to convince the lords nearby to join our cause," Gladstone said. "They control the majority of the cataphracts in the entire kingdom."

"We need to call on them," Ralph said, "and convince them to join our side before it is too late."

"What do you mean, too late?" Colonel Gillies asked.

"If we succeed in starving Volplane out of his siege, the lords who are waiting to see which way the wind blows will miss the opportunity to be on the winning side," Ralph said. "That will lessen their influence in the future, won't it?"

"The problem will be convincing them that we will win without them," Gladstone commented.

"Volplane's alliance with the Skamorrans will not influence them?" Ralph asked.

"He has probably already denied it," Gladstone said. "Still, they haven't heard our side of the story."

When Ralph and the army drew within sight of the capital, they could see the earthworks thrown up by Volplane's soldiers. Volplane had already surrounded the city walls. Gladstone established camp at a comfortable distance away from the enemy and assigned different sections of the enemy line to his different units.

They used the Skamorran prisoners to begin digging their own set of fortifications. Just beyond arrow shot, the prisoners began to work. Gladstone also sent patrols out, looking for the arrival of the supply wagons. Their orders were not to engage but to report back immediately. The second day after their arrival, they spotted the first train of carts.

Gladstone ordered Colonel Nadeau to take his unit and intercept the wagons. Ralph rode along to observe. Nadeau's command numbered just over seven hundred mounted soldiers. Most were archers.

The supply wagons were escorted by roughly four dozen cavalry. Nadeau instructed his people to leave the wagons and their drivers alone and focus only on the cavalry guarding them. In less than five minutes, Volplane's soldiers were dead. The drivers were trying to run away, but Nadeau sent his people to corral them and direct them back to the loyalist camp.

"It's bad enough to have your supplies cut off," Nadeau explained earlier, "but to see them go to feed the enemy is even more disheartening."

"After darkness falls, we need to be sure our people communicate to the enemy lines that we captured their food," Ralph said to Gladstone when he returned to camp. "Most of their soldiers are militia, like ours, right?"

"Sure," the general replied, not understanding Ralph's point.

"How do they benefit if Volplane wins? What consequences do they face if he loses?" Ralph asked. "If the answer is that it doesn't much matter, we need our people to talk to them after dark. I mean, if my liege lord is asking me to risk my life only to assuage his vanity and lust for power, I might not be too eager to stick it out if things turn against my side."

"I understand your idea," Gladstone said, "but it won't work. Volplane and his people treat their people much more harshly than you might be accustomed to. Not only would someone attempting to desert be killed, but his whole family would probably suffer as well."

"We should still—"

"Oh, I don't disagree with that at all," Gladstone said. "Just don't expect it to generate much in the way of visible results."

For three weeks, Stan and the duke remained inside, figuratively licking their wounds. The duke's armsmen had found the other group of Palace Guards lurking on one of the roads out of town and dispatched all four of them. The head men and women of the towns and villages in the duchy came to the manor during this time. Eric instructed them to warn the militia that conflict was coming. Midway through the fourth week after the attack on the road, the duke received a letter from the Earl of Courtenay.

"He says that his men already discovered the 'blackguards,' as he termed them, before he received my letter warning him," Eric said. "His men chased them away. The earl agrees that the chancellor wants war. Our most pressing issue is whether we summon the militia now, to gather in force at key locations, or wait. He suggests waiting, even though there is a chance we might be caught unprepared."

"I hate to say it, but he has a valid point," Stan said. "Pulling the militia away from home and hearth in the middle of winter, then requiring them to march for days, will be unpopular. And in addition to that, there is the uncertainty about supply, and there is a real possibility of losing our army before the first battle. We thought the chancellor might be moving too early. I am beginning to think it would serve his purpose if we mobilized right now."

"The earl is not as direct, but I believe he has the same thought," Eric said. "He agrees that Varenna is a likely place to expect the Skamorrans, in addition to increased activity on the border. The earl also believes he knows who shared your identity with the other side."

"Who is the traitor?" Stan asked.

"Not a traitor so much as a fool," Eric said. "Lord Blakeslee is young and still has friends who I believe are in contact with some members of the 'Degeneracy Council.' The earl thinks Blakeslee was indiscreet and may have mentioned that the source of our suspicion regarding the chancellor was a member of the Palace Guard."

"That would have been enough," Stan commented. "What will you do about Blakeslee?"

"We need Blakeslee," Eric said. "He will command between seven and eight hundred soldiers. The earl has written him, advising him to be more careful in what he says and to whom he speaks."

"Will that be enough?" Stan asked.

"Blakeslee is, in my opinion, a good man—just young and inexperienced," Eric said. "Of course, none of us has any experience in dealing with the aftermath of a king's assassination and a missing prince, but we know not to flap our gums."

"Eric, if—or should I say when—we defeat the chancellor, who should take the throne?" Scott asked, entering the conversation for the first time.

"Well, there are several—"

"I understand that there are second and third cousins," Scott said, waving his hand dismissively. "Consanguinity aside, is there someone else you feel is more qualified?"

"I don't understand."

"Who is the best person for the job of ruling Boreas?" Scott asked. "Is there someone in your peer group you can point to? Don't consider whether there is any blood tie. Evaluate only on the person's experience, character, and judgment."

"Hmm," the duke murmured as he pondered the question. "I'm going to say, Viscount Huntington."

"Not the Earl of Courtenay?" Stan asked.

"No," Eric said, shaking his head. "He's a good man but too irascible. He reacts too quickly to provocation when he should respond after due consideration. The earl almost always apologizes, but we need someone steadier. The viscount, on the other hand, is a careful man. He thinks things all the way through. As a result, when he speaks, most of the rest of us listen carefully."

"Now, of those who are blood kin to the late king, who is the most acceptable candidate?" Scott asked.

"Wexler," Eric replied immediately.

"Do you think you could convince Wexler to support Huntington?" Scott asked.

"That will be difficult," Eric answered.

"Why?"

"Because Wexler is probably thinking of himself as being the best of those related to Philip."

"Does he want the job, or just the title?" Scott asked.

"That's a clever question," Stan remarked.

"Yes, it is," Eric agreed. "Wexler would want the title—there is no doubt of that. Shouldering the responsibilities that go along with it—I think he would be happier in his current position."

"Would Huntington be a better choice than Prince John if the prince somehow reappears?" Scott asked.

"I'm going to say no," the duke said. "They share many of the same qualities and strength of character, but John would be a more vigorous leader. But why are you asking all these questions?"

"The Regency Council should decide who will succeed Philip before you take up arms against the chancellor," Scott stated. "If you don't, your efforts will lack unity of purpose. If there are multiple people who are trying to mark out their claims to the throne, your military efforts will fracture. Even if you manage to defeat the chancellor in the face of this disunity, Boreas will immediately plunge into another civil war between the victors."

"So, I should get the rest of the council to agree on Huntington before the weather improves," Eric noted.

"And you need to begin with Wexler," Scott added.

"John, you look particularly melancholy today," Phoebe remarked. "What's wrong?"

John's first inclination was to deny there was a problem. Since it involved his relationship with Cia, he did not feel terribly comfortable discussing it with her mother. Still, he remembered someone telling him that a problem shared is a burden lightened.

"Phoebe, I'm torn," he said.

"Between what?"

"There is something I am meant to be doing," he said, "back in the world. I don't know who I am, or even if John is really my name, but I can't escape the feeling that I have weighty responsibilities and obligations back where I came from."

"John, you know that no one who has attempted to leave has been successful," she said. "We would know if they were because a ship would appear. Whatever your duties back in the world, you will never be able to attend to them."

"I know, but that is only part of the problem. Did I leave a family behind?"

"Everyone has a family, John," Phoebe said gently, "so I'm sure you did."

"But a wife? Children?" John said with a bit of a moan.

"Ah," Phoebe said. "This is about Cia."

"Yes. She is the other part of the problem," John admitted with a sigh. "It would not be fair to her to deepen our relationship if I am already tied to someone else, and yet, she enthralls me. I am in love with your daughter, Phoebe. I wish to make her mine—in every way a man can join with a woman."

"John, I understand," Phoebe said. "And I can see that Cia shares your desires in every way. The only advice I have for you is what I said before. Daubmer Island has been cut off from the rest of the world for generations and generations. Now, I cannot promise that a ship will not suddenly appear on the horizon, but up to this point, there has been no ship. Even if a miracle should take place, and a ship does appear, who is to say you must leave?"

33

I t was another six days before Mira rode into the loyalist camp. Naturally, Ralph was tied up in a meeting. She waited patiently for him to emerge from the tent.

"Mira!" Ralph said, crossing to her quickly and embracing her. "I'm so glad to see you. Please! Come!"

Ralph clasped her hand and nearly dragged her to his tent. He ducked inside quickly and retrieved the ring from his saddlebag. When he came outside, he took her hand again and dropped to one knee. Seeing him in this posture, those nearby stopped to watch.

"Mira Grimble, although I am unworthy of you, please allow me to present this token of my love for you. I offer this gift without obligation, desiring that you will agree to be my wife. How say you?"

Mira's reactions were varied and followed one another rapidly. At first, when she realized Ralph's intent (and that people were watching), she blushed furiously. When she saw the ring, she gasped. She stood stunned as he attempted to slide it onto the fourth finger of her left hand. The ring slid on easily—it was slightly too big.

The surprise and shock stole her power of speech momentarily. Ralph looked up at her with a helpless expression, waiting for her answer. She shook herself like a wet dog and regained her senses.

"Rise, Colonel Fitch," she said with a calmness she did not feel. "I accept this gift representing your love and affection. It is indeed my fond desire to marry you and be your wife."

"Thank you, Mira Grimble," Ralph said with a broad grin as he stood.

"Kiss! Kiss! Kiss!" the onlookers began to chant.

With another look at the beautiful ring on her finger, Mira jumped onto Ralph. She wrapped her arms around his neck and her legs around his waist. Their lips crashed together, and their tongues slipped in the other's mouth for a bit of wrestling. Those looking on cheered the amorous display.

"Where did you get the ring?" Mira asked. "It's magnificent!"

"Your fairy godmother," Ralph said. "I went to her only to ask where I might find a jeweler, and she pressed this on me. She would not allow me to refuse. By the way, if the band does not fit, she will take you to get it adjusted."

"I wondered," Mira said. "Though you are a man of many talents, I know the state of your purse, and it could never come close to buying something like this."

"I would have done the best I could," he said, "but you're correct—it would not have been anywhere near as grand as this."

"How nice for us both that Vicki has adopted us," Mira remarked.

"When and where should we have the ceremony?" Ralph asked.

"Soon, and nearby," Mira replied. "You need to obtain the actual marriage ring. If I visit Vicki to get this ring adjusted, I will order it. You will need to pay the man and collect it. I will arrange my routes to return in a couple of weeks. I will ask my father to join us if he can. We can have the ceremony then."

"What is your father doing?" Ralph asked. "And are Paul Escamil and Sven still with him?"

"They are overseeing the work in Chartage, managing the Skamorran prisoners," she said.

"It does not trouble you that I have no home?" Ralph asked. "Other than the ring, which was a gift from Vicki, all I possess are my uniforms, Bob, and the inadequate contents of my purse."

"You have made yourself invaluable to General Gladstone," Mira replied. "Even when you defeat Volplane, they will keep you in service to the realm. Your future is secure."

"And what about you?" Ralph asked. "I do not see you living the idle life of a court gossip."

"With the Gods favoring us, we will have children," Mire said with a smile. "And you will find us a place in the country where we will raise them to be strong and independent. When they are small, I will be their mother. Once they are older, perhaps I will ride for the Royal Courier Service again."

"I can see you doing that even with a babe in your lap," Ralph said with a chuckle.

"Don't tempt me," Mira warned.

"Caleb, may I have a word?"

"Certainly, John. What's on your mind?"

"Your daughter," John said bluntly. "I have the strongest of feelings for her."

"You are considering making her your wife?" Caleb asked.

"I am. Though I am still uncertain regarding who I am, I know for sure that I want Cia as a part of my life from now on."

"Well said," Caleb commented. "Have you managed to put your misgivings aside? Phoebe shared the content of your discussion with me."

"I am still troubled by the gnawing feeling that I am failing to meet my obligations back in the world we left," John said. "At the same time, Phoebe pointed out that I have no way of fulfilling them. And though I worry that there might be a wife, I do not think I ever experienced before what I feel for Cia."

"If, by some miracle, a ship would come?" Caleb asked.

"I would take Cia with me if we decided to leave the island," John said.

"She would be eager to go, if I know my daughter," Caleb said with a chuckle. "If you are seeking my blessing, you have it, John."

"How do we become man and wife? Is it as simple as my asking Cia if she will join me?" John asked.

"It can be," Caleb answered with a smile. "In the world we left, it was more involved, but here on the island, it can be as simple as you described, or you can have a ceremony. We don't have any priests, and our memories of the proper wording are growing hazier every month that passes, but if you—"

"Simpler suits me, but I will ask Cia," John said.

"Wise decision," Caleb agreed with a laugh. "If she agrees to be your wife, we will need to build you a house."

"We leave in the morning," the Duke of Roundel announced.

"Where are we going?" Stan asked.

"To call upon Lord Wexler," Eric said. "I acted on Scott's advice and wrote him, asking if we could meet. He just responded, inviting us to visit. We will travel to meet with Wexler and convince him to yield any claim to the throne."

"And you think you can persuade him of this?" Scott asked.

"I must," Eric stated. "Viscount Huntington is clearly the better choice to lead us out of a civil war and restore the country. Wexler is proud, but not so blinded by that pride that he cannot admit Huntington is the man for the job."

"You seem confident," Stan noted. "Are you too confident?"

"There is one other important factor in Huntington's favor I failed to mention," Eric said. "He is childless, and of an age where producing an heir is unlikely."

"Ah!" Scott said. "He will need to adopt a successor. Who is the next most qualified candidate?"

"Lord Wexler," Eric said triumphantly. "And if all goes well, he will have ten years or more to learn the role from Huntington."

"Can you promise this?" Scott asked.

"Not without discussing it with Huntington, but I believe he will agree," Eric said.

"What about your peers?" Stan asked.

"I believe Courtenay will be on my side. If Wexler agrees, and the choice is Huntington, the only people opposing us would be the Degeneracy Council— and we might be able to eliminate them along the way."

"Colonel Fitch, General Gladstone asked me to find you," came a voice from outside the tent.

"Is it urgent?" Ralph asked.

"I believe so, sir."

"I'm sorry, darling," Ralph whispered to Mira.

He untangled himself from his bride-to-be and dressed quickly. Ralph wondered what was so important. He was present at the staff meeting after breakfast and there was nothing new, so he went to steal a few pleasant hours in Mira's arms before she needed to leave.

Ralph followed the orderly to the general's pavilion. As he drew closer, he saw what he thought was one of the teamsters they captured with Volplane's supplies. Ralph wondered what that meant.

"Ah, Colonel Fitch," General Gladstone said. "I apologize for interrupting, but I believe you will thank me when you hear what this man has to say." Turning to the teamster, the general asked, "Go on. Tell him what you just told me."

"I come from Merriam, on the eastern shore," the teamster said. "Now, jes' before I left, there's a fantastical story spreading through the county. A man in a little boat, name of Rathburn or summat like that, sailed smack into the port of Boother in this little boat, not much more'n a skiff. This Rathburn says he come from some island in the middle of the eastern sea. From what I heard, he says there's over a hundred people living there, almost all from shipwrecks. Rathburn was born there, according to the story I heard. This feller say people have tried to leave the island and sail back west before, but I guess no one ever made it. Rathburn says they never returned to the island, so they was lost in the ocean, I guess."

"Skip ahead to the part that got me excited," the general urged.

"Right. Well, Rathburn says that a few weeks before he shoves off, a feller washed up. This feller was dressed real fancy, had an impressive sword and all. I guess this feller was hurt but bad. Head was bashed somepin awful and he didn't remember who he was."

"What was the man's name?" the general prompted.

"Well, according to the story they tole me, he din't rightly know, ya see," the teamster said. "At least, he din't remember his family name. He thought his first name was John. Since he din't know his last name, one of the fellers who carried him from the beach where they found him complained he was nothing but a burden, so they calls him John Burden."

"General, I need to go see this Rathburn immediately," Ralph stated firmly.

"Colonel, I understand," Gladstone said. "And I would let you go except there are a few problems. Count Martinson, who controls Merriam, is probably only a few hundred yards away from us right now. He is one of Volplane's closest allies. That makes Merriam enemy territory. You have nothing to prove as far as your courage or skill, Ralph, but you would not survive the journey. Even if you did, and learned enough from Rathburn to convince you that this John who washed ashore was your missing prince, you would need a ship to take you to find this island in the middle of a vast ocean. That, in and of itself, will be no easy task. The only one who can give you a ship like that is the king. And though I am sure he would help you in an instant, at the moment we have no way of communicating with him. So, as exciting as this news is, I don't think there is anything you can do about it in the immediate future."

Ralph returned to his tent where Mira waited. The look on his face told her his news wasn't good. After crossing to her, kneeling down, and taking her hands in his, he shared what he had just learned. He did not gloss over the uncertainty of the information.

"Even with the improbable nature of what the man said, I must investigate it further," Ralph concluded.

"We," Mira said firmly.

"What?"

"*We* will investigate it further," Mira stated, standing up and glowering at him.

"Mira, I can't ask you—" Ralph tried to protest as he stood to face her.

"But we cannot begin until the war here is over," Mira ignored his attempted objection. "And when the war here is over? If we go and if we find your prince?"

"Then I will return him to Boreas and see him take his rightful place on the throne," Ralph said.

"*We*," Mira stated fiercely. "*We* will return him to Boreas."

"Mira, this is not your quest," Ralph said without conviction.

"Did you not mean it when you asked me to be your wife?" Mira argued.

"Of course I meant it," Ralph said.

"Then we will do this—together," she said.

"Arugh!" Ralph shouted in frustration, raising his fists to the sky. "Fine. We will do this."

"Good," Mira said smugly. "And afterward?"

"And afterward, we will marry, and Gods willing, make a family, Fitch said, grinning.

Mira threw herself onto Ralph. Wrapping her arms around his neck and legs around his waist, she kissed him passionately. When they broke for air, Fitch's face resumed a somber look.

"What?" she asked.

"Finding John and starting our family is in the future," he said soberly. "We have a war to win first.

ABOUT THE AUTHOR

John Spearman has been a Fortune 500 sales and marketing executive, a Latin teacher and coach at a prestigious New England boarding school, and is also an author. He lives in coastal Maine with his wife and their dogs. He began writing because his wife challenged him. He was lucky enough to find an audience and has not looked back (except to fix the mistakes he made in the early days!).

This book is the first of a new series. Spearman has five other book series, all but one in the category of military science fiction. The one that is not, the FitzDuncan series, is in the fantasy genre, and won First Place in the Fantasy Series category of the 2023 Chanticleer International Book Awards.

If you enjoyed reading this book, please consider leaving a positive review on amazon.com or goodreads.com. It will help other readers like you find books they might enjoy. To learn more about the author's different works, please visit www.johnjspearmanauthor.com.